OGRE'S PASSING

OGRE'S PASSING

paul melniczek

king's way press

ATLANTA
2016

King's Way Press
3721 New Macland Road
Suite 200-141
Powder Springs, GA 30127
http://www.kwp-books.com

Limited Edition Printing

ISBN: 978-0692677872

Artwork Copyright © 2016 by Wayne Miller
Interior Design by Kate Freeman Design

OGRE'S PASSING

a chill wind blew in from the west, gently swaying the high grass bordering the grain fields of Sarion's farm. Arms folded across his solid chest, Sarion stared past his own lands, pondering the black rumors circulating the countryside. Stories of outlying homes being broken into, the families taken away in the night. The destruction of property, the loss of cattle. Peddlers traveling along the dusky roads spoke in low tones about the unrest, an increasing number of them staying away from outlying areas as they made their way to the more secure larger towns and villages of the central kingdom. Many tales, all of them troublesome.

A dark cloud hovered ominously over the collective conscience of the durable men and women who lived in this region, and Sarion felt it as well, creeping slowly over his own heart and mind, a growing menace, a warning of ill times to come. Something evil was encroaching on the borders of his homelands, the kingdom of Trencit. Sarion lived at the westernmost fringe of the domain, close to forsaken lands ruled by dangerous and malevolent creatures. And now a nameless entity was terrorizing the peaceful frontiersmen, plaguing their nightmares and threatening all who dwelt nearby.

He stooped down, grabbing a huge bale of hay, his brown, shoulder-length hair catching some of the individual straws. It smelled fresh and pleasant to him, a mundane aroma of peace and order. The cooler season was not too far distant, and this was a busy time of year for the household.

"Uncle Sarion, a group of horsemen approach."

He turned around as his young nephew Edward came towards him, the boy's cheerful face thoughtful as he pointed down the dirt lane leading to the farmhouse. Dust rose in trailing clumps as the party made their way steadily towards them.

"Yes—and they're warriors, I see. Thirteen strong." Sarion replied, a note of surprise evident in his clear voice, as he held a hand over his keen blue eyes, blocking out the late afternoon sun.

"How can you tell from here?" asked Edward. He lifted his curly blond head up excitedly. There were few armed companies in the region as they were seldom required, except as routine patrols. The king's royal armies were needed in the east, where a war was being fought against their enemies, the Devlents.

"Hmm, perhaps they were sent to investigate the raiding. It's probably not large enough to be part of a major division."

The group approached at a modest gait, and Sarion waved a hand in recognition. The men were dressed in with a minimum of armor, looking more prepared for quickness and stealth, the common attire for a small scouting party. The horses were tall and broad, bred and raised in service of the kingdom's fighting force. Coming forward was a lightly bearded man of brown hair with a hawkish face wearing a helm of steel, a crimson eagle on his breast. Sarion knew it to be the symbol of a captain in the Trencit Home Guard. He raised his eyebrows in response, genuine surprise on the handsome face. It was unheard of to see one of the king's own elite commanders outside of the eastern provinces, their numbers being very few. Unusual indeed…

"Well met, my good captain. It is not too often we see any of His Majesty's finest in our lands. What brings you so far from the capital?"

The man signaled for his squadron to halt, expertly reigning in his own steed, steel glinting in the fading sunlight.

"Greetings also. You're obviously familiar with royal insignia. I'm Captain Grundel, leader of this company and an officer of the Trencit Home Guard."

Sarion made a short bow. "My name is Sarion, and this is my nephew Edward. You and your men are welcome, and at my service. Whatever supplies or information I have is at your immediate disposal."

A sharp look passed Grundel's weathered face, quickly disappearing. "Our thanks to you."

"Could I ask what it is you seek? The sight of your group is encouraging, and I'm sure you are well aware of the recent events. The people of the countryside have appealed directly to the king. There is a nameless force which threatens the region."

Grundel dismounted from his great steed, a black mare that frisked with scarce contained energy.

"And that is exactly why we are here. To offer aid and to find answers. My assignment is to seek out the source of danger, eliminating whatever is preying upon our people."

Sarion nodded. "The popular belief is obvious, of course. Something has crept in from the wilderness, and is terrorizing the countryside. But this isn't the work of bandits, or common men at all. No, my belief is that it hails from the Grammore Lowlands."

"And if that is where our mission takes us, then it will find us ready and determined." Grundel's eyes were quietly intense.

Sarion frowned. "Is there a larger group being dispatched?"

The captain shook his head.

"Surely you don't mean to go yourselves?" Sarion did not attempt to mask his pessimism.

"I think our farmer here knows little of the king's guard." A huge man on an enormous horse trotted up. He looked oversized, even for the magnificent steed. A thick red beard covered half his face, and he jumped off his mount. "I hope that you do not question the prowess of our company." It was a statement, and the man loomed before him in an obvious pose of intimidation.

"This is Rundin, my second," said Grundel, who made no offer to appease the anger of his fighter.

But Sarion was undaunted. "I question no one's ability. You do not know the dangers that lurk beyond these borders, unless you were born a frontiersman. Little knowledge reaches the king's city, or those who fight in the east."

Rundin towered over Sarion, who was over six feet tall himself. The man had the visage of an awakened bear, eager to confront anything that threatened. He licked his lips, scowling.

"And there are many who are so far removed from battle that they forget the valor of the men keeping the peace." Rundin tapped his chest.

Sarion shook his head in defiance. "Some, perhaps. Maybe many. But not all. Sacrifice comes in a variety of forms. The touch of loss plays no favorite tune." A dark look crossed Sarion's face, and Grundel nodded to himself in approval, the sea-ice eyes narrowing a hair.

"Rundin, you shouldn't be so quick to judgment—or anger. This man speaks much truth. And, he is not what he appears to be..."

Edward stared at his uncle, innocence reflected on the ten year old's face.

The captain continued. "It is not by accident that we came to this farm. And this is no ordinary farmer standing before us."

Rundin looked questioningly at Sarion.

"I seek out someone who served in the Western Watch, now seven years past. This man was the greatest tracker and swordsman on the frontier."

Rundin's mouth opened, realization dawning on him.

Grundel continued. "A captain in his own right, he once led a company into the wilderness, fighting back a band of marauding Glefins. Fifty men were sent. Out of that sizable force, only three returned, one of them lost to his own mind, the other gravely wounded, passing away shortly after entering our lands. The third man stands before us—Sarion, who slew the Glefin leader himself."

Sarion's eyes grew dark with the memories. "You awaken black thoughts, captain. Ones I would rather keep forever from the light of day."

Grundel sighed deeply. "The need of our kingdom outweighs many reprieves, I'm afraid. For it is you who I have searched out for help."

Gesturing with his arm, Sarion pointed towards the west. "Death and madness. This is what waits beyond the hills." He paused. "My experience I will gladly lend, however terrible. Although I am one of the only men to have traveled within the Lowlands, I can't guess at the source of trouble myself. But I'll provide whatever information which still remains of that disastrous journey."

The captain lowered his voice. "You misunderstand my intentions. We need someone to lead us into the wild, and help to determine the source of unrest. You have been there before, and your skills are required once more, although you would wish it otherwise."

Sarion stiffened, feeling Edward's eyes boring into his face. Was this the shadow which he had felt clutching at his heart recently? Now come to reality? He stared across the gentle fields, feeling a sudden sense of foreboding at Grundel's words.

"You ask much, captain. There are nightmares beyond description past our safe lands. And now you want me to leave my farm and nephew behind?" The two locked gazes.

Grundel nodded in sympathy. "The war demands the bulk of our men. There are few left to spare. We must be enough. If the danger grows larger, then the king needs to gain knowledge of what it is which menaces his people. Failure is unthinkable. Things are grim now. But it may only be the start of worse to come."

Sarion gripped Edward's shoulder, a frown of disapproval on his youthful face.

"Help see to the men's comfort. We'll put them up in the barn, if that's all right with the captain." He turned towards Grundel as the boy hurried away. "My hope is for the lad to have a better future for himself, along with all the youth of our kingdom. Too many have died sharing that same dream. Brave fighters, my countrymen and kin."

Grundel replied, his voice low. "And many more await their own grave as evil grows stronger. Come, I am sorry to have brought this upon you, but the need is great. We're all tired, and the end of our path is nowhere in sight. A warm bed beneath even a barn is a comfort to weary fighters in the field. You know this too."

"Perhaps a glass of ale can bring a good night's rest to your men. And you're right, but it's been a long time since I've slept under the trees and stars. Such service to the king-dom allows for little relief. You deserve better."

Rundin snorted as Sarion led them away. "We all might be dreaming and remembering your pleasant farm here in the weeks to come."

⚜

The small cabin was hazy and dimly lit, as the figures of two trappers sat around a modest ring of burning embers, the open roof vent drawing out the lingering smoke. Several stars glittered downward from the vast heavens in the clear sky. Mixed hardwood tress huddled against the small structure, moss covering the bark, a carpet of twigs and leaves blanketing the great roots.

"Been pretty poor lately, don't understand it." Rigel puffed on a long pipe and he looked over at his companion Dustan, who had worked with him for the past two years.

"You think we should push a little deeper?" Dustan's bushy eyebrows clung to his forehead like caterpillars as he squinted at the older man.

"I don't know, with all the talk I've heard. People are pulling back, getting away from the border. We're probably the last ones on this side of Hawker Peak anymore. Can't remember when things were this bad." Rigel took a swig of ale, wiping his mouth on an already stained shirt sleeve.

"Aye, but we have a great pack. Some of those others work on their own."

Rigel agreed. "Those old dogs have a lot of spark in them, don't they? Well, I've always fed them good, and you need hunting dogs in this part of the world. There's creatures past this mountain that'll freeze your blood. I've seen some of them. Moving out of the shadows in the evening, coming out to greet the darkness."

Dustan shuddered. "What about the stories? Do you know what it could be?"

The other trapper cleaned some mud off his leather boots, scraping the dirt with a wicked dagger. "Could be a lot of things, but I'd rather not speak of them." He whispered. "They say that you can attract evil sometimes, just by naming it... I'll tell you what the problem is, though. The king's forgotten about this frontier with the war going on back east. He's let the Watch pull in, left it for the locals to protect themselves. But this much I do know."

He crouched over the fire, moving closer to his friend.

"There's more death that sleeps in the west than anyone dreams about. Older than the hills, and deadly. Things were here long before men came around. And..." He paused for effect, peering through the window. "...every once in a while, something wakes up, comes looking for fresh territory, and food. That's what I think."

The cabin seemed to press in on the two men, and Dustan wished he were back home in more hospitable regions. A few more days, and they would have enough skins to take back. Just a few more was all. He could manage.

"Well, let's start early tomorrow. I'll be happy when we leave these woods behind. They're not too friendly anymore, if you take my meaning." Dustan straightened, yawning as he stretched his lean arms back.

Rigel nodded. "I feel that way too sometimes. It's good having four warm walls around you, and a spirited pub within walking distance... and a few wenches strutting about," he added with a wink.

His smirk quickly vanished as a loud baying erupted outside the cabin. The trappers stared at the doorway anxiously, every trace of humor drained away. They had brought eight dogs with them, the pack now tied up at a makeshift rail in front of the cabin. Their howls were terrible to hear.

"They smell something bad out there. Grab your weapon." Rigel picked up a battle-ax, and a short sword leaning against the wall. The other trapper fingered his own blade, apprehension gripping his chest at the frightful wailing outside.

Rigel opened the door, gesturing for Dustan to take the large oil lamp which sat on the eating table. "I've never heard them carrying on like this. Whatever's out there can't be very friendly." They locked gazes for a tense moment, both of them unwilling to give voice to the terrible seed of fear which waited to sprout open into the breathing night.

They rushed outside, the small clearing illuminated by sets of torches set strategically around the cabin. The hunting dogs were in a frenzy, leaping against their chains, the mixed wolf breeds greatly resembling the wilder strain of their bloodline. Some of them were clawing madly against the ground, snuffling in the dirt, attempting to break free.

"Shades! What do they smell?" Dustan peered into the shadowy eaves, his head darting in all directions as he tried to locate any movement, but all was still. "Should we unleash them?"

The older trapper hesitated. It might be better to have them free, he thought. They had no idea what lay hidden in the trees.

"Loosen half of them. I don't want to have all of the dogs roaming around at night. I don't like these woods. They feel bad."

The men were barely able to unfasten the metal collars. The wolf hounds snarled madly, jumping to break away. As the dogs were unleashed, they bolted straight into the forest, angling west. Four animals ran with reckless speed as they sought their quarry. Tense moments passed as the trappers waited for any indication of what lurked out of sight. The other dogs carried on ferociously as their kindred went to the hunt. The trappers remained on guard, nervously fingering their weapons. Dustan spat, more an action to ease his own apprehension than anything else. Time dragged on agonizingly.

Without warning a dreadful noise shattered the clearing. Erupting out of the night was the sound of a great hunting horn, ringing harshly like an invitation to battle. The echoes fleetingly drifted through the forest, and then everything was silent. The woods remained still as the men stood transfixed by the frightful call.

All at once a terrible yelping broke out. The men listened in shock to pure cries of anguish, ones which scorched them to the very bone.

"By the Devil's tongue! They're being slaughtered!" Dustan grabbed Rigel's jacket collar, a look of disbelief on the older trapper's face. "We've got to leave. The horses!" Dustan pulled Rigel, but the man was immobilized by his terror. He dashed away, his own mind made up.

Dustan threw down the lantern and went to the back of the cabin. The horses were tethered, neighing in agitation. The trapper saddled the larger of the pair, gathering the reins from the other horse with one hand. Rigel had not followed him, and Dustan was worried. The man seemed to have lost his senses. Kicking his mount forward, he gained the front corner of the cabin. One of the dogs had broken his chain and was gone. Rigel was standing motionless, staring into the woods, an intense look on his face.

"Come on, we've got to leave now!" Dustan halted next to the older trapper, willing him to break out of his inaction.

"You can't escape, it's coming." Rigel pointed into the trees, where branches cracked as something huge approached. It was all Dustan could do to keep from being thrown from his horse.

"Rigel! Now, there's no time left." He clutched at his friend's collar, but the trapper only watched in fascination as another dog became free and ran quickly behind the cabin, vanishing into the forest's maw. Dustan was about to leave when his horse kicked its legs high, throwing him to the ground.

Everything went black for a minute and he felt himself being dragged away. Rigel had snapped out of his confusion and was pulling the other trapper to the side of the building. The remaining two dogs were howling in agony behind them, and Dustan staggered to his feet.

"Run, run. I'll try and hold it back." Rigel pushed Dustan and held up his ax. "It's my fault—I'm an old fool. But I'll gain you some time."

Dustan didn't argue, and stumbled into the cover of the trees. He ran off, hoping to find one of the horses. If he didn't, the prospect of walking long miles through thick woods faced him. An extremely unpleasant possibility. There was ample starlight to guide him, but it wasn't enough to allow the man to move forward with any sense of confidence.

Several minutes passed and he scrambled through the brush, leaving the cabin behind. His breath came in ragged gasps, and he wondered as to the fate of his friend. After long minutes he paused, leaning heavily against a hoary oak, when a chilling scream echoed through the night. He faltered, listening to the hideous cry. There could be no doubt as to the source. It was Rigel. The trapper was gone.

Terror gave him renewed strength and he plunged ahead, nearly falling into a ditch edged with loose dirt and rock. Dustan tried to stop, his hands waving madly, and he plummeted head over heel, crashing to the bottom several feet below and into a churning brook. The water was ice cold and he felt searing pain in his ankle. He knew immediately that it was twisted.

Cursing in fear and frustration, he limped downstream, trying to keep due west, although his situation made all paths seem murky. If the attacker still pursued him, the water might throw off his scent, and it was all he could hope for. Dustan had no idea what followed, and didn't want to know. He wondered if Rigel had somehow known the identity of their antagonist because of his strange reaction. The old trapper knew a lot about the surrounding wilder land and its legends.

Dustan shuddered from the horror and cold. He fell into the stream several times, bruised and weary. He needed to rest, so he collapsed under a willow tree, its gnarled roots sprawling down a bank and offering shelter from any prying eyes. The trapper pushed himself as far back as he was able and huddled there, regaining his breath and wits. The last hour had been a harrowing experience, and Dustan was convinced that he'd only narrowly escaped Rigel's fate. All around him, the forest was silent. There seemed to be a genuine lack of insect and animal noises, which was unusual. He could hear his own heart beating—methodical, and heavy in his chest.

Dustan heard something then...

His head lifted, and he stared upstream. It was unmistakable—something was coming. It seemed that the hunter had not abandoned its prey after all. Indecision gripped the man. He was in no shape to continue the race. His ankle was unsteady, and if he needed to sprint, the end of the chase would be certain.

Dustan waited, not daring to breathe.

Something large approached, footsteps crashing down on brambles and rocks, snapping branches and kicking dirt. Hearing the commotion only made Dustan more afraid. The hunter made no effort to even hide its coming. A low snuffling came from nearby, as of a predatory animal in pursuit of fresh meat.

Dustan willed his teeth to cease chattering, the sound magnified in his ears. The trapper wished he possessed the power to sink into the dirt behind him, disappear with the worms and grubs. Suddenly, a huge shadow appeared from the bend of the stream. Dustan could make out a dim form through the interlacing roots of the willow tree. His blood froze.

It was a creature like he'd never imagined, monstrous in size. Well over twice the height of a tall man, it lumbered forward with one arm hanging low, swinging it like the limb of an ape. In the other arm it carried a long club tipped with cruel spikes. An animal skin covered most of the brute's body, and now the head came into view.

A living nightmare.

Wicked eyes glared from side to side as the grotesque head searched for the hidden prey, nostrils flaring, trying to pick up the scent. Tusks protruded from a drooling mouth which had recently feasted on flesh, and now craved for more. Old stories and fables swam through the maelstrom of Dustan's head. Dark tales of the evil inhabitants that roamed the wild lands. And here was one scant feet away from him, death held in its foul grip.

It was an ogre.

His fear overwhelmed him. The ogres were extremely rare, but few legends spoke of a more dangerous and horrific creature that walked the world. Possessing the strength of a score of men, they were cunning and relentless, fearing nothing, and now Dustan was being stalked by such a monster.

The ogre trudged along the far side of the creek, nearly opposite from Dustan's hiding spot. The trapper braced for the crucial moment when the ogre would be across from him. It continued, taking great strides forward. The creature splashed water as the large feet stomped into the stream bed. It was now directly opposite the terrified trapper.

Dustan didn't breathe.

But the ogre never stopped moving, instead shuffled along, sniffing the air every few moments. When it was over a dozen yards past the willow tree, it slowed, then stopped completely. The scent was confused. The monster's head made a circle, sweeping the surroundings, the body remaining motionless.

Dustan was drenched in sweat, and his chest felt like it was caught in a vice, squeezing the precious life out of him. When he was certain that the ogre would start back, it suddenly let out a low growl, but then pivoted, continuing downstream. Only when the creature was clearly out of sight and sound did Dustan begin to feel a glimmer of hope.

Luck had been with him, he thought, crawling out from under the bank which had spared him. Fortune for him, at least for the moment. No man could withstand such a beast, and he was no warrior himself.

He scanned the forest. The evil one was gone. Eyes darting madly in every direction, he crept onward, his body shaking from the almost fatal encounter. Dustan headed back upstream, his chapped lips parting in silent rambling as he ignored the numbness of his ankle and the ache in his bones. The trapper's instinct's kept him moving, the body blindly following the silent command to flee from danger.

Instinct was all Dustan had left as his mind swirled in darkening confusion, his logic and intellect consumed by madness.

"A good vintage."

Grundel held up the goblet, smacking his lips in approval. He basked in the warmth of a cheerful fire, watching while Sarion poked the embers with a pair of iron tongs. Two stacks of wood were piled neatly to either side of the hearth. Kettles, roasting spits, and ash buckets were placed in careful arrangement within nooks or sitting on one of the several shelves perched upon the wall. The entire house was simplistic and fundamental in design, and immaculately clean. It was clear that the master of the property was someone who respected order and appearance. A pair of hunting dogs lay nestled on a large throw rug, both of them wagging their brown tails when Sarion spoke or moved.

"It has been a good year for crops and vineyards." Sarion raised his own drink, his face becoming serious. "But let's go back to why you're really here. You're telling me that this token force is all that could be spared from the Royal Armies?"

"For now, this will have to do. Unfortunately, our ranks are stretched out all along the border. The war is pulling in an increasing amount of warriors. If things get any worse, stronger measures will be implemented."

Sarion let out a deep sigh. "A calling of former soldiers, then an outright draft. It's worse than I thought."

"Indeed it is. This is happening already in the east and central parts of the kingdom. Word carries much slower to the borderlands here in the west. But don't be misled...The king has not ignored the rumors and activity, but his attention must be fixed to the closest problem at hand, and quite a large and protracted one at that. And I'm afraid that your problems are not entirely unique."

"Oh?" Sarion raised his eyebrows. "Meaning?"

"Meaning... that other parts of the western border have complained also, of infringing raiders, marauders in the night. The king fears that something else may be brewing."

"These are ill tidings," replied Sarion thoughtfully. "The king cannot afford too many distractions from the war in the east."

"Exactly. So that is why I need your help. Not only in this excursion, but to perhaps offer you a place in the Guard itself. Your actions have not been forgotten."

Sarion pushed himself away from the table. He looked at the stone walls of his kitchen, soaking in the warmth and security. Home. He'd never asked for more. Never desired anything else besides a roof over his head and his household, peace for the country folk. Simple hopes for common men. And now everything was in jeopardy of being lost to him. The dark clouds of war and death threatened everyone within Trencit, and could eventually find them all, to the most secluded hamlet or small farm, over hill and dale.

He clicked his teeth. "Edward would be devastated. He's already lost his parents to marauders—I'm the only family he has left." His voice was sad, knowing that his nephew would bravely accept the circumstances, although the boy's proud face would conceal his pain, his eyes would speak the truth. Inside he would be certainly be crushed.

The captain leaned forward in his chair. "I'm terribly sorry about all that, but it's not an unfamiliar tale. You must act for his future, and the kingdom's as well. We all have much to lose. I have family back east, and haven't seen my wife and children for close to a year."

Sarion stared into the captain's eyes, seeing the anguish held tightly. He nodded to Grundel. "A bitter fate, the life of a warrior."

Grundel followed quickly. "But one that I readily accept, knowing that I fight for the freedom of friend and kinsman."

Sarion paced along the floor, absently scratching the head of one of the hounds. "Well spoken, captain. But tell me, what of the king's right arm? They say that General Charadan has had great victories over the invaders, and as long as he remains leading the armies, the king will never be defeated. Even in the west, his name is golden. The people have great admiration for the champion of the land."

Grundel rubbed his callused hands together. "Yes, the people follow his leadership. Hopefully, he can hold courage together and find the means to bring final victory to Trencit. But who can truly know? The enemy is devious, and deter-mined. The challenge monumental."

Sarion knelt to the floor as the other dog fawned for at-tention. He stroked its head. "They say he is always at the heaviest point of fighting, remaining in the field. Without his charisma, the leadership would be greatly diminished." Sar-ion rose, and sat down again, slumping into a wooden chair.

"Then let us hope that fortune stays with him." Grundel looked down at his drink, gazing more into himself than the sweet liquid.

Sarion rubbed his eyes and spoke, his voice laced with resignation and sadness. "All right, tomorrow it is. You can rest in my chamber tonight, captain. I will be up late making arrangements for the servants. There is a lot of work needed before the harvest, and Edward will not take this lightly."

Grundel waved him off. "That is unnecessary—I'll lodge in the barn with my men. There will be many nights ahead in the country, and a comforting bed takes the edge from the discipline that we are used to."

"Good night, captain Grundel. I have to talk with my nephew."

Sarion walked away, his heart flooded with emotions as he went to Edward's bedroom.

⁘

Edward sat at a small mahogany table in the corner of the room. His eyes were moist, thinking about the company of men and what they were asking of Sarion. A light rapping struck against his door, followed by the tall form of his uncle.

"How do you feel? You heard what the captain said, about the need of our people. I'm sorry."

There was little else he could say. The boy was exceptionally bright for his age—too bright at times, yet so young and fragile. Sarion tousled Edward's hair, his stomach feeling empty inside.

"I know. There is so much danger in the world, Sarion. And especially the Lowlands." He shuddered. "You've always told me about the evil that lives there, and now you have to go. Is there no other way?"

Sarion gently shook his head. "I'm sorry."

The boy looked down. "Please...be careful."

Sarion sat down next to him. "You know I will. Don't forget, I've been there before, and know better than to become careless. Here, look at me."

Edward turned around, staring at Sarion with deep green eyes.

"I'll return—I promise. Do you believe me?"

The boy hesitated, then nodded his head.

Sarion knelt in front of his nephew. "As you get older, you'll learn that difficult decisions confront us at every turn, and you never know when the unexpected will happen. A man needs to be prepared, and make sacrifices for others who might not be able to fight back the darkness. I go, but to protect our village, and all the other towns and cities. A war is being fought in the east. Right now there are brave men dying somewhere, alone in the night, to protect us. It's time to help them out, too. They deserve it."

"I will practice my weaponry twice as much when you leave."

Sarion smiled. You'll be the best someday, lad. You're already a match for the older boys. Let's get some sleep. We'll both have our hands full in the days to come. I'm relying on you to help out on the farm, and Jergen will need you while I'm gone. And remember, after every night the dawn never fails to arrive. You must always hope." He raised himself up. "Good night, I'll see you off in the morning."

He kissed the boy on the head and slowly walked out.

Edward stared after him.

"When I grow up, I want to be just like you, Sarion. Just like you."

The boy's voice was a whisper, but Sarion heard it after closing the bedroom door.

A tear trickled down his eye.

It was late morning, and the company rode down a dirt track leading away from the border village of Gristor, stopping for fresh supplies. Members of the king's guard had the right to take what they needed, but were not allowed to abuse the privilege. The villagers spoke grimly of outlying homes and farms being ransacked, with demons roaming the countryside at night. A few households had already been abandoned as families relocated to more populated regions deeper within the kingdom, although most would stay, defending their homesteads if necessary. These were stalwart folk, and not easily moved from their lands. Many had lived here for generations, and nothing would change that.

Throughout the trek, Grundel conferred with Sarion concerning the geography of the area. The rolling farmland soon gave way to forested hills and valleys. They were approaching an uninhabited country where trappers and hunters made their livelihood, but hesitated on venturing too far into the west, and less hospitable lands. The captain rode with the former soldier, explaining the current strategies being waged in the east. Several other patrols had been sent to the western frontier, and a campaign was underway to enlist more men for the Western Watch. Some of the unused outposts were to be reoccupied in the coming weeks as well—if they could find the men to occupy them.

"So King Gregor has definitely noticed the unrest." Sarion steered his mount away from a pit in the road.

"Let's just say that his eyes are focused on the war, but his ears listen to all points of the kingdom," answered Grundel.

"That brings some comfort, then. The king is a good man, and the people revere him even this far from Daregil Keep." Sarion paused. "I also think it would be a good idea to send scouts ahead from now on...to make sure nothing catches us off guard," he added.

"We're still within the confines of Trencit here. Do you anticipate trouble already?" The captain peered into the surrounding countryside, his keen eyes missing nothing. Birds sang in the trees and small woodland creatures scurried away from the armed company. A narrow brook tumbled quietly to their left, high reeds thirstily drinking in the moisture.

Sarion adjusted his belt. "There have been many strange tales coming out from this territory. I don't know what to expect anymore. Haven't traveled here recently. I roamed the entire westland in past years, and there is much to see. But when skirting the eaves of the Ridgeline, nothing is certain."

The captain nodded, scanning the rough woods which were now becoming denser. He gave a quick whistle signaling a pause, and went to the front of the party. Jumping off his horse, Sarion grabbed a leather water sack from his saddle to quench his thirst. His broadsword rattled at his side. Despite being out of the Western Watch for nearly seven years, he'd honed his fighting skills, working on new techniques constantly. Practicing every day, he was quicker than a cat with both blade and dagger. A long knife was strapped beneath his jerkin, and he kept the weapon there even while working on the farm. A warrior's instincts never left you, he knew. His skill with the bow was unrivaled. Sarion was a weapons master in every sense of the word, and had quickly risen through the ranks in his previous service to the land.

He watched as Rundin walked over, giving him a curt nod.

"Please forgive my tone when we met, Sarion. My cynicism grows deeper with age." He stroked his beard while holding a stick of smoked meat in the other hand. "Care for a bite?"

"Thanks, on both counts." Sarion tasted the offering, the saltiness giving rise to his thirst once more.

Rundin grinned. "Strong, isn't it? Gives one sustenance on the battlefront."

"Have you seen much fighting?" Sarion chewed on the morsel, watching as Grundel sent two men on ahead.

"A lifetime's worth, I'm afraid. Too many friends and comrades have fallen to the Devlents. There is no respite on the front, only intervals of give and take, with neither side intent on making any major undertaking. There is talk that our enemies have enlisted the aid of others, but as yet there is no sign of this."

"That would surely set the scales in their balance."

"Aye," replied Rundin. "And that is the king's greatest fear. The unrest in the west is a cause of much concern. Our country is vast, but flesh and bone have their limits."

The afternoon sun slipped behind a cloud, and the bright day swiftly grew gloomy. Sarion looked at the quiet country around them. It seemed hard to believe that a war was being fought on the far corner of Trencit. A world away.

"Tell me, though," said Rundin. "What are the dangers of the land we ride into? You guessed right yesterday. I was born in the east, and the enemy is readily seen there. But here..."

Sarion's face was grim. "It's the exact opposite in these lands." He pointed to the encroaching hills. "One needs to be wary of the unknown. A peaceful forest by day can be transformed into a hostile environment at dusk, prowled by creatures born from nightmares. There may be bands of Glefins yet, although none have been seen in the seven years since my company tracked the last group. But other, much greater horrors dwell in the west."

"Can you give them names?" Rundin pursued his questioning. "At least what can we look for?"

"It is not so much that we saw many other creatures, but the signs were there. Glimpses, tracks, noises." His words were ominous, and Rundin leaned closer to the man.

Sarion's eyes drifted down roads of dark memories. He stared at the warriors, some of them resting, others milling about. A guard was already in place as well. He continued. "The howling at night. Decayed bones, footprints left by unknown animals. Even strange plants with a taste for living creatures. It's like another world, and I have only set foot within the edge of the Grammore Lowlands, where not even the bravest trapper would dare go. You'll see it, feel the life there. And the hostility. It's almost as if our two lands are separated by an invisible veil. Chaos and death rule there. No help is to be found. Hopefully our path will not lead us into that terrible country. The creatures of the Lowlands feed on fear and weakness. We must offer them neither, and need to maintain our vigilance."

Rundin crinkled his eyes, pondering Sarion's words.

"And so we will, my friend. So we will."

The afternoon passed uneventfully. Long shadows stretched outward from the hills that thrust up before them, and the air grew chill. Grundel had sent two men to scout the way, and periodically he would send out another pair to relieve them, coordinating the timing and location. The idea was to keep abreast of any lurking dangers on the road ahead, and to look for signs of potential trouble.

They had seen a handful of trappers all day—most unusual for this part of the country. The men were surprised to see the king's warriors, but readily offered what information they could. All were nervous, and spoke of demons walking the forests at night. Even the sight of an armed company of the king's guard did nothing to ease their worries. The trappers were all seeking safer grounds to work. Hawker Peak now loomed in the distance, and the road had turned into little more than a narrow trail as the trees pressed closer. Grundel had Sarion ride next to him, inquiring as to a suitable campsite.

"There are cabins scattered all about these woods—we should come across one before nightfall. Normally a safe land, although it does lay close to the shadow of Grammore."

Grundel seemed satisfied by the answer and rode on silently, the men following the lead of two warriors, Chertron and Halgur. Chertron was quiet, but had kind eyes, sharp as an eagle's. Tall and lean, the man was a proven woodsman. Halgur looked similar to Rundin, with a red beard but smaller in size, although still a large man.

Sarion did not recognize all the soldiers' names yet, catching snatches here and there. Tarral was the oldest, his weathered face criss-crossed by numerous scars, his voice low and penetrating, as if speaking from a well. Cerestin was clean-shaven, with bright, humorous eyes, quick to laugh or lend a hand. He wore a silver helm, marked by several dents. Another was Areck, tall and lean, with light blond hair, cropped short for battle. His hand was always fingering the hilt of his sword, anticipating danger at every corner. Sarion failed to catch the names of the others. He concentrated on the land around him, trying to maintain his bearings and recall the terrain. Years had passed since he'd last entered the region, but nothing had changed. The going was smooth, despite the road narrowing. Sunset was soon upon them and the scouts returned, reporting immediately to Grundel. A mile ahead was a small cabin, unoccupied, they said. The men could stay there for the night. The group hastened as Grundel ordered a swifter pace, and the company reached the cabin shortly.

A wooden building sat beneath the branches of a tremendous oak tree. The ring of a fire pit lay in front of the structure, consisting of a circle of round stones. A single door led inside, with two windows on separate walls. The captain gave orders to set up camp, and the warriors immediately went to work. Two instantly patrolled the rim, while others gathered kindling or saw to the horses.

Sarion observed the fighters going about their tasks. There was no lack of discipline in the group, he thought. The king's guard had not grown lax in the years since his own departure. Grundel's commands were never questioned, the men's loyalty strong. He was a genuine leader. But Sarion had realized this when they'd first met.

It wasn't long before a warm fire had been started, and a light meal was broken out. They would certainly not lack for food in the area. Sarion knew of the ample game and edible fruit. Beyond Hawker Peak it would be different. Anything on two legs was considered prey, themselves included.

Sarion retired inside with Grundel and several of the soldiers. Rundin and another took first watch. The floor of the cabin was solid, the timber fairly new. A basic trapper's lodge, providing warmth and shelter. Sarion eyed the room cautiously, his natural instinct for danger always present. He turned his head to the center of the chamber, but surprised the company when he whipped his sword out from its sheath in a blinding flash.

The men were startled, some grabbing for their own weapons, but Grundel held up his hand.

"What is it, Sarion," he hissed?

The tracker crouched like a cat, pointing to the far corner of the cabin.

"There's a trap door in the floor." Everyone followed his gaze.

"And something's down there."

⌣∵∾

Gesturing with a curt nod, the captain sent Chertron over to the trap door. The other men took postures bracing for quick action, with weapons held ready. Another soldier, who Sarion now knew as Kalen, moved opposite Chertron. Kalen's dour face never showed any emotion Sarion had noticed since the trek started. He was middle aged, with a shock of black hair and trimmed beard. The two men locked stares, and Kalen lifted the seam of a carpet which concealed the wood flooring beneath.

A metal rung revealed the hidden enclosure, and Kalen grabbed it with strong hands. The pair glanced over at Grundel, who signaled them for action. As Kalen lifted, Chertron pointed a sword, guarding his comrade from potential violence.

Sarion detected a gentle rustling. Whatever lurked below made little effort to hide its presence. Kalen flung open the trap door, and another soldier held a lantern next to his shoulder to penetrate the darkness. There was a short gasp, and a voice trembled from the compartment.

"Please, I mean you no harm, don't hurt me."

The warriors poked their weapons at the head of a disheveled man, who looked more like a drowned rat than anything else. It was difficult to judge his age, and his garb was in the traditional brown of a trapper.

"Who are you, and why do you hide? We are the king's guard—come out at once." Chertron waited for an answer to his command, but the man was reluctant.

"You don't know, the danger...the horror." His voice drifted off, his hands held to the side of his head, waving at nothing.

"If you are a citizen of the land, then there is nothing to fear from us." Grundel came forward, measuring the man with his gaze. "I am Captain Grundel, of the home guard. Why do you hide? From us?"

The man crawled out, and Kalen lent him a wary hand. Sarion knew that the soldiers took no chances—a sign of the seasoned vigilance of fighting men. His own blade remained within his grasp.

"My name is Dustan, I'm a trapper. There is a great evil in these woods." His voice was a whisper. "Rigel was right..."

He covered his face with hands marked by scratches. "Rigel, poor Rigel."

Chertron offered the man some water and a wafer of bread. "What do you mean? Speak more of this."

The trapper was ravenous, consuming the nourishment. He had obviously been through a black time, and his eyes were wide and feverish.

"Leave, we must leave." Dustan stared at the cabin entrance. "It's getting dark."

A chill went down Sarion's spine. It was almost night, and the surrounding forest took on a more threatening aspect as the sun departed. The land was being terrorized by something. Had this man seen it?

"What is it you fear? You are safe with us." Sarion crouched down next to Dustan, who now huddled in the far corner of the cabin.

"I will not speak of it! Rigel knew. He knew!"

Chertron threw a blanket over the trapper, who closed his eyes and shivered. "Captain, this man has a fever on his brow. Sick, of mind, and maybe spirit as well. He could be delirious."

Sarion drew close to Grundel. "He saw something terrible, perhaps what we now seek. The horror is etched into his eyes and his heart. Something deadly walks these woods."

"Yes, and he looks to be of little help to us at the moment. I can't leave him alone in such condition, or take him with us."

"Can you send him back with someone?"

Grundel frowned. "My mission restricts choices in such a matter. We are a small group to begin with, and I have great reluctance in breaking up the party in hostile areas, especially with an unknown enemy nearby. We have no knowledge of this threat, and I fear we will know only when faced by it.

We'll let him rest for a while, and hope that he calms down."
Grundel walked over to Dustan.

Sarion considered the captain's words, trying to work out a satisfactory plan himself. It was a day's ride to the nearest village, and that would set them back twice as long waiting for someone's return. And Sarion had the feeling that time was pressing down on them, and events could unravel quickly, although there was no justification for his grim thought.

But then again, Sarion had survived on his instincts in the past. Instinct had saved his life before. He paced around the cabin, perusing the scant furnishings. Such buildings dotted the woodlands, serving as resting spots for trappers or travelers passing by. Since the area was considered a border region, no one could stake an actual claim to the property. It was a courtesy to share the modest lodges, regardless of who originally built the structure. Most of them had existed for decades. In one of the corners, several high-backed chairs surrounded a long wooden table marred by cuts, and Sarion settled into one. The warriors spoke quietly, some among themselves, others to Grundel and Dustan. Seating himself, he wondering about the trapper's unusual demeanor, curious as to what he'd encountered. He knew with deadly certainty that it was something fierce, native to a much more hostile country. They were too close to Grammore and its horrors.

Without warning a harsh cry of alarm sounded from outside the cabin. Sarion immediately sprang up, and the warriors diverted their attention from Dustan to the cabin entrance. Grundel barked out orders as all but one of the fighters ran to the entryway. Sarion followed the captain's tall figure, both men eager to see what was afoot. As Sarion burst from the door, he saw the fire blazing hungrily upwards, sparks flying like miniature comets. Several stakes had been set all around the immediate perimeter as the warriors took nothing to chance. They knew the country was unfriendly and were ready for anything.

The horses were tethered at a low bar fronting the cabin, and were now kicking hysterically. Rundin and another fighter had taken positions near the edge of the forest and were staring intently into the dark recesses. The animals possessed keener senses than their human masters, and the warriors were wise enough to take heed. Sarion felt a shiver snake down his back. The evening was deathly quiet—even the night insects seemed to have forsaken the clearing.

"What is it?" Grundel shouted over to Rundin, who stood motionless, eyes scanning the tree line.

The fighter's voice was low, barely more than a whisper. "Something is out there. A wild beast perhaps. I've never seen the horses this troubled, captain."

The warriors spread out in the clearing, posturing for maneuverability and position. Sarion listened with straining ears, but the forest revealed nothing. And that struck a warning nerve in his mind.

"The woods have grown silent. Rundin is right—we are being stalked."

Chertron was nearest to Sarion, and he pulled out a great longbow which was strapped to his back. "Whatever manner of creature is out there, my arrows will make it think twice. Just give me a target, and I'll teach it the meaning of pain."

Sarion hefted his own, holding it ready. With the force of men guarding the edge of the clearing, he would be of greater use sending shafts at any attacker, he knew. The horses became increasingly agitated, and one of the fighters stood nearby to protect them. They couldn't afford to lose their mounts. Grundel crouched behind the foremost men, stooping low to the ground. Sarion watched the captain's face for any expression, but the man remained unreadable. He held up a hand for silence. The tension was maddening, and Sarion felt his heart beating excitedly within his chest. Inwardly he was calm, though, focused on his surroundings. His eyes sharp, his weapon ready. The fighter's instincts were in his blood.

Without any warning, a tremendous blast rang through the forest, shattering the night. It was a war horn, and no one doubted what it signified—a battle cry. Meant to crush the confidence of an enemy. But these men were the pride of Trencit, no common fighters, and would not be easily dismayed.

A yell echoed from the cabin as Dustan peered outwards, hysteria glazed within the trapper's eyes.

"It comes!" He shouted the warning and ran back inside, the terror striking him senseless.

A loud crashing erupted from the trees in front of Rundin, and the warriors watched as a huge shadow appeared, lumbering purposely forward. No one spoke as the creature moved closer, and several heads shook in disbelief at the monstrous size of the hunter. The fighters were used to combating other men—they were not prepared for the sight of such a nightmarish enemy. Several oaths were uttered, hands gripping weapons even tighter.

"By the three serpents—what a monster!" Chertron held his bow ready with notched arrow, astonished at the sight of the unexpected assailant.

Sarion had never seen one before, but he knew instantly the nature of what confronted them. An unforgiving brute—

what it lacked for in wit, it made up for by its strength. Cruel, barbaric, and a legendary dweller of the Lowlands.

"Grundel, an ogre! They have the power of twenty men! I don't know what brought it here, but the beast is savage!"

The captain recognized the creature also, and was quickly thinking of a way to battle the monster. The ogre stood at the edge of the clearing and hesitated, holding a large spiked club in one arm.

"Arrows! It must be driven off." Grundel shouted the order for action.

"Have a care, it's going to charge!" Sarion released his shaft as he screamed the warning, and Chertron fired his own arrow.

The singing of bows filled the night and the arrows flitted gracefully towards the beast, Chertron's piercing the ogre's shoulder and Sarion's plunging into the right arm. The creature was furious, roaring in unbridled rage and pain. It loped forward, directly at Rundin.

The clearing swarmed with movement as the warriors sprang into battle.

Rundin knew better than to stand his ground and dove to one side, narrowly escaping the sweep of the brute's club. Two more arrows shot out but Chertron's was well off mark, and Sarion's glanced off the creature's tough hide without effect. One of the warriors slashed at the monster's leg as it ran by, and Grundel screamed out a warning.

The ogre possessed surprising speed and slapped the man a crushing blow with one arm, knocking him hard to the ground. Two other warriors pressed the creature before it could finish the wounded fighter, and Grundel managed to drag the man to safety. The fighting was getting close, and using the arrows would endanger the men. Sarion drew his own weapon and hurried forward.

One of the fighters cut into the ogre's leg, but suffered a kick to the chest as he pulled away too slowly, and crumbled to the ground where he lay unmoving. The ogre dwarfed the warriors in size and strength, shrugging off the few wounds it had received. It swung the club in huge arcs, keeping the men at bay. Sarion saw that it was making a line straight at the horses, which neighed wildly in fear.

Grundel charged the creature from the rear, attempting to create a diversion. Sarion watched in amazement at the lightning speed of the captain's sword. He cut into the monster twice, and the beast bellowed its wrath at the elusive fighter. Chertron found an opening and fired another volley, scoring the ogre's arm once more.

It swung the club in Grundel's direction, then suddenly turned to the left unexpectedly, charging right at Halgur. The brave warrior saw his peril and desperately slashed at the ogre's leg.

The brute brought the club around and Sarion watched as it caught the helpless man wickedly in the side, tossing him into Kalen and knocking both to the ground. Four of the warriors were now down, and at least one was seriously injured. The ogre showed no sign of weariness, howling as the fighters backed away. Sarion faced the mighty creature now, and waved his sword at the enemy, taunting it forward. He needed to gain time for the wounded men to be carried off.

"Watch the club, Sarion! Back off!" Grundel circled the monster from the other side, trying to catch its attention.

The ogre started at Grundel, then swung the club around towards Sarion. Grundel moved closer, thinking that Sarion would be impaled by the blow. Instead, Sarion waited until the last second and dove beneath the deadly spikes, rolling swiftly and sinking his blade deep into the meaty thigh of the ogre, which for the first time felt real pain. Sarion bounded to his feet and scurried away, trying to regain his breath.

"Well done!" Chertron shouted support to Sarion, and the wounded men had been quickly pulled to safety.

"I don't think we can hope to kill the beast, but maybe we can drive it off." Grundel gestured as Chertron and another warrior launched more arrows at the ogre, which seemed to be uncertain. As another round was fired it roared, swinging the club at the nearest man, then lumbered back into the forest, swallowed up by the trees and vanishing into the night.

The fight had lasted scant minutes, but it seemed much longer. Grundel pointed for Rundin and Kalen to guard against the ogre's return, then went to the front of the cabin where Chertron was tending to the wounded men. Sarion came close, and winced at the hard look on Grundel's face. The warrior who had been kicked by the ogre lay still, his eyes closed.

Sarion had not even learned the man's name.

Halgur was covered in a blanket, the fighter groaning in agony. He had suffered deadly wounds from the spiked club, and Sarion knew that the veteran fighter would not be returning to his family. Grundel knelt next to the man, whispering words of comfort in his ear, holding onto his arm. Halgur coughed up blood, but there was nothing the warriors could do for him. Seconds later, he dropped his head back, his body racked by convulsions, and then lay still. The brave warrior was gone.

Grundel moved away, talking to the two others that had been injured, while Chertron wrapped one of them about the ribcage.

"A few broken bones, but I think that is it." Grundel nodded as Chertron finished with the man. Barthuk was the other wounded fighter, as Sarion caught snatches of the man's name. He was fairly young, with several scars on his arms, and some ugly bruises as well. Sarion helped to take the wounded men into the cabin, where they would try to find some much needed rest. He took out a small leather pouch from his pack, handing it to Chertron.

"Give this to the men," he said.

"What do you have here?" The warrior gave him a puzzled look.

"Roots of healing, they will help to ease the pain, and bring them swifter to the forgetful corridors of sleep as well."

"Thank you, Sarion. My heart grieves to see my comrades in such distress." He walked away.

Sarion sat at one of the chairs, and Grundel disappeared for several minutes to check on Rundin. He also wondered what had happened to the trapper. There was no sign of him anywhere. Perhaps he had fled when the ogre attacked. Grundel returned shortly, and approached Sarion, who spoke words which contained little comfort. "I'm sorry about your men, captain."

Grundel's face was impassionate. "They were brave fighters, loyal to Trencit and its people. They gave their life in noble service. The loss strikes me like a blade, but it is a risk we all take. Regardless, the sting of death never dulls."

Sarion nodded sadly, but there was little else to say. He was no stranger to violence and death himself.

Grundel sat down. "The nature of the threat has been revealed. Who would have believed such a monster prowls the very borders of Trencit."

"There can be little doubt as to where it came from—the Lowlands." Sarion's thoughts drifted back in time, to the harrowing expedition against the Glefin's, and the forbidden dark country they'd entered in pursuit of the cruel marauders. "But why would an ogre travel here in search of prey? There is no record of any being seen for hundreds of years, at least according to the royal archives." The captain took off his gloves, rubbing dry hands together.

"You have heard of this creature too, then?" Grundel looked over to his men, where Chertron was keeping an eye on their rest. Some of the other warriors had gone outside.

"There exist many legends of the cursed land, and the borderland folk are ripe with tales for speaking around fires and taverns. Whether the old wives' know more than the common man I can't say, but we have seen enough to learn the truth."

The captain pressed him. "What of our immediate plight, though? Do you think the creature will return?"

"No." Sarion took out his hunting knife, sharpening it with a gray stone. "I think that the ogre did not expect to find such resistance, and will head straight back to its lair. The Grammore Lowlands."

The captain paused before replying. "In the morning we will pursue the creature."

Sarion was startled by Grundel's statement, and raised his eyebrows. "You mean to hunt the ogre?"

"That is my plan."

"A dangerous scheme indeed. Maybe we've managed to drive it away for good."

"My orders are to determine the origin of the intrusions, and to take appropriate action. We have uncovered the nature of one enemy—now we will seek its destruction. And there are too many stories and incidents to blame it all on any single creature, no matter its ferocity." The tone of the man left no doubt in Sarion's mind as to the captain's resolve. Grundel matched his gaze. "I know what you think, but I cannot allow this monster to roam freely on Trencit's borders. We will find a way to destroy it."

Sarion carefully replied. "I mean no offense, but this is a creature unmatched in the experience of your men, or anyone for that matter. A lesser group would have been slaughtered."

The captain lowered his voice. "Your words are true, but that is my order. You are the best tracker in the west, you can follow the beast."

Sarion shrugged. "Yes, the trail will be clear, but isn't this a reckless plan? It is my belief that it travels primarily by night, and will head straight for Grammore."

Grundel rubbed his hand across the table. "Surprise and cunning. I don't think it will expect to be hunted, either. The element of secrecy will be on our side this time." The captain shifted as Rundin entered, having been relieved by another warrior.

Sarion followed his stare. "And just how far do you intend on tracking the ogre?"

Grundel's eyes were steel. "Until we catch up with it. And then we finish it off. I don't know how many of these creatures even exist, but even one is too many for the future safety of our borders."

Frowning, Sarion replied "Our party is diminished, of course. What about the wounded men?"

"Barthuk and Lerion will head back with our fallen comrades, returning to the fortress of Nighton, where you served years ago. It is our main bastion in the west, and word will be sent to King Gregor. Perhaps more fighters will be committed until this threat is vanquished."

For the first time, Sarion wondered whether Grundel knew more than he admitted. He let it go for the moment.

"All right, but it certainly is a hazardous venture ahead of us. The further west we go, the more comfortable our quarry will become. We will be the trespassers—entirely on our own. Help will not be found in this part of the world, and there are a lot of unpleasant creatures living in Grammore. Some far more dangerous than the ogre."

"That is as it may be. Good night, then. I must see to the watch." Grundel stood up.

"I'll help, of course," said Sarion. The captain made a gesture to wave off Sarion's offer, but he insisted. "The next turn, have someone rouse me."

The captain nodded before leaving.

Sarion managed to catch some sleep before being awakened by Kalen, and he gazed into the quiet forest as his mind recalled the country that lay before him, and what manner of evil stalked the night unseen. Memories unbidden whispered to him in the twilight, and terrible visions grappled onto his consciousness despite his efforts to throw them aside...

"Sarion? Trullik and Baren can go no further. The poison seeps through their veins and steals their life away."

Sarion looked across the still marsh, frustration giving way to a feeling of helplessness and anger. What to do? Turn back and let the Glefins escape once more, to return on their own time and ravage his people again? But his orders were firm. They were to pursue their quarry until they were all destroyed, to the last creature. And he couldn't forsake Captain Quelm's party either. They were late for their rendezvous, and Sarion had a growing suspicion that something terrible had happened to the other group. The mission had been disastrous so far. Even on the edge of the Grammore Lowlands, it was clear that they were in a much deadlier situation than their leadership had anticipated. The Foresters had not foreseen the savagery of this country, failed to give any faith to the tales and rumours.

They were true.

As he wrestled with such grim thoughts, he spun around, his hand moving to his weapon as shouts rang out in the night, and something dreadful bellowed its fell call, seeking easy prey in the gathering dusk…

Sarion crouched down, resting on one knee. He sighed, reliving some of the nightmares from his venture into Grammore, a place he never wished to look upon again in his life. And now it appeared that fate had something else in mind for him, and all paths were clouded in uncertainty.

꧁꧂

The next morning dawned cloudy and cool, as the two warriors rode off with the slain men strapped to their horses. There had been no sign of Dustan since the fight with the ogre, so Grundel concluded that he must have run off into the night, his fear overcoming him. No one had seen him leave. And who would hold blame for his actions after what they had seen, and survived?

Sarion led the group of nine with Chertron by his side. The trail was easy to follow as the ogre left large imprints on the moist ground. Drops of blood were visible for several hundred yards, then disappeared. The trees were not dense, and the way was easy on horseback. Leaves lay scattered on the forest floor, and thousands of acorns crunched beneath the feet of their steeds. The air had the bite of morning coolness, but it was not uncomfortable for riding. The company continued after the ogre's trail for the early part of day, stopping only once for a brief pause. Sarion had no trouble tracking the monster, which appeared to be headed due west—directly to Grammore as he had anticipated. As the afternoon waned on, Grundel conferred with Sarion about the landscape ahead.

Sarion tried to describe the region to the best of his memory. "The terrain gradually slopes, as you may have noticed. The trees grow denser, and the undergrowth will become difficult. There's a great ridge at the crest of the forest, and on the other side at its feet is the very edge of the Lowlands. Grasslands mark the area in places, serving as a border against the wilderness itself. We'll reach the ridge by early tomorrow, if nothing unforeseen occurs."

The captain nodded, and Sarion read the unspoken words in the man's eyes. He knew they both shared the same feelings—a sense of foreboding about the approaching land ahead. Anything could happen once they reached the dangerous region.

Evening fell early as high clouds moved in from the west, and the company settled around a rocky hillock for camp. The place offered protection from intruders, with piles of large boulders clumped together and forming a sizable mound. But the structure was unusual, and had not been created by nature—this was clearly evident, and Sarion only shook his head when questioned by Grundel.

"It's very old, and the purpose is a mystery. There are said to be many strange and ancient structures within Grammore and around its borders. The royal archives may even speak of such, the old maps which I've heard about. I haven't seen any sign of recent activity except for the ogre's passing. We draw closer to the creature, but it travels swiftly, fearing nothing in the wild."

They turned their heads at a shout from Kalen, who had scaled the high point of the rocks, and now waved for them to approach. The two men leapt over jagged boulders, amazed by the vastness of the stones. Whatever had placed them here possessed incredible power.

Kalen pointed down, and the pair examined what he'd found. A perfectly round hole opened up from the top of the small hill, and a shaft led into the structure. The opening went right through the rocks. Kalen let out a low whistle, lighting a brand to penetrate the darkness. The bottom was beyond their sight, and could only be guessed at. The men were quiet for several moments, exchanging glances. The captain drew in a short breath, his eyes gleaming with excitement.

"I've seen rough pictures which are liken to this. Yes, the formation is just as described..." He peered downwards, running his hands across the edge. Grundel's voice was low, cautious. "Unless I'm mistaken, this is the abandoned lair of a Killworm."

They men stared at him in silence for long moments, until Sarion responded. "That's incredible. They were said to exist over a thousand years ago." Sarion recalled hearing tales of the ominous and deadly creatures in the past, and he felt a slight shiver that this could possibly be the ancient lair of such a monster, which existed only in legend.

"How do you know that it's abandoned? Kalen backed away from the opening, looking nervously around. He fingered his weapon.

"Well, for one thing, the ogre passed by here," replied Sarion.

"And if the Killworm was alive, the ogre would have long been dead. With us to keep it company within the creature's lair," added the captain.

"What manner of creature is this Killworm?" Kalen dipped the torch lower, revealing nothing.

"Was the Killworm," answered Grundel. "Long thought to be extinct—if it ever actually existed—it was said to have possessed the form of a great, sinuous spider, able to secrete a vitriolic acid that could bore through living rock. It would lay in wait for victims, hearing anything that moved for hundreds of yards in every direction. It then spun a network of webs, snaring the hapless man or animal that walked within sight of its lair. Even the webs were coated with some type of chemical, causing drowsiness. The Killworm liked fresh meat, and the unfortunate victims were dragged below, still alive, to await the hunger of the monster."

Kalen shuddered. "That's ghastly, to suffer such a horrible fate. But how were the rocks moved here then—by the beast?"

"No. The tale goes that an ancient race of giants used to dominate many parts of the region, and they placed the creatures at strategic points, guarding the borders of their homelands, thought to be Grammore."

"I've never heard the full story before," said Sarion.

"You haven't gained access to the royal archives either, my friend." Grundel clapped him on the shoulder. "But this find here is of immense historical importance, confirming the old scripts, if it is indeed such a den. It was also said that great treasures could be found within the lairs, gathered from the countless victims."

Both Kalen and Sarion stared at the tall captain as he continued.

"And I mean to go down there."

꧁꧂

"You're serious? Down into that hole?" Sarion gazed at Grundel in disbelief as the captain nodded.

"Kalen, I will need several lengths of rope, and some more torches. Alert Rundin as to my undertaking, and let Chertron know as well." The warrior bounded off.

"Are you sure you want to do this?"

"We know the Killworm is long gone, so there is no real danger that I can think of. I'm fascinated as to what may be down there."

"Maybe something else lives down there now."

Grundel shrugged, but said nothing.

"How deep do you think the hole is?" Sarion peered downward, a growing uneasiness creeping into his heart. The thought of descending into the lair of such a creature—dead or not—was unnerving, and a risk not worth taking, even for the chance of precious gems.

"No one recorded that detail. Anyone who ever saw a Killworm never lived to report it." Grundel's words had a profound effect on Sarion, as he visualized the horror of such a monster. The Grammore Lowlands were steeped in legends of countless mysterious creatures and their terrible habits— and appetites.

Sarion stared into the opening. "The Lowlands have always been extremely dangerous. Who knows what still dwells there yet? We spotted some of the lesser creatures seven years ago. It was to our fortune that the deadlier predators did not come across our trail, or I wouldn't be standing here right now…But what we did encounter was enough to decimate our ranks. I left behind many nearly all of my comrades."

"That may be true," replied Grundel. "How far from here did you enter the region?"

Sarion looked to the north, then pointed. "I would say a few dozen miles from where we now stand, although my recollection is clouded. The ridge was fairly steep, and we ventured inside only a mile or so. The Glefins fell prey themselves to something shortly after going in as well, despite being native to the Lowlands. Lucky for us that half their party was killed by the time we met up with them. We found out too late that they were being pursued, and they determined us to be the lesser threat. What does that tell you?"

"Too much, and not enough at the same time." Grundel turned as Kalen came toward them, followed by Rundin.

"Captain, is this true what Kalen has told me?" The warriors placed their supplies onto the rocks, and Rundin gave Grundel a hard look, his bristling beard not lending any softness to his stern face.

"Yes, and I need you and Kalen to support the rope. I'd rather not be trapped in the lair. Tie three lengths together—make the knots strong. I'll take several torches along."

The men obeyed and Sarion gazed across the landscape, the moon climbing high overhead, the white radiance complimented by the distant fires of a billion stars.

"I think it would be best if I accompanied you down there." Sarion stared at the captain for a moment, who actually grinned in return.

"Although I appreciate the offer, it is my idea, thus my risk. I need you to stay here, and if anything happens, they'll come to my aid." Grundel hesitated before continuing. "Or if I find something too dangerous, take the men and leave."

The three men looked at the captain, weighing his words. Sarion was beginning to understand this man better, and he knew the fighters admired him. Grundel demanded respect—he was a man to be trusted. One did not rise to the Homeguard without earning the position. Charismatic and fearless, Captain Grundel was a natural leader. Sarion felt that the loss of his fighters had struck him deeply, but his loyalty to the king was unwavering. He obviously felt that such a discovery called for investigating, and he now took the risk himself instead of setting it upon one of his company.

"Tie the ends fast, under that rock." He pointed to a long boulder, and the men grabbed the rope, pulling it around the one jagged side.

Sarion tossed one of the lighted torches into the hole. Grundel stood beside him and they both watched the glare becoming dimmer and smaller. A few seconds passed and it reached the bottom of the shaft.

"A bit of a drop, but not too deep." Sarion scanned the captain's face for a reaction, but there was none.

"Wish me luck, my friend." Grundel knotted one end to his waist, grasping onto the sturdy coils with gloved hands. "All right, lower me slowly."

Rundin and Kalen obeyed his orders, and the captain entered the shaft, holding a lantern with one arm. The two warriors eased him down, and Sarion watched Grundel's shrinking form, the illuminating lantern emitting a ghostly light as he descended.

⌣∶∾

The shaft was smooth, and Grundel was amazed at the perfection of the hole. There were no flaws visible in the sides of the circular tunnel, or rocks jutting out. The captain looked up and saw the top of Sarion's head as he peered down at him, and then he disappeared entirely. Light now flickered beneath his feet from the brand as the bottom drew closer. In a few short moments Grundel reached the floor of the shaft, and he tugged on the rope a few times to let his men know he was all right. He raised the wick on his lantern, dispersing the shadows and revealing a spacious cavern. Objects gleamed dully from the floor of the cave.

They were bones.

Thousands of them.

The entire floor was littered with remains from the Killworm's victims. And judging from the grisly scene before him, there had been countless. They also seemed remarkably well-preserved. Grundel shuddered at the thought, chiding himself for his nervousness. The Killworm was long dead. The bones were most likely preserved by the secretions that the creature used to entrap its prey, and it appeared that the monster had been quite successful.

He moved cautiously through the cave, crouching down as he examined the piles of bone fragments. But what surprised Grundel the most was the variety of skeletons, the majority not even human. He didn't know what species the bones came from, but it pointed to a large selection of creatures, many coming from the Lowlands in all likelihood. They were now at the very edge of their frontiers, in a region where man was the intruder, and unwelcome. A lesson in biology as well as diversity could be learned from examining such specimens, he mused. Grundel continued his search, partly to gain insight about the lair of the legendary Killworm, and also to satisfy his own pangs of curiosity. The cavern stretched away for dozens of yards—it was much larger than he'd first imagined. Bone fragments crunched beneath his feet as he paced about, the sounds making him wince. Even the idea of such a creature living in the hole centuries ago made him feel uneasy.

What a monster it had been.

He walked on, and the ceiling overhead became lower, angling down sharply as it reached the wall. The bones were less thick here, and Grundel noticed another tunnel ahead. There was a new shaft, this one leading into a different section. He bent down, poking the lantern inside. He couldn't see the end of it. And to go any further meant untying the rope. It took him only a moment to decide, and he loosened the coils holding him tight. Grundel soon had to crawl forward on hands and knees to continue.

The tunnel was musty and damp. He wondered if it led to the former resting area of the creature. It occurred to him that he might be the first person to ever venture inside the lair of a Killworm—a dead one, of course. It stretched on for over a dozen yards, and then the sides fell away, the cavern mouth yawning open.

Grundel's eyes widened in shock.

Reflecting off his light were piles of gleaming objects. Gold and metal trinkets were scattered about. The treasures of the Killworm's victims. All the discarded belongings of the unfortunate creatures had been dragged into this chamber, being of no use to the Killworm. The captain stepped forward, examining the assortment of items. Old coins, helms, shields, and armor were pushed into a pile against the wall. Artifacts of a long-lost age. Etched into the weapons were strange designs, unfamiliar to him. One shield had a serpent coiled about a tree, another was square, carvings of an ancient language emblazoned on the front. Grundel eyed the objects, marveling at their unknown origin.

Another item caught his eye. It was a small obsidian rod, the top ending in a red orb. For a moment, he thought the orb flickered with energy, the depths coming to life, but it happened so quick that he couldn't be sure if it was his imagination. He picked up the shaft, expecting it to be cold to the touch. To Grundel's surprise, the rod felt warm in his hands, despite the thickness of his leather gloves. It appeared to be something of some value, but as to what purpose it served he could only wonder. As he stuck it into his pouch, he then noticed something else. At the far side of the cavern lay a pile of ebony shards, but they were not skeletal remains. He made his way over to the heap to take a closer look.

It was a large egg.

Cracked apart.

⌁∶∾

"What's taking him so long?"

A worried look creased Rundin's face, and he gently tugged at the rope.

"He reached bottom a while ago, that much we know. Maybe he found something of interest." Sarion offered an explanation, but didn't feel too sure himself. "If he doesn't come back soon, I'll go down after him."

"It's not your place to do that. The captain gave me strict orders to see to your safety, under any circumstances." Rundin gave Sarion a stern but honest look.

The two warriors stared at him, and he was certain of one thing—that all of them wished there would be no need for any of them to go into the shaft and search for the captain.

⌁∶∾

A shudder ran through Grundel's lean form.

An egg!

It was not possible! After all these centuries, and something had yet survived in the lair? He backed up, as quietly as he could, eyes darting for signs of what had been hatched from the egg. There was no telling what manner of creature it might be.

Sword in hand, Grundel looked warily at the tunnel, now dreading the close confines. Whatever had crawled from that egg was very likely down there with him now, perhaps in another offshoot from the main cavern. He again crept into the tunnel, silently wishing that nothing would surprise him. He managed to gain the main cavern after a few harrowing moments, and he retraced his earlier progress, wincing at every crack of an old bone fragment as he spotted the line.

The captain hurried to tie the rope again, placing it firmly about his waist. His mind raced wildly. What had been born from that egg? Another form of predator maybe? It was certainly conceivable. Some other creature might have found the lair to its liking, and now lived there, finding it an ideal location. An extremely unpleasant thought...Grundel cursed himself for ignoring such a possibility.

Grundel approached the torch, the flame still giving off a smoky glow. He watched the curls of vapor drifting upwards, ready to ascend, when he stopped in his tracks...

Beneath a pile of bones lay a long figure, his boot almost touching the motionless body. He held his breath, staring at what rested before him, shrieking inwardly at what he'd nearly stepped on. And Grundel had no doubt as to what the result would have been.

A long, sinuous creature lay in slumber, several sets of legs attached to its side, each appendage ending in massive talons. Two feelers fronted a bulbous, hideous head. Curved pinchers rested below a pair of eyes, protruding on short stalks. Pieces of shell clung to the creature's hairy body, which pulsed in a steady pattern of deep breathing. Grundel had never seen a picture of one before, but he recognized it instantly.

It was a Killworm...

A Killworm!

Alive, and recently hatched. A baby. And the size of it already.

How had he not seen it before? Did it just come out from another hidden chamber? Maybe the creature heard his movements, and came to investigate, still tired from its infancy.

Grundel didn't have an answer, knowing only that he must somehow get by the sleeping monster. He stared down at the certain death that waited before him, debating his course of action. For one rash moment he considered trying to kill it, slicing into its head with his sword, but he quickly banished the thought. There was no way of gauging the strength of the creature's hide, which appeared to be tightly scaled, a natural form of armor. And he remembered the legends about the monster, although many of them were most likely half-truths or fancy, concerning the creature's strength. It was said to be magical in nature, unable to be killed with steel or fire. Fables or not, he didn't want to test their merit. Scarcely daring to breathe, Grundel moved around the young Killworm, treading lightly on fragments, each step sending new waves of fear throughout his frame. He hoped the creature was resting deeply, because it was impossible for him to circle without making any noise.

The utter terror that Grundel faced within that lair would have been too much for an ordinary man, who would have broken from the horror and met a gruesome end, but the captain was no ordinary fighter, his training and experience

unsurpassed. Step by tortuous step, the he moved on the tips
of his boots, a cat on two legs, and he crept towards the shaft.
More than once he stopped, breath held, as the creature shifted in its repose. Those were truly frightening moments, and
he feared the end several times. He felt a cough rising in his
chest and he nearly choked on his own wind.

Grundel never took his eyes off the monster, and he'd already decided to strike at the Killworm's head if it indeed
roused from sleep. Grundel believed he might be able to get
one jab at the beast, and perhaps not even that. There was
also no way to judge the Killworm's speed.

He tried to will himself into his surroundings, every fiber
of his body focused on silencing his movement. Despite the
frailty of his situation, he finally managed to reach the torch,
pulling at the rope and taking the dwindling flare with him.
Immediately he felt himself being hoisted upwards, and the
ground fled below him. Grundel's feet passed through the
narrowing shaft, and as he moved higher, a sound caught his
ear that froze the very blood in his veins.

There came a soft rustling from the lair. Had the Killworm awakened?

He was pulled up soundlessly, and couldn't dare risk calling out. If the creature suspected that its lair had been invad-
ed, then it would swiftly clamber up the shaft and find him
helplessly exposed.

Time crawled agonizingly by as the captain moved closer
to the surface. Sarion's head appeared above him, and Grundel gestured with his arms, hoping that the man would recognize that something was wrong. The hole opened up, and
the three men pulled him out, seeing the captain's sharp gesture for silence.

Sarion knew that something was dreadfully wrong by Grundel's expression. The captain quickly pointed down to the other warriors, one hand to his lips. Kalen led the way down, and the men carefully picked a path among the strewn boulders. Only when they had reached the bottom did Grundel voice his intentions.

"The horses, swiftly. Gather the men, we leave now. Make no sound." The warriors obeyed wordlessly, and the posted guards were signaled to head into the forest, away from the clearing.

While the fighters grabbed their belongings and hurried off, Grundel gazed back at the top of the hillock, awaiting any indication of movement. With luck, they might yet escape before the creature came to the surface. Most of the men started away, and Sarion returned to Grundel, leading two horses with him.

"What is it?" Sarion hissed to the captain, but the man only shook his head in return.

The company left the grassland, and Rundin's vigilant form waited for the pair to catch up. The sky was cloudless overhead, the moon nearing full splendor as it illuminated the clearing in a radiance of milky brightness. Sarion hazarded a glance behind his shoulder, his mouth aghast at the movement he saw on top of the rock pile as something large emerged into the night. Grundel noticed the stare, and they urged their mounts forward as a shrill noise broke through the area—a high droning sound.

"Captain, make haste!" Rundin held his hand up, pointing to their former resting area.

The sky over the clearing glinted silver, as the moon glow reflected off strands of vast webbing that issued forth from the creature. The trees were a few yards ahead of them and they kicked their steeds for speed, knowing that death descended from above.

"Hurry!"

Rundin gestured frantically, his own face pale as he realized what was happening. The landscape looked surreal, eerily beautiful as the webbing rained down from the sky, glistening and deadly, falling quietly and clumping onto the ground below. The two men raced desperately forward and their horses bounded into the forest as the strands descended only a few feet behind, narrowly missing them.

Rundin turned his own mount as they finally reached him and all three entered the trees at once, storming into the forest as they escaped the deadly net of the Killworm.

෴

Sarion gazed at the orange glow from the young fire, seated next to Grundel's crouched form as he chafed his hands together, stealing the warmth.

"Fortune smiles on you tonight, captain."

Well over an hour had passed since the near escape from the Killworm. The company had bolted into the forest, not stopping until the captain was convinced they were out of danger. They had no idea if the Killworm would pursue them, but Grundel guessed that it would stay near the lair, especially since it was newborn. Two guards were posted as Sarion and the captain held deep discussion, the other warriors attempting to catch a light sleep. The group had to settle for a treeless stream bed, which offered little protection but gave them a clear view if anything approached.

"Good fortune for all of us, my friend." The captain leaned back, weariness settling into his lean frame.

"Maybe it was a good thing that you searched the lair. The creature might have risen during the night, catching us off guard. It would have certainly been the end." Sarion pulled his cloak around his shoulders, fighting the cool night air.

The captain paused. "A horrible thought, but you may be right. I shudder to even think about it," he replied. "What worries me even more, though, is the fact that such a monster still exists. And outside Grammore yet. After all these centuries?"

Both men stared at the burning embers, and Sarion caught a glimpse of a warrior pacing at the edge of camp, vigilant in the night.

"I'm afraid there is no easy answer to that question, captain. And if there is one still living, then perhaps there are others. You saw only the one egg?"

Grundel nodded, his eyes closing.

"I can't believe the incubation period could last for so many generations. Something is gravely wrong here." Sarion absently brushed against the stubble on his chin, mind grasping at the dark implications that fluttered through his mind like bat wings.

"If we're to believe the ancient records, the Killworm is a long extinct species," said Grundel. "The relic of a dangerous and wild age. Hmm, I wonder what else will be proven false."

Sarion lifted his head up, staring into the sky. "That is my own fear as well. And I have a sinking feeling we'll know a lot more about Grammore before our journey is finished if we fail to reach our quarry in time." He was quiet for a moment. "More than we would ever care to know," he added.

"I'll take the next watch, you should find some rest. There will be little for any of us in the next few days. We should see the Lowlands sometime tomorrow."

Sarion stood, peering westward as his mind wrestled against fears of the unknown, and the threats that awaited them in the days to come.

He knew there would be many.

⚜

The next morning dawned a cheerless and gloomy day, dark rain clouds hovering over the boughs of the forest, brooding and heavy. Routine took over as the fighters quickly packed their belongings and secured their weapons, with the full knowledge that they were entering a fierce and unpredictable wilderness, danger now behind and in front of them. The ogre's trail had been lost to them, and Sarion suggested they cut northward, angling in the direction where he believed the beast was most likely to travel, but admittedly it was only intuition. He hoped to catch the creature before nightfall, if luck was on their side, although he didn't trust to such things. Those who relied on fortune would likely end up in an early grave, especially traveling inside such harsh country.

Sarion rode at the head of the company, the reliable Chertron by his side. The two men scanned the terrain, searching for any movement or traces of the ogre's passing. Sarion took in everything around him, consuming the sights and scents of the region. The instincts of a tracker were highly refined, adding an additional sense to those with mastery. And Sarion was one of the select few bestowed with such talents. He'd worked ceaselessly in his pursuit of learning the art and it had come to fruition at an early age for him, but he never stopped trying to improve. Just like with his practice of weaponry. These were skills that needed constant honing, and despite his relatively quite life on the farm, and he sparred regularly with members of his household and others from the near-by village, although his prowess was unmatched, and many came to him for advice on training, especially those entering the Western Watch.

Conversation was subdued, the fighters still unnerved by the previous night's harrowing escape from the Kill-worm. Gradually, the ground started to rise as they reached the line of hills that stood above the Grammore Lowlands. Sarion pressed the captain for the group to remain quiet and alert as they approached the edge of the increasingly dangerous region. Anything could happen, he told Grundel. And at any given time...

The day crawled on without event, and by early afternoon a chill rain began to fall, dampening their clothes and spirits alike. They brought out their cloaks, hardening themselves against the dismal and unfriendly weather. Upwards the ground rose, steeper and rockier. They took only one brief pause, and Sarion urged the captain for greater speed, know-ing that the ogre was getting closer to its homeland, and the advantage would soon be on its side.

By late afternoon, the rain had progressed into a steady downpour, and it became difficult to see far ahead. The el-evation continued to increase, noticeably higher as the day drew on. Faced with a choice, the company traveled along the higher edge of a heavily wooded gorge, deciding to pick that path over the easier vale below. Grundel rode in the middle of the company, a position from which to exercise the greatest control while affording him the maximum protection, although it was more from the stance of protocol than his personal desire for safety.

Sarion turned around, looking back at Forlern, who rode in front of the captain, his shifty eyes peering at the surrounding thickets. He was the youngest in the company, but had served exceptionally in the recent wars in the east, Grundel had told him. A longbow was strapped to his back, along with a sword, and twin daggers were pouched on each side. His mastery with numerous weapons made the dark haired man a valuable addition to the company, and Sarion recalled the look on Forlern's face when the ogre had attacked. Not surprise, or fear, like the other men, but almost an eagerness for battle, to test his skills. He had been the one assigned to guard the horses while the others fought, but Sarion had read the disappointment in the man's face after the skirmish.

Forlern had craved a fight with the ogre—Sarion was sure of it, and he wondered how such a confrontation would affect the man, when and if it occurred. Self-assurance was one thing, but recklessness had serious consequences for all of them. But still, the fighter possessed an aura of confidence that was striking.

Sarion started, turning his head to the side, and he spoke to Chertron, the company halting behind them. The men quieted their horses without being told. Moments later after conferring with Sarion, Chertron dismounted and approached the captain.

"What is it?" Grundel whispered.

"Sarion heard noises—in the vale below, not far off." The captain's eyes narrowed.

"Our quarry perhaps?"

Chertron looked uncertain as he looked up at the captain. "He heard several cries, but doesn't believe they were human. Some type of beast, he thinks."

"That is certainly reason for concern then. Come with me, I'll share the lead now." Grundel pushed his steed forward, with Chertron in tow.

Sarion had left his own horse and now peered down the brink of a steep ravine, the slope clustered with mixed oak, maple, and tall ash trees. Small rocks were scattered along the cliff, some in large clusters, others jutting out in wicked points. The forest below was hidden as the evening grew darker, and the day would soon be lost in shadows as a premature twilight descended. Heavy drops of rain splattered onto the branches above, and every man was wet and uncomfortable.

"Sarion, what..."

"Listen." Sarion held up a hand. "Down there."

The three men gazed into the vale, at first hearing nothing. Then a short yell pierced the air and Grundel's face turned sharp. Again the noise rang out, a howl of unknown origin echoing mournfully across the shrouded hollow. They all knew it could not possibly have come from any human lung.

"Any idea what that could be?" Grundel dismounted and leaned next to Sarion, searching his face for a telling reaction. "Is it the ogre?"

Several long moments passed, and Sarion stared down the slope. He turned his head about and looked at the two warriors.

"I'm not sure if the ogre is making the noise, because there are several different sources." He paused. "But one thing I do know." Sarion licked his lips.

"They're coming this way."

Grundel was a silent statue, his ears straining for the sound that was sure to come. He soon heard it—several howls, louder than before. A few of the horses nickered softly, restless from the predatory cries. Even if he doubted his own ears, their instincts were not to be ignored.

"Well, we have a decision to make, captain. Wait here, and confront whatever draws near, or go forward and hope to avoid any unnecessary conflict, but with the knowledge that we may be hunted into the night, perhaps attacked later, and in worse circumstances." Sarion angled his head, a brown hood covering most of his face. "Poor choices either way."

The warriors all wore thick cloaks, trying to keep out the relentless downpour. Made from a weather resistant fabric, the outfits proved remarkably reliable against the adverse conditions, and Sarion had been given a spare as well.

Grundel responded swiftly. "We move on, quickly and quietly. There's a good chance that this rain will wash away our scent, and avert attention to our presence. Let's move."

He gestured to the fighters behind him and returned to his own mount. The pace was slow, but they were careful to avoid sending any loose rocks down the ravine. Sarion veered away from the edge itself, but wished to stay close. It would be much easier to defend against an approaching enemy from their superior height. Occasional howls pierced the air as the company rode on, but they didn't appear to be getting any closer. Grundel remained behind Sarion and Chertron, desiring to confer with the tracker. Sarion had proven his fighting and tracking skills in the few short days of the excursion, and already the warriors regarded him with a healthy respect.

After traveling for over a mile, the captain halted the company. After speaking briefly with Sarion he ordered Rundin and Kalen to stay behind, and report on the prowling creatures. It was risky, but he needed to determine if the group was being hunted. The two warriors did not question the order, understanding the rules of the field all too well. They remained on guard, their unmoving figures vigilant to the surrounding forest as the others went forward.

The terrain grew rougher, with dense thickets cropping up between the large trunks. Sarion kept away from the deeper woods, turning the group always back towards the cliff. To their right, the ravine now became treacherous, and a drop of over a hundred feet awaited anyone unlucky enough to fall. But it also shielded them against attack from that direction. Darkness now covered the countryside, and Sarion informed the captain that they were nearing the peak of the ridges that looked over the Grammore Lowlands.

"Our chances are slim of finding the ogre, but I think you know that by now."

Grundel stared ahead, taking in every shape that loomed out of the night. The rain had slowed considerably, and a sluggish mist rolled out from beneath the eaves of the forest.

"There is always the hope of finding our quarry on the other side of these hills, maybe catch it in the open grassland."

"Who can tell?" replied Sarion. "The land slopes steadily downward, behind the ridge line. The Lowlands begin a few miles below as the ground levels out. There the woods thicken, and in many spots becomes marshy. As I said before, we were further to the north, and didn't venture very deep. No one really knows what lurks inside."

"We'll stop soon—I want to give Rundin a chance to catch up."

They continued on for a short march before the captain called for a halt. Three warriors went on immediate guard. One ahead, another behind, and a third man at the edge of the bordering forest. Spirits were low as they hunched down against the weather, anticipating the return of Rundin and Chertron.

Time dragged on and the men failed to arrive. The fighters muttered among themselves, worried about their comrades. Ever since the skirmish with the ogre, and the flight from the Killworm, there had been a subtle change in their collective attitude—they were still confident, strong, and unwavering in their loyalty, but Sarion saw in their eyes what they kept in their hearts—a growing sense of dread. They were on the edge of a wild and unpredictable hinterland, where nightmares walked the earth and held dominion. It was a daunting reality.

But right now Sarion was more concerned himself with the overdue fighters, and he fidgeted with his weapon. He was about to suggest going back to search for them when light voices carried up from the rear. The warriors appeared through the veil of mist.

"Captain, it took us a bit longer than we thought." Rundin leaped off his horse, handing the reins to Forlern, who was in charge of seeing to the steeds when the company rested.

"Are we being followed? Did you hear more from the creatures in the vale?"

Sarion observed the captain, wet and disheveled like the rest of the men, but somehow his stature was never diminished. Regardless of the circumstance, Grundel was always relaxed, and in control. Sarion was well aware of the fact that when the two spoke, the captain would bring out Sarion's true feeling on things, and gauge reactions that were conveyed by him from more than just the obvious words. He tried to read his emotion, and even his unspoken thoughts. And Sarion was also convinced that the captain knew a lot more than what he'd revealed to him. Sarion couldn't quite bring himself to distrust the man, but there would be a time for answers. Maybe soon...He listened to Rundin.

"We waited, and the howls continued, at times seeming to draw closer, then fading away. The valley was silent for a spell, and we decided to head off. Scarcely did we move on when a new sound wailed in the night." Rundin paused, his face ashen.

"A great bellowing erupted from the vale, followed by the most blood-curdling screams I've ever heard. Something met a horrible end down there—of that you can be certain."

Sarion's skin crawled at the warrior's description.

Rundin continued, shaking his head. "My guess is that whatever made the first noises confronted a foe that was far greater. Almost as if a pack of wild creatures was on the hunt, and became the hunted themselves. What do you make of that?"

Sarion answered. "Well, it sounded to me also that some beast, or group, was following prey. And maybe you're right, a stronger creature went after the animals. The Lowlands are beyond the ridge, well within hunting distance of predators. It's not out of the question for such creatures to roam these hills. We've already seen this to be true. And many beasts constantly migrate, looking for new grounds. With Grammore, it happens to be the home of things which are extremely dangerous, and unknown to us living within the confines of civilized regions."

Grundel looked at them both. "I can only consider us fortunate to have stayed higher, as the valley below conceals hidden dangers. It is best to avoid such encounters, although we may not always be so fortunate. We will move further ahead. My wish is to put as much distance between us and the hidden lurkers as possible. See to the men, Rundin."

The warrior nodded, and Sarion felt distinctly uncomfortable with their location.

"You know, captain, we have enemies behind and in front of us now. I had hoped to see the land on the eastern side of the Ridgeline safer than this, at least until we reached Grammore, but that wish has proved false. If larger predators are roaming further into the borderlands, then the ogre might be part of a much larger problem."

"That is my fear also," answered Grundel. "Part of my mission is to look into that possibility, regardless of the hazards. That is why I take certain risks, but you no doubt have guessed that already."

The captain packed his own items, and readied for departure. The company soon proceeded on, the visibility limited to a few yards in all directions. Their pace was laborious at times, but both Sarion and Grundel felt the need to push forward.

After a time, it became apparent that they were near the summit of the hill, and Grundel called for them to make camp. The higher elevation would offer more protection during the night, with the lower valleys more accessible to the nocturnal hunters. Sarion sat on first watch with Forlern, his back to a fallen ash tree. An occasional sound would break the silence, but these were the normal sounds of active beasts. Night insects droned in the distance, and birds piped from hidden branches. These noises comforted him, and he knew they were harmless. It was the unusual cries he listened for, ones which announced the approach of something danger-ous and unknown. Vigilant, Sarion attuned his senses to the dark forest, trying to become one with the night, although his mind tried to drift on its own accord.

A heaviness crept over his heart at the thought of what the next day might bring.

ᴧ.ᴎ

A cheerless dawn greeted the warriors as they broke camp for an early start. The night had proven uneventful. Rundin looked ragged and worn as he walked over to Sarion, who was feeding his horse. "Will the sun smile down on us today, my friend?"

"Not to dim your hopes, but the Grammore Lowlands are as bleak and inhospitable a region as you could ask for." Sari-on grinned at the scowl on the man's face. "Now why should such things bother a stalwart fighter like yourself? Burden-some thoughts hinder the acts of an otherwise strong body."

Rundin appeared puzzled, then he let out a throaty laugh, his face rippling with mirth. Some of the other warriors looked over, Sarion noticing several puzzled smiles on the tough faces.

"You've reminded me of something I'd forgotten, Sarion."

"Oh, and what would that be?" Sarion replied, mirroring the man's sudden merriment.

"Humor, laughter. When one is too long in the field, and far from home, it is easy to become acquainted with grim thoughts. Dark notions blacken a true heart if left unfettered. Remind me if I falter again."

Sarion clapped him on the arm. "You have my word, Rundin. And we will certainly need a lot of mirth in the next few days."

The fighter nodded, his smile lessening, but his eyes remaining bright.

Grundel rode over and gestured to Sarion. "Can you tell me what to expect when we breach the hill?"

"Only the unexpected… If you are asking about the layout, then it is somewhat the same on both sides. Woods, and a gradual descent, until we reach the Grammore Lowlands. There might be a few short miles of grassland, then we are faced with a swampy, dense jungle as the climate turns much warmer. Let us keep our wits close by."

He mounted his steed, and the party started off. They struggled over loose rocks and scrub thickets, and the ravine was behind them as they climbed the hill. The trees were less thick, but the sky overhead churned in turmoil, gray and threatening more rain.

Another hour found them at the peak, and the trees suddenly opened up to a rocky clearing. The company stopped as Grundel and Sarion looked out over the country in front of them. A line of ridges jutted up as far as the eye could see, to the south and north, a natural barrier holding down the vastness of wilderness at their footstep, and below, still several miles away, stretched the forbidding edge of the immense and terrible Grammore Lowlands.

It was an ominous sight.

A dense jungle lay before them, hidden beneath a misty shroud, impenetrable and menacing. The entire westland was encased within gloom and vagueness, and they could only guess at the sprawling size of the immeasurable, hazardous wilderness. The warriors stared in mute silence, the old tales of nightmares awakened from childhood memories in many of their minds, pricking at their vulnerabilities, teasing insinuation. Chertron came forward, eyes glazed over by the awesome, horrifying spectacle below.

"It looks evil—you can almost sense it. The home of nightmares to tell children before bedtime. But it's real, and we're at the doorstep."

Sarion tilted his head in agreement, sharing the man's feeling, and he spoke in low tones. "It's like a huge, black maw, waiting to swallow the unwary. Mysterious and deadly, home to the most fearsome beasts in the world. There is no room for mistake down there—of that you can be absolutely certain. Creatures roam the Lowlands that are unaware men even exist. To most of them we're just another form of prey for the taking. I don't think I need to remind everyone to be alert, for anything and everything. Sight, sound, or even smell down there. Trust nothing—listen to your instincts."

"Let's go." Grundel urged his horse forward, with Sarion directly behind him.

Rundin remained at the rear of the group, and Forlern and Chertron came after the leaders, the former warrior scanning the horizon with a look of quiet suspicion, even trepidation. The horses picked their way down the gentle incline, sending tiny fragments of splintered rocks ahead. They seemed to be the only living things on the hill for most of that morning. The piercing shriek of an occasional hawk would scald the air at times, but no other creature came within sight. Overhead, the thunderclouds slowly drifted eastward, and the prospect of rain soon ended. The sky was sullen, a lofty companion to the forsaken country ahead.

By early afternoon, they had left the line of ridges behind, and the ground leveled off, becoming softer and easier to negotiate. It was a good sign for the men, eager to leave the disquieting hills, but Sarion felt the tension as the day wore on. At times he would speak with Grundel, making small observations as to their location, but the captain said little. Sarion questioned him again on his objective, with the ogre being lost to them, and he answered only that it was still necessary to scout the area.

"But how far into the Lowlands would you have us go? Surely not much past the edge?"

Grundel replied, pausing briefly. "I have my mission—but need to stay alive too, if that's what you are wondering... No purpose is served if we all perish out here." He grinned wryly. "We go in, try to pick up the ogre's trail without becoming entangled too deeply in the wild. Then quickly get out again in one piece."

The company carried on for the remainder of the afternoon, and they eventually entered a shallow ravine, the bottom filled with brush. Sarion hesitated, finding tracks in the light dirt and gesturing to Chertron. He crouched low to the ground, holding back the others with a wave of his hand. Pacing along a narrow stretch, he came across fresh prints.

"Good fortune again. The ogre passed through here—the markings are unmistakable. And not too long ago."

"During the day?" Grundel scanned the far rim of the depression, alert eyes missing nothing. "Look, there's something up ahead." He made a curt gesture, and immediately Forlern and Chertron rode forward, weapons held ready. The pair moved toward a figure that lay crumpled on the ground.

"It's dead."

Forlern prodded at the shape with his sword, his clean-shaven face eyeing the carcass suspiciously, his natural look, and Chertron rode further on, in case of a trap.

"I've never seen such a creature, Captain Grundel." Forlern stared back as they approached, his dark eyes unwavering. "It looks like it was dangerous, before meeting its end."

They joined him, examining the remains. On the ground was a lean creature, the body black and covered in a makeshift hide of some unknown animal. The long arms ended in sharp talons, and the feet were similar to a great cat, furred toes with sharpened claws. The most striking feature was its head, though, with brown tufts of hair, long whiskers surrounding a large mouth filled with wicked incisors, and long oval eyes now permanently closed. Ugly wounds covered its torso.

"I have no idea what manner of creature this is," said Sarion.

"Maybe it is one of the beasts that prowled in the vale last night." Forlern examined the torso of the creature. "Look, deep puncture wounds in the side. Crusted blood. Can't be very old, the vultures have not feasted yet."

"Hmm. It would appear that it met up with our quarry, and formidable as it looks, was no match for the strength of the ogre. Few creatures are." Grundel fingered the hilt of his weapon.

"I think you're right. All the signs show the passing of the ogre, and of a struggle as well. See, broken branches over there, in the bushes. Confused prints. There may have been more of these beasts here also." Sarion pointed at several spots on the ground, and the others nodded.

The captain whistled sharply. "We should make haste. I fear that once in the Lowlands, our chance of overtaking the brute are slim." Grundel agreed with Sarion's remark, and the company left the dead creature behind.

It was becoming evident that Grammore was near. Mist rose from small bogs that now appeared, and the air wafted lazily by, bringing with it the unpleasant stench of old and decaying vegetation. The ground was softening, but not wet. They followed the ogre's trail, and Sarion was confident that it was not far off.

"It could very well be nursing fresh wounds." Chertron's voice drifted up to the two leaders who were intent on the footprints, clearly left in the dirt.

"That might make it even more dangerous. An injured beast is always the most deadly and unpredictable. And desperate." Grundel looked warily ahead, but his companions were silent.

As the company rode on, clumps of trees became thicker, and Sarion mentioned to the captain that the men should avoid speaking unless absolutely necessary. He felt a chill of warning crawl along his spine. Here once more, he thought... After all these years. Black memories reared up in the back of his mind, sinister and powerful. Faces and names. Emotions.

Anguish.

Dispelling the bleak thoughts, Sarion continued. "From higher up, the lowlands are fairly distinct. But along the border, there are numerous copses that protrude from the main forest. We will have to decide as to where we stay for the night. At the edge, or within the Lowlands themselves."

They passed through an overgrown area of tall grasses and directly in front of them appeared a swampy lake, the waters fading away into a deepening mist. Cattails and reeds lined the banks, and unseen bullfrogs croaked eerily in the distance, along with unfamiliar insects. Grundel reined in his horse sharply, holding a gloved hand up for silence.

"Maybe we won't have to," he whispered.

He pointed to the water. A rocky outcropping jutted out into the lake, partially obscured by high weeds. Boulders lay scattered about, offering a natural barrier against the grass itself. Stretched out on the rocks was a huge figure.

They had found the ogre.

᠅

Grundel motioned everyone to back away, and the horses were restless. The air was blowing behind them, the ogre's scent not having reached the sensitive noses of the war horses. Chertron dismounted, flattening in the concealing grass to keep watch. Grundel took no chances, and led the warriors a good distance before calling a halt.

"Over hill, and through treacherous woods, many miles. We have caught up with our prey once more. This time there will be no stalemate."

A humorless smile etched the captain's face, and Sarion read the hurt and anger inside—along with the determination. The loss of the warriors ran deeply through his veins.

"I will tell you now the rest of my orders—our mission."

Sarion's eyes darkened, surprised by the captain's statement. The warriors watched their leader with unquestioning eyes, the only exception being Rundin, who took guard after they'd stopped.

"It's not only for revenge that we have pursued this beast, although it deserves retribution for the loss of our companions. No one here would question that fact."

His gaze never wavered, fixing on Sarion's attentive face.

"King Gregor suspects a growing evil in the west, and many incidents have validated his fears. The marauders, signs of prowling creatures...and I believe the discovery of the Kill-worm was no accident. Something has stirred up the denizens of Grammore, and I was sent to locate the source, even if it means penetrating into the Lowlands themselves. There is a reason that the ogre cannot be permitted to escape."

None of the men showed any hint of doubt. They were loyal to Trencit, and Captain Grundel, to a man.

"It's my belief that the creature is under the power of some other, and is headed there now. If our presence is detected, then we may be faced with enemies too strong for us to overcome. Indeed, if there is a single force behind the unrest, it will seek us out immediately before we return to our homeland. We must not fail."

Sarion stepped forward a pace. "Has the King expressed any opinion as to what is stirring Grammore from slumber? Perhaps the Devlents are responsible?"

Grundel hesitated for a moment, then shook his head.

"No, that is not his belief. He feels it is unrelated, but nevertheless, the consequences could be devastating. The Western Guard has been steadily depleted, with no more warriors replacing the ones called away. This makes our position extremely important to the King."

"And what is your plan for the ogre?" All heads turned towards Forlern, who fidgeted with one of his daggers.

Grundel folded his arms, gesturing for them to move nearer.

"We have it enclosed, and couldn't ask for a more perfect location to assail it. Now is our chance. And this is what we shall do."

⌣∴∾

The ogre lay still, as yet unaware of the encircling company of men, who were quietly plotting its end. Both Grundel and Sarion agreed that once the ogre awoke, events would become chaotic. There was no margin for error against such an adversary.

Several of the warriors set torch to the scrub brush that served as a barrier against the pond's edge. All the men were on foot, as Grundel was unwilling to risk the element of surprise from a skittish horse. Chertron and a few of the others knelt a short pace behind the burning thickets, arrows notched with flaming tips. Sarion, Grundel, Forlern, and Rundin stood with swords ready to hold back the ogre if it tried to break through. Sarion wondered if they would be enough, though. The creature had proved incredibly fierce in their earlier pitched battle.

Despite the general dampness of the area, the bushes were soon smoldering, the fire catching. The captain carried with him some kindling oil, and combined with a collection of well-placed deadwood, succeeded to enhance the blaze. All eyes watched as the flames spread, and the ogre roused from sleep. It was confused, and sprang up onto the rock pile, glaring at the strengthening fire, the orange flames licking the tops of the bushes. The slitted pupils fixed on the motionless forms of the warriors, recognition crossing its surprised face.

Bellowing in rage, the ogre picked up its huge club and lumbered forward, realizing the trap which had been set.

Grundel gave a shout and the bows sang, shafts of fire arcing through the darkening air. The smoke proved more of an asset to the warriors as the wind drifted gray curls straight at the enemy, but the archers found their mark. Several of the shafts plunged into the tough flesh of the creature, the pointed tips still burning.

"Again!" Grundel screamed to his men as the ogre ignored the pain and neared the flaming brush, intent on going forward. Arrows rained down on the hulking form, and now it hesitated, one of the shafts driving into its massive neck. It howled in fury and pain, pulling the shaft out. The warriors fired volley after volley and the ogre retreated, unable to breach the wall of fire or arrows.

"We have him! He's trapped!" Forlern stamped his feet, sword slashing empty air, anticipating a swipe at the creature.

The fighters moved as close to the fire as possible, the smoke making it hard to see. The ogre had retreated to its former resting place, swinging the club in defiance. Sarion said nothing throughout the interchange, as he tried to foresee what action the ogre might take. And then, to the surprise of all, it suddenly jumped onto the highest rocks, grabbing the great war horn with one ham-fist.

"Shoot the horn!" Sarion yelled to the others, going for his own bow.

Chertron was the first to see the danger, and let fly a perfect shot which embedded itself in the ogre's horn, knocking it straight into the waters below. The creature seemed stunned at the loss of the horn, still clenching a cruel hand, now empty. Loud coughs broke out around the fire, and some of the men moved back, the vapors stinging their vision.

"Look, Captain. It attempts to escape." Rundin ran over to Grundel, and they all watched as the ogre crouched over the water's edge, a drop of several yards. It suddenly jumped down, a loud splash shattering the serene surface, and disappeared. The visibility was poor, and the captain shouted for someone to bring the horses forward, scattering the warriors to either side of the lake. Sarion sprang past the clumps of strewn rocks and fallen logs on his side, shocked that the ogre would attempt to swim the dark waters. Several minutes of confusion ensued as the warriors brought the mounts up, a few of them unwilling to go close to the blaze.

Sarion peered out at the murky waters, eyes straining for any sign of their quarry. The waters were flat, nothing broke the surface. High reeds and other moisture-thirsty plants clustered along the edge, but further out was only a listless void, mist shrouding the deeper areas, reducing sight to only a few dozen yards. On this side at least, the ogre was nowhere to be seen.

Rundin and Forlern rode up, bringing Sarion's mount with them.

"Any sign of the beast?" Rundin's shaggy face was streaked with grime and sweat, and Forlern scanned the shoreline.

"No, it should have surfaced by now. I didn't think the ogre could swim out past our sight."

"Maybe it sank to the bottom," replied Rundin.

"I'm not certain," Sarion replied. "We need to patrol the edge without putting too much distance between us. What of the others?"

"Captain Grundel rode around to the other side with three men, leaving the rest at the blaze. He told me ride back in ten minutes if we failed to find the creature."

"Let's go a bit further, but from here it's impossible to judge the size of the lake. The fire might alert any nearby creatures as to our presence as well. Let's keep our eyes open and wits clear."

A look of concern covered Rundin's face. They all remembered the other hazards of the region. He nodded, and they continued onward. The trio paced along the shore, avoiding soft, treacherous pits which marred the ground. Sarion rode with his head downward, finding no trace of the creature. After a short while, he realized that the ogre could not have swam such a great distance already, and he became increasingly worried that Grundel might have found it, with only a handful of men to fight the beast. They turned around and bolted towards their earlier position, the scent of smoke heavy in the air.

Upon returning, they found the three warriors who remained on guard, none of them having seen any sign of the ogre. Sarion relayed his fears and the company all set out in search of Grundel and the others. They rode scarcely a hundred yards when Sarion spied horsemen approaching.

"Hail, Captain! Did you find the beast?" Rundin shouted ahead as the two groups reunited.

"Nothing...I take it your result is the same as well?"

Sarion answered, leaning forward on his mount. "Aye. So there are but two possibilities. The ogre might have sank to the depths of the lake."

He paused, looking out at the swirling fog.

Grundel finished his line of thought. "Or, the beast defies our expectations, and is making its way to the far shore even now."

"Either way, we've lost it." Sarion frowned, the prospect of a night beneath the eaves of Grammore now an unpleasant reality.

⋌⋮⋋

The company skirted the lake's edge, Grundel making the decision to continue searching the side where Sarion had met up with him. It was evident that any tracks would be missed, as nightfall arrived and the mist deepened. The ground was soft along the edges, and the lake proved to be much larger than they'd originally thought, dotted with numerous small coves, and a few streams trickling into the sluggish waters. Insects buzzed throughout the region, and black water herons glided lazily above the surface, disturbed by the intruders. Their sense of direction was muddled, and Sarion didn't trust the increasingly soft earth.

"Captain, it seems that the lake is breaking down here, and even now starts to develop into treacherous swampland. The risks are great. I think we should call a halt."

Sarion waited as Grundel stared ahead, contemplating the wisest choice. He held up his arm and the men behind understood the signal to make camp.

"The land doesn't offer much in the way of protection. We'll stay near the water's edge—at least there is some measure of security here." The captain dismounted and cocked his head to one side, hearing a distant sound.

"Yes, the night predators are awakening." Sarion patted his horse, feeling weary from the day's events. "Probably wolves, and similar prowlers. We won't have to worry much about them. It's the strange noises, or the creatures that are silent, which concern me."

Kalen stood nearby, a look of discomfort crossing his face. "Like that beast we found earlier?"

"Yes, and others. I can't offer much knowledge on the things that dwell in Grammore—as I said before, we didn't go too far into the deeper forest. But it becomes a vast and terrible jungle. The air has become much warmer already, the terrain wetter. I can only guess that the diversity of life will increase the further we travel."

Kalen nodded.

Warriors milled about, settling in for the night, with two men instantly on guard. There was a tenseness reflected in the eyes and movements of the fighters as they felt the wilderness rising from slumber about them. They were within the borders of a dangerous no-man's land, a country that brought fear to the brave and rekindled nightmares to children and adults alike.

Sarion slumped down next to a bank of loose dirt, reading the subtle change in the warriors. Except for himself, the men all were from the east, an area much more populated and currently embroiled in a fierce conflict with an enemy which had sworn to conquer Trencit. But they were trained to fight human enemies, and now found themselves battling creatures which were known only in old tales and legends. Against the ogre they'd displayed remarkable courage, and Sarion trusted their collective abilities without question. But what did fate have in store for them next?

With lingering doubts swirling in his mind, he drifted off into restless sleep.

***

Sarion awakened, Rundin's grim face greeting him as he held a torch in one hand. A long hunting knife instantly appeared in Sarion's grip, quickly put back in its sheath.

"A fighter's habit is hard to break." Sarion felt a twinge of doubt as lines of worry creased the warrior's bearded face. "What is it?"

Rundin held up a long finger, pointing out at the misty depths of the water. Both the men stared into the murkiness, Sarion listening intently, searching for an indication of whatever had caught Rundin's notice.

"I heard something, moving in the bog. A light splashing, several minutes ago. Then again, right before I wakened you." He spoke in a whisper and Sarion crouched forward, facing the impenetrable haze moving sluggishly above the stagnant waters.

"Areck watches yonder—against that twisted stump."

"Only two? Another should be guarding until we leave this cursed region behind," Sarion murmured. "I'll stay up, but no more talking." Rundin nodded, creeping forward to his earlier position at the front of the sleeping men.

Sarion picked his way to a suitable spot where he found a fallen tree covered with damp moss, and there he sat. His senses keyed outwards, he failed to detect anything unusual in the shrouded night, the fog hanging heavily above the putrid water. The region teemed with life. Insects buzzed angrily over the swampland, and the sound of bullfrogs echoed forlornly through the musty air, the lowlands a warmer climate than what they'd left behind. From what he'd read, the larger part of Grammore stretched southwest of Trencit, and the Ridge Line protected the Lowlands from cooler weather, acting as a natural buffer against the northern winter. Waiting there in silence, his mind wandered back to the farm, and his young nephew.

Edward was tough, and responsible. He'd learned how cruel the world could be after losing his father and mother to the Glefins. A marauding party had attacked the little settlement they lived on, pillaging the homes, and brutally killing all who they found. A hidden trapdoor was all that had saved the boy from his parents' tragic fate. When Sarion slew the Glefin leader himself, no one would have rebuked the man for savoring in sweet revenge. But that was not Sarion's purpose, or nature, and he'd felt nothing but emptiness after the act, focusing only on returning home, knowing that his people were safe from the threat of the Glefins and their malice. A pang of sorrow seared his chest, setting off old, painful memories, and a bleakness in his heart which could never be entirely healed.

The sound of quiet splashing erased the trail of Sarion's recollection, and he chided himself for drifting off. Second chances were not to be found in Grammore. Raising himself, he looked out into the water, then over to where Rundin stood as he leaned against a thick, barkless tree, one with gaping roots snaking out greedily towards the bog. The warrior had also heard the sound, gesturing in the direction of the noise.

Sarion was suddenly struck by the solitude of their surroundings.

A deathly silence fell across the dismal fen, the amphibians and insects strangely hushed. The air felt tense, triggering inner alarms inside Sarion's mind. He moved towards the sleeping figure of Grundel, but the captain's eyes were already sharp and alert, staring into the night.

Without warning the surface of the swamp exploded, sending waves of green water cascading for yards in every direction.

The two men gave the call to their comrades, and the confused fighters sprang up from their disturbed rest. Sword held ready, Sarion bounded over to where a large shape broke through the water, elongating into a nightmarish figure, swiftly closing in towards Kalen, who was still shaking off the throes of a deep slumber.

"Kalen, get back!" Grundel's voice was shrill, and he was on his feet instantly, trying to protect the men and determine the nature of what threatened them.

All eyes watched in astonishment at the unspeakable creature which burst from the water. A long, twisting body churned out from the bottom of the swamp, green and armored with scales, slime and muck oozing from its plated torso. Bog plants fell off its form, species which thrived within the hidden depths of the murky waters. An immense head swayed from side to side, hideous and knobbed with a trio of pointed horns, fronted by a slavering maw lined with rows of countless teeth, each one a wicked dagger several inches long. It was a behemoth of vast proportions, with seemingly no end to its barreling trunk.

Sarion charged ahead, a stricken feeling in his chest at the sight of Kalen only scant yards from the approaching monster. He knew that the fighter was too far away even as he struggled desperately to reach his side. The brave warrior waited until the head was almost upon him, and he dodged to the left, rolling in the moist ground.

Hope flitted through Sarion's heart as it appeared the man was quicker than the raging creature, but with incredible agility, the monster's snout pivoted to the side, hungrily snatching the helpless warrior up in its open mouth. No one was close enough to give aid to Kalen, and the fighters watched in utter horror as the beast quickly withdrew back into the swamp and plunged beneath the dark waters with a tremendous splash, a single, lingering wail of anguish escaping from the warrior's lips before both were gone.

Sarion felt a sickening knot in his stomach as he stared in disbelief at the rings of water, the only indication as to the disastrous end of Kalen.

"Get the horses, back away from the edge! The beast might yet return!" Grundel's commanding voice snapped the men out of their shock, but Forlern and Sarion remained at the swamp's edge.

"Kalen's gone—just like that! By my sworn oath, this is a land of devils!" Forlern's sword gleamed dully from the distant torch light, his jaw clenched tightly in rage.

"Let's go, we can't fight such a monster here. Hurry." Sarion grabbed the fighter's arm, pulling him towards the others.

Forlern stared into Sarion's face, a smoldering fury burning in the orbs like hot coals. "To go like that, without even a chance."

"We must live to fight another day, Forlern. I know your anger. I saw nearly fifty of my companions fall prey to Grammore."

The fighter breathed deeply, then went with Sarion, eyes still fixed on the silent waters. Several of the men were on horseback already, the others scrambling to follow. The captain beckoned to Forlern and Sarion, and they hastened over.

"We must go inland, and put some distance between ourselves and the swamp." Sarion leaped onto his steed, a bitter scowl creasing Grundel's face. "I should never have trusted the water's edge, it's my poor judgment."

"No—don't blame yourself, Captain," Sarion snapped. "There are no safe regions in Grammore. There was nothing any of us could do. Who would have thought such a nightmare lived in the waters? Nothing prepares one for the evil in this land."

Grundel reined his horse forward, motioning at Chertron. "Sarion, go ahead with the lead, see if we can find somewhere to spend the rest of the night, then we stop. Forlern and I will guard the rear. My guess is that the creature will not wander from the swamp's edge. There must be deep waters to harbor a monster of that size, and it will not be so protected on land."

"More bad luck as well," Rundin called over. "Kalen's steed broke loose during the attack. Lost like its master..."

Sarion rode forward, the company waiting in mute sorrow, their hearts darkened by the death of their brave comrade. They trotted the animals forward into the night, black thoughts weighing heavily on the company from the loss of another comrade-in-arms, and they eventually settled down in a grassy clearing, where there was little chance of being taken unawares. No one felt like sleeping, and it was a long time before any lay down to rest. Conversation was fragmented, and they gazed into each other's eyes, all of them realizing they could be the next victim to fall beneath Grammore's mighty and unforgiving violence.

The hours stretched by without mishap as the men took turns at watch, the surrounding landscape pierced with distant howls and cries of unfortunate creatures, constant reminder as to the nature of the hostile region where they dared to travel as unwelcome trespassers.

꧁꧂

Dawn arrived, sullen and gray, promising little cheer to the band of weary fighters. The inhospitable weather served to dampen already aching spirits, as the waking men were assaulted again by the horrors of the past night. Sarion sat on a flat rock, an out-of-place structure in the clearing. Saddened by the loss of Kalen, he pondered the end game facing Grundel and his warriors.

The captain approached, trying to instill words of encouragement to the dour-faced fighters.

"What thoughts have you now, Captain Grundel?" Sarion read the hidden pain in the man's eyes, a hurt that needed to be repressed by the unwavering call of duty. To do any less would be a failure to his calling as the King's own.

"My orders remain, of course, but much has been learned by our venture thus far. I think we make a sweep around the edge of the swamp, circling in hopes of finding the ogre again, although I admit the chances are slim."

"The beast is at home here," Sarion answered. "If it does indeed serve another, then it might be in our best interest to return to our lands, soon, and you can convey our knowledge to King Gregor. As for what he intends to do with the knowledge, you would be the better judge."

"Additional patrols, enlistment preparations for the western provinces. Such things are in motion as we speak."

Sarion nodded. "Looks like I won't be returning to farm work for a while."

Grundel clapped him on his shoulder in a gesture of comradeship. "You have far proven your worth, Sarion. Needless to say, I'll be personally recommending you for reinstatement in the Western Guard. With men such as yourself, Trencit has much to hope for."

Kicking his muddy boots, Sarion grimaced. "Thanks for the kind words, Captain, but first we need to complete this journey. We'll need fortune smiling on our backs to return alive."

They stared at each other in silence, grim-faced and apprehensive, their thoughts darkened by the loss of Kalen. It would be a long time until either man could lift the black cloud weighing heavily on their hearts.

The warriors skirted the edge of the fen, staying back from the deeper pools and softer ground. There was no desire from any of them to tempt the denizens of the swamp once more. Sarion rode at the lead, Chertron's stern face gazing ahead in every direction—looking, listening, and concentrating. Sarion himself wondered as to the length of the great swamp, which showed no sign of dispersing. He knew that Grammore was filled with bogs and dense forests, but no actual map existed in defining the mysterious land. It appeared as little more than a name on every one he'd ever looked over, even while serving in the Western Guard. A white area of unknown size and terrain, a wilderness of mammoth proportions. How large was it?

Dawn was long past, but the sun would remain elusive yet again, Sarion thought, staring at the stifling cloud cover overhead, which was barely visible through the ever-present rolling mist. The fog pressed down on the men, oppressive and uncomfortable, speaking of harbored secrets, hidden threats. The land was vocal there, the droning of insects mingling with lonely cries of marsh birds. Scavengers and rodents scurried in front of the horses, including swamp rats larger than any Sarion could imagine. Chertron's horse stumbled, and the warrior nearly lost his seating. He gasped as the animal pitched forward, neighing loudly.

"Steady, steady!" Chertron grabbed the reins, patting his horse, which grew increasingly agitated.

Sarion held up his hand for a halt. "Chertron, what is it? What's bothering her?" He backed away, his own mount excited. The warrior's efforts to calm the horse were becoming desperate, and he was in danger of being thrown off. The animal was now prancing in circles, kicking wildly in the air.

"Something's wrong here! Chertron, jump off!" Sarion kept his own horse at bay, handing the reins to Rundin. He tried approaching Chertron, but the enraged animal was kicking savagely at the surrounding vegetation. It was then that Sarion saw the cause of the horse's distress. A long snake slithered past the animal, heading into a clump of grass.

"A viper—she must have been bitten." The horse was foaming at the mouth, and heaved the warrior about. It was too much for him, and he went flying to one side, crashing hard on the ground, but luckily rolled with the fall and quickly regained his footing.

The horse continued bucking, braying in pain from the wound. "Chertron, have a care! The snake was in that grass."

Chertron hurried away from the area, reaching Sarion's side. "Curses. Bitten by a snake. What misfortune will strike next?"

Grundel was now up front with the men, and they watched as the horse carried recklessly into the brush, making a tremendous commotion.

"We should put her out of misery—whatever bit her was lethal. Notch an arrow, we can't save her." Grundel gestured to Chertron, and he quickly pulled out his bow. Sarion followed suit, but the horse already was moving out of range, thundering behind a group of thick, gray trees, with sprawling roots and a canopy so packed with foliage that the tops were obscured.

Chertron and Grundel moved ahead as the horse nickered loudly. "Hurry," whispered Sarion. "Such a disturbance may alert nearby predators." Chertron crouched down on one knee, sighting with his eye.

Sarion stood behind him, and Grundel searched the forest, clearly anxious by the animal's disruption. Chertron aimed the arrow, his fingers on the verge of release. Sarion stared suddenly at the odd trees, his mouth opening in a gesture of recognition.

"Wait," he hissed. "Hold your shot."

His warning was too late and the shaft flew confidently through the air, slicing directly at the horse's breast. Above the horse, in the shrouded branches, there was a flash of movement. A pair of crooked, hairy arms burst downward, long and gnarled, grabbing at the animal and snatching it into the air.

The men watched in astonishment as the arrow connected into one of the hideous appendages, embedding deep into the crusted flesh. A cry of anguish bellowed from the tree's heights, and the horse was impaled by several more of the unseen creature's limbs. They darted out madly from the branches, stabbing into the limp animal again and again, a frenzy of blinding attacks, mistaking the arrow as a wound inflicted from the horse. Sarion pulled the other men with him, putting a finger to his lips for silence. Grundel backed away, staring at the flurry of limbs that still struck blows at the dead animal, dozens of appendages ripping chunks of flesh from its bloodied coat. The men were quiet until they reached the rest of the fighters. Sarion pointed south, away from the swamp and the monster ahead.

"I've never seen such speed in all my life." Chertron's eyes reflected his horror. "What was that creature?"

"I don't know, but we lost four men in that same manner." Sarion shook his head, his memory going back seven years ago to another part of Grammore. "They were taken and dragged into the trees. Back then, we were too startled to make a connection, but now, after seeing the same trees, I realize that the monster makes its lair there, up in the dense foliage. The cries of the horse brought it from slumber, or maybe it waits for such a thing, I know not. Either way, the creature is incredibly deadly."

"We have to be on the watch for the trees. Hopefully, they live only in that species." Grundel organized the men for a change of route, and Chertron stared back from where they had escaped the creature's notice. "I shudder to think if they start to change habitat."

"If they do, it could very well spell the end for all of us. Let's not even think about that prospect." Sarion watched as Tarral and Areck shared the same mount, Grundel stating that it was more important for Chertron to remain sole rider of another horse as he was the only tracker from his company.

The captain talked to the warriors, ordering them to remain vigilant to everything around them, on the ground and overhead. "Fortune favors no man in this forsaken country," he said. "In the east, you can see the enemy, guess at the attacks, prepare for conflict. In this land, every shadow, any movement, can bring swift death. We all know this now. Our mission is quickly drawing to completion, for the king himself would not want us to continue risking our lives in Grammore. We'll push on until tonight, and if our quarry still eludes us, then our task is done—no more can such a group accomplish. I need a hundred men at least to go much further in this country."

"Even so," replied Sarion, "a larger force may offer protection to some extent, but word could spread quickly, and the more organized creatures of Grammore might move against us, with the potential for us to be fighting every step of the way. We don't know anything for sure."

The captain absorbed Sarion's words for a moment, with-holding any comment. He positioned the fighters once more and they started off, with one less horse and surviving yet another harrowing brush with disaster.

ᴄᴉᴄ

In the lead again, Sarion and Chertron picked a naviga-ble path for the company, the latter constantly peering in the boughs overhead, as if in dreadful anticipation of coming within the grasp of the deadly monster that had carried away his former mount.

Sarion was not quite as concerned about this prospect compared to any other threat, but his watchful eyes missed nothing, above or about. His senses were refined to the point of making him quite possibly the greatest tracker in the west-land. His skills were unparalleled, as much from raw instinct as to years of training in the field. But unknown to the others, he kept some observations to himself. In the past several days he'd noticed many signs which had secretly alarmed him. Footprints of predatory beasts, various creatures both harm-less and dangerous alike, large and small. The majority of the deadlier species were nocturnal, stalking the night for the unwary. They inhabited every corner of the Lowlands, every varying terrain. Always present, working their way through the jungle in search of food or prey. But Sarion especially looked out for droppings, for the strongest of Grammore marked their individual territories with their own leavings and scent. So far there had been no sign.

This matter concerned Sarion far greater than anything else.

He knew with chilling certainty there existed powerful beasts which claimed huge regions as their own hunting ground. To venture into such an area would pose a tremendous peril to the warriors. He didn't want to alarm them further, but the creatures they had encountered so far were the normal kinds, dangerous enough, but living within a limited, narrow range. The real terrors of Grammore held vast miles of wilderness under their sway, attacking any poachers with stunning ferocity. He was fairly sure that the group would not enter into such a territory, as yet being on the edges of the Lowlands. But the possibility existed.

When the company paused for a brief rest, Sarion decided to talk openly with Grundel about his fears, especially if they were to push much deeper into the interior.

"Do these monsters stray beyond the borders, I wonder?" asked Grundel.

"I would think not, unless driven away by something more formidable," answered Sarion. "A stronger predator, or lack of game. Or to increase its territory. I know little, but guess at much. Based on the vast diversity of wildlife, the unique species inhabiting Grammore, it seems a plausible conclusion."

"Ah, but your assumptions hold greater weight than most people's knowledge, and you've more than proven your worth, Sarion. Many times over. If not for you, we would all have been lost, a long while back." He rubbed the growth on his chin, a far-away look in his eyes. "The King sorely underestimated the evil of Grammore." Grundel hesitated. "And myself, for that matter. Brave men have met their end because of our shortsightedness."

Sarion disagreed. "You can't blame yourself, Captain. There's a threat to Trencit from the west, and the nature is of great concern to King Gregor and his counselors. It was the correct decision to track the ogre, and like you, I'm eager to understand the reason behind its actions. I think you're partly right about a larger purpose, but I'm not quite sure it will be what we expect."

"Meaning what?"

Sarion looked back at the men, speaking in hushed tones, several on guard. "I wish I knew that answer for you. This land holds many secrets, and doesn't give them up very easily."

Grundel nodded lightly and stood, preparing to move ahead, but a sharp look from Sarion froze him in his tracks.

"Captain, try to act normal. In the bushes behind you, about twenty yards away." Sarion turned his head, not staring directly at the spot.

"We're being watched."

～∴～

"Act disinterested—whatever you do, don't give us away." Sarion's voice was low, a whispered warning to Grundel. He casually stretched his arms back, yawning deeply, and walked towards Forlern, who was busy sharpening his blade. The captain followed the man's lead, pretending to adjust one of his boots, muttering under his breath, and turning in the direction of the watcher. Sarion was closer to the forest edge, discussing something with Forlern.

Grundel restrained himself from approaching the lurker, trusting in Sarion's instincts. To the shock of Forlern, and several of the fighters as well, Sarion spun around with catlike speed, moving so quickly that even Grundel looked amazed.

Sarion drew his bow, notching an arrow and pointing it with deadly purpose into a section of bushes only yards from where he now stood. There was a slight rustling from the thickets, and the only sound was Sarion's voice, speaking to whatever lay hidden in the undergrowth. He stepped forward, eyes never leaving his mark, Forlern a pace behind him, a sword gleaming in his hand.

"Step out slowly, or you'll be without the use of an eye—that's a promise."

There was no answer and the warriors held their breath, tension clutching everyone's heart at this new threat. Several long moments passed, and Sarion nodded at the intruder which slowly made its way out of the cover. All eyes watched in disbelief as a humanoid creature shuffled into view.

Two pointed ears sat on top of a scaly head, mouth open slightly, revealing rows of sharp fangs. A forked tongue slithered between thin white lips, probing the air in agitation. The creature stood taller than even Rundin, lean and muscular, its chest covered with reptilian scales, wearing a short sash around the waist. The legs were leathery, mottled with gray hide, and a short tail twitched angrily. Its feet ended in sharp talons, just like the arms. To the last man, the warriors knew it to be a deadly creature.

"What the blazes is this beast?" Forlern broke the silence, ready for any move by the thing, which now faced a number of arrows pointing at its head.

"Well, Captain Grundel, Grammore gives up another little mystery here, it seems." Sarion's face was grim, and he refused to let down his guard.

Grundel signaled two of the warriors forward, carrying coils of rope.

"Hand over your weapons. Now." Sarion's gaze never wavered as he locked eyes with the creature. After a moment of hesitation it conceded, pulling out a strange looking knife from the pouch. It was long and thin, with two handles.

"I wouldn't say you're fortunate, Captain, but this is a rare treat. Rare indeed, and one which I thought never to see again. You're looking at one of the craftiest dwellers of Grammore."

The men bound the creature's arms and legs, wary of any movements, but it didn't fight their efforts.

"It's a Glefin."

⌣ː∾

Forlern let out a low whistle, while a few of the fighters tightened grips on their weapons. Grundel came forward, staring with great interest at the bound creature.

"A Glefin," he purred. "So, this is what one looks like— I've often wondered."

"Extremely cunning, highly intelligent—and, of course, dangerous." Sarion lowered his bow, still locked in a staring match with the creature, neither one willing to break first.

"Can it speak?"

"Definitely, if it so wishes. They have their own tongue, but know ours. There was a time in the past when they traded with trappers and frontiersmen, until they became hostile. I'll admit being surprised at seeing any still left. I thought they were all dead."

"Indeed," answered Grundel. "Rundin, I want you in charge of watching the Glefin. Two men at all times will be guarding it, is that understood?"

"Yes, Captain. It won't catch us sleeping."

Rundin and Cerestin checked the ropes binding the creature, motioning for it to sit on the ground. Grundel took Sarion aside, conferring about what they would do with the captive.

The captain whispered. "You say it can speak, but only willingly, of course. I am very interested to discover why it was trailing us, if that was its purpose, or could this be a chance meeting?"

"I doubt it is any coincidence," replied Sarion. "These creatures always have a purpose in mind. Maybe it found our trail and was naturally curious. A group of armed men in Grammore is certainly uncommon, you know."

"True enough, but my main concern is for our mission, and the safety of the men. It is an added burden to have it with us. We are tired enough without the need to guard a dangerous creature."

"I know. The Glefin could lend us some valuable information, though. It would know of any disturbance here in the Lowlands, and even the reasons behind it, possibly. It may very well have the answers to what we are seeking."

"Do you propose to entreaty it, then? Offer freedom, for giving us information?"

Sarion looked back at the Glefin. "Unfortunately, I don't believe it will be that easy. There is no love lost between our races, and if anything, it will attempt to undermine our mission in some way. We can't trust its intentions, regardless."

"All right. We'll take the creature with us, but at the first sign of trouble, it will be dealt with. I don't kill anything in cold blood, but if it gives me a reason..."

His sentence drifted off, and Sarion nodded. He knew what the Glefins were capable of, having tracked them seven years ago, putting an end to their rampage. It hadn't been pleasant.

Grundel walked among the warriors, giving orders, and seeing to preparations for the trek ahead. He spoke softly to Rundin especially, making sure the Glefin was properly secured and watched. Rundin would ride behind the creature, while Chertron, now horseless, would walk in back of it. Sarion thought it was a good idea to keep it in the lead, knowing that the creature would not foolishly endanger itself. He told Grundel that it might also give the Glefin a chance to communicate with them, if it believed they would let it go at some point. Grundel addressed the creature, telling it his offer. The Glefin stood attentively, but remained silent.

They started off again, riding and walking forward in the gloomy forest. Sarion looked up, wondering if he would ever see the sun again, a lost friend in the forsaken Lowlands. The company saw no sign of the swamp as they now traveled in a region of increasingly dense woods. Sarion looked for tracks of predators, but saw nothing to catch his notice. He found himself constantly watching the Glefin for any reaction. As long as it seemed content, then Sarion believed they were in no immediate danger.

The afternoon progressed without incident, and the land gradually sloped downhill, the trees strangling each other for space. The forest was quiet, and Sarion wondered as to the lack of noise. The air felt heavy, stifled somehow, and he kept his senses keyed for anything out of the ordinary.

"What is it?" Grundel rode beside Sarion, noticing his apprehension.

"I'm not sure," he answered, his voice a notch above a whisper. "The forest has grown silent, and it has me uncomfortable. The Glefin shows no sign of worry, though."

"Could it be leading us into a trap?" The captain glanced over his shoulder, his eyes meeting Forlern's own, the fighter never missing a beat.

"I've considered it, but I don't think the Glefin would put itself in danger along with us. Perhaps it is thinking the same thing as I am."

He pointed ahead, and for the first time, the Glefin appeared agitated. Its tail whipped back and forth, the reptilian head probing the trees in a slow, calculating stare. The green tongue flicked in the air, and the creature lifted its nostrils, sniffing for odors beyond the ability of humans to detect.

"The Glefin tracks with eyes, ears, and scent, like many of the creatures in Grammore. That is one reason why men can't survive here long. Our senses are not finely tuned, instinctual. We're no match for the native predators."

Grundel tapped his arm. "Ah, but that is where our intelligence and quicker wits come to play. Men have proven to be superior to the wild beasts in this manner."

"There are numerous creatures in the Lowlands which possess great powers of reasoning as well. Those are the ones that really worry me. He pointed to their captive." Sarion rubbed the back of his horse, his eyes fixed on the Glefin.

"True enough," replied Grundel.

It became increasingly obvious that the creature was growing more uncomfortable in the minutes that followed. The Glefin crouched lower at times, flexing its talons as if testing the binding ropes. Sarion knew that if the Glefin could loosen the cords, it could easily tear through and free itself. They needed to be vigilant in case the creature was bold enough, or desperate enough, to try and escape.

The terrain grew denser as they passed unknown species of trees, some with massive girth to their mossy barks, others tall and slender, the jungle canopy shrouding the ground below in perpetual twilight. Bright-green ferns and exotic flowering shrubs became more prevalent, replacing the more familiar foliage they could identify.

Knowing the dangers of plant and beast alike facing them, Sarion keenly observed the Glefin as it walked with Chertron at its heal, a coil of rope attached to Rundin's steed to prevent any mischief. Sarion watched several times as the creature purposefully steered clear of a particular type of plant, keeping a safe distance from the odd-looking petals. He commented to Grundel concerning this, and the captain nodded, taking mental note.

They were descending into what appeared to be a huge depression, with the ground angling steadily downward, taking them into the deeper parts of Grammore. Although the day lacked noticeable changes in lighting, it was turning into early evening, and Sarion knew that Grundel would be making a crucial decision soon—whether to abandon the expedition and return to their own lands, or change his mind and continue onwards. Sarion had little desire to test fate any longer in the Lowlands, after narrowly surviving numerous brushes against disaster. And yet, he couldn't shake the feeling that even if they managed to return unharmed, that little would have been accomplished. True, the group had discovered the creature responsible for perhaps some of the raids, the elusive ogre, but neither himself or Grundel believed the incident to be isolated. The scope of marauding clearly argued against it. They would come back to their lands feeling incomplete, faced with the knowledge that the true nature of evil remained hidden, lurking behind the impenetrable walls of Grammore.

Did the answer lay before them now, he mused, in the form of the Glefin? The creature was cunning, and knew much. And Sarion was certain, that even if it didn't know the reason beneath Grammore's unrest, it was well aware of the disturbance, and much closer to the truth than they might imagine. Pondering these things, Sarion was ready to suggest a halt, when a distant rumbling sound echoed in the forest ahead. It was a faint rushing noise, as of something moving.

After a few moments, Grundel and Chertron exchanged glances, but the captain merely gestured towards the Glefin, which seemed unconcerned with the new sound.

"Water." Sarion spoke to Grundel in a tight whisper. "There's a river ahead of us, and from the sound of it, this could be an obstacle in our path."

The captain peered ahead. "We shall see, then."

The fighters rode onward, and Sarion felt the air becoming heavy with moisture, as lazy clouds of mist began to curl about the legs of the horses. The noise grew louder, changing into a muffled roaring, and the ground was rapidly sloping downward, most likely towards the source of water.

"We have to be nearly on top of the river by now," said Grundel. He let out a low whistle, signaling added caution for Chertron ahead. The warrior inclined his head, checking his grip on the Glefin. The trees broke open in front of the company, and suddenly the leaders came to a halt.

"Captain Grundel, you won't believe this, by the Three Serpents!"

Chertron gestured back to the others, the churning water a ceaseless, low rumbling. Giving orders to secure their position, Grundel dismounted, handing the reins to Forlern. Sarion immediately jumped down from his own horse, following the captain's lead, while Forlern narrowed his eyes at their departure, appearing restless for action. But nothing could have prepared the men for the sight which lay below them, as they stood perched on a high ridge overlooking the source of the water.

Hundreds of feet beneath them was an immense waterfall, a deluge of clear-blue water issuing forth from the living rock of a gargantuan cliff, the steep sides dotted with leaning trees and loose stones, angling sharply down into a huge lake, the shorelines nearly invisible in the fading light. The view was staggering—the landscape before them an unheralded spectacle, a forbidden realm opening up its primeval arms as the gateway leading into the black heart of Grammore. It was both moving and frightening in the same breath, and they all felt the almost magical allure of the scene. And despite the magnificence of the vision at their feet, it paled before the horror of what they saw on the surface of the lake.

Dark objects moved slowly along the water's rim, appearing and submerging at varying intervals. Splashes broke the stillness in numerous places, revealing the emergence of horn-crested snouts. Sarion's face became grim, his thoughts chilled by what he looked upon.

The lake was teeming with a host of water monsters.

⌣⁙⁚

The fighters stared in amazement and dismay, as if looking through a window and seeing an alien world on the other side. And to Sarion's eyes, Grammore was indeed such a place. Although he was a survivor of the disastrous journey into the Lowlands seven years ago it left the same impression now—the region inspired awe and emitted an overwhelming sense of foreboding within its shrouded forests and vales, the territory imbibed with a sense of dread and dominance that defied understanding. Even the seasoned warriors could not shake the feeling of trepidation that slept beneath every rock and blade of grass in Grammore, the entire landscape waiting patiently to spring upon the unwary and consume them whole.

"An unbelievable sight. Incredible..." Chertron mumbled, keeping the Glefin in front of him, careful not to step too close to the edge.

A fairly steep drop opened before them, but it was not impassable. The rocky descent was broken up by scrub bushes and outcroppings, with certain areas offering shelter and easier footing. Grundel rubbed his chin thoughtfully, and Sarion knew he was torn by the decision to go back, or proceed further and risk even greater danger.

"Look at the water beasts," said Chertron. "From here they appear small, but I think they could be enormous, some of them. Crossing that lake is impossible—we wouldn't last beyond a few minutes before one of them would attack."

"Without a doubt," replied Sarion. "They may well be even larger than the muck dweller that took Kalen. The deeper into the wilderness we go, the more common such beasts become, it appears—larger, and more dangerous, as well."

"It would take an army to clear a settlement of men here," answered Chertron, still shaking his head at the sight below.

The Glefin made a barely audible snort, but Sarion heard the sound, taking it as a rebuke to Chertron's words. The others hadn't noticed, and Grundel remained silent. Tarral and Areck fanned out to either side, making sure they were adequately protected against any surprise attack. Cerestin and Forlern waited in the rear, and Grundel whistled a signal to make camp, choosing not to speak any further for the moment.

The sky was dark overhead, and stars were visible above the mist, which lessened above the vast lake. Sarion looked upon the waters and valley at his feet, admiring the pristine beauty and wonderment of the Lowlands. Grammore was a marvel to behold, encompassing such opposing qualities in the same breath, of unparalleled sights and wonders accompanied by lurking, treacherous creatures. It was a paradoxical existence, unlike any other region of the known world.

The men settled for the night, not daring to light any fires which would reveal their presence, and Grundel sat with Sarion in conference. The Glefin was tied fast to a tree within hearing distance of the two, a suggestion Sarion had made to the captain earlier. It was his belief that the creature might break its silence if the opportunity arose.

"So, Captain. It is decision time. Have you made up your mind yet?"

Grundel sat with arms folded, unusually quiet since reaching the lake. "No, but I will before the night ends. All hopes of finding our quarry seem fruitless at the moment. The trail is lost, we have no knowledge if it managed to survive the swamp, and a seemingly impenetrable obstacle lays before us. What other recourse do we have?"

"It would seem little, yet you hesitate. I echo your reservation, Captain." Sarion matched Grundel's gaze as he shifted his head, probing the meaning behind the spoken words.

"Oh, in what way?"

"We have identified one part behind the raids, certainly not all of them, for that matter. The ogre didn't just decide to go randomly on the hunt, so far past its own lands, knowing that our people would pursue and slay it without hesitation. If we go back now, what will King Gregor make of our excursion? It seems that for every answer that is uncovered, deeper questions emerge. Despite all this, I have no steadfast advice on the next course we take."

"You have proven to be a man of great resourcefulness and wisdom, my friend." Grundel's face twisted into a smirk. "The army was reduced when you went on to other pursuits. It is no great mystery as to how you entered Grammore before, and were the only one to return intact."

Sarion glanced over at the Glefin, tilting his head ever so slightly.

The creatures eyes were glistening, as it listened with interest to their conversation. Sarion knew these creatures well enough from past experience—he was sure that the Glefin understood their motives in keeping it near their discussion. Schemes and deadly games we play, he thought...His mind drifted back to the rolling hills of his farm, where Edward would be working with Jergen and the others to till the fields. The boy would miss him sorely, but that couldn't be helped. Edward showed much promise—just like his father. Sarion winced at the memory, and looked over at Grundel as he spoke again.

"It seems as if we've been in this forsaken land for months, doesn't it?" Grundel yawned, fingering the knife at his belt. "And it's only been days, very long, and sorrowful days." His voice trailed off wearily, and Sarion felt the weariness leak into his bones.

"I guess I'll share the late watch, maybe the sun will rise tomorrow and show her face. I expect surprises and danger at every turn in this land, but I'll admit, nothing prepared me for the sight of this lake. No maps exist detailing even the fringe regions of Grammore. We're on our own."

Grundel nodded. "The water beasts are a suitable deterrent for any passage—by craft, at least."

He left the statement at that, but it sounded unfinished to Sarion's ears. Was the captain implying a trek onward? Alluding to continuing the expedition, in the hope of uncovering more information? Inside he argued against something which seemed so foolhardy, and he wished to return immediately, leave the darkness of Grammore behind, its secrets deeply buried. Another part of him looked at the greater scheme of things, and saw merit against abandoning the quest—the portion of his mind that craved knowledge and adventure, which could prove reckless as well, but was reinforced by the nagging belief that the warriors and himself were caught up in a larger plan, one that was swelling like the waves beneath an angry wind, churning helplessly wherever the storm would take them. And to what end, he asked himself? What paths lay before him and the fighters—how many more would share the fate of brave Kalen? He hadn't known the man very long, but it was enough. A noble warrior, and someone to call friend in the brief time they rode together in harsh lands.

Trencit needed such men—the world needed such men.

Sarion drifted slowly into slumber, where he became entangled in nightmares, finding himself on a small boat pursued by a horde of savage creatures.

⋅:∾

Sarion was awakened in the late-night hours by Cerestin, the young fighter's face impassive in the torch light, the small stick in his hand the only permitted flare. A full blaze would be an invitation for any nearby creature to investigate. They certainly didn't need to tempt fate any further. Normally cheerful and light-hearted, Cerestin had become subdued like his comrades during the hardships of the past few days. There was little humor to find in Grammore. It was Sarion's turn to stay near the ledge, and keep a wary eye on the captive Glefin. He watched as a thin membrane moved over the creature's pupils, and realized that it served as protection, since it lacked the eyelids that men possessed.

"You choose to yet remain silent?" Sarion challenged the creature, not expecting any reply. "Unlike your breed, we honor our given word. Freedom for useful knowledge—a fair exchange. You have nothing to gain by holding out on us. If you think to ensnare us, I will tell you this, Glefin. Do not try it…Whatever scheme you have in mind will be discovered. Don't underestimate Captain Grundel, or myself." He leaned closer to the captive. "I think you know who I am."

He bent down in front of the creature, his eyes unblinking, his face confident. The Glefin returned the gaze, the tongue waving menacingly in the air, then disappearing quickly.

"We bear no love for each other, but survival necessitates strange alliances. Think over my offer. Give us the information we need, and you'll have your freedom."

Sarion straightened, looking around the camp perimeter. Most of the men were sleeping, their breathing steady and comforting to Sarion's ears. Areck and Rundin were posted further off in the woods—they could have been granite statues beneath the forest boughs, listening and watching the night. Far off in the distance a loud yelping broke out, which Sarion believed to be from several beasts in hunt, and the noises ended after several seconds. Having grown accustomed to the low roaring of the waterfalls, Sarion was alert for sounds from behind, where they had traveled earlier. At least for the night, that would be the area of greatest threat.

He leaned against a hoary tree stump, the rotted bark festered with lichen, and stayed that way until daylight finally broke through the lingering mist.

⌣∶∾

The men gradually stirred from sleep, their limbs weary and aching from days spent without the warmth and softness of home or bed. Sarion missed both as well—adventuresome treks in the field were never as glamorous in the doing, as opposed to the reading of such heroic tales in print. Grundel stood at the lip of the hill, peering through the mist with his own clouded vision, deep in thought. He turned around as Sarion walked over to him, the face confident and intense.

Sarion knew that the decision had been made, and he felt a twinge of excitement, realizing that he would feel strong emotions from the man's decision, no matter the course of action. Forlern guarded the captive, eyeing the creature suspiciously as he fingered his knife.

"We are at a crossroads, Captain Grundel," said Sarion, joining him on the ledge. "By the look in your eyes the choice has been made. Are you going to make me guess for the answer?"

"Am I that good at masking my thoughts?" Grundel smiled at him, appearing more sadly resigned than humorous.

"Indeed you are—at times."

"Well then, let's go over to the men. All ears should hear my decision."

The pair greeted the fighters who were busy at breaking their light camp. Several wore puzzled looks on their faces, but Rundin and Forlern were expressionless. Tarral was the lone watch as he stood facing the forest behind them.

"It seems that our mission has reached a pivotal point," said Grundel, staring at the attentive warriors. "King Gregor was firm in his orders—to seek out information on the raids, discover the source if possible. We have been partly successful."

Sarion glanced at the Glefin. The creature was looking straight at him, taking in everything it heard.

"The ogre has disappeared into Grammore, and with it the answers we need. There are signs we might take as unusual from our travels, things which play some role in the unrest facing the borderlands, and now, in this realm, we pass as unwelcome intruders, and have suffered the loss of several worthy comrades in the fulfillment of our duty. I am not blind to our danger though."

He paused, eyes boring into the men, gauging their reaction. Their loyalty was unwavering.

"I have been entrusted with a grave decision. King Gregor has commanded me to return with knowledge of the threat from Grammore—if indeed it hails from this treacherous land—and if I go to him now, I will have failed in my mission."

Sarion caught his breath...

"We must continue forward, making a sweep of the Lowlands, hoping to uncover the information that will benefit the kingdom. I have led you into peril. We are at risk every second we spend here. And our path goes even deeper now, with no certainty as to the end of our journey. It is much to ask, but you are the finest caliber of men for such an undertaking. You have all been handpicked because of your talents. The weight of Trencit may very well rest on our shoulders."

"Captain." Sarion stepped forward a pace. "Do you mean to attempt the lake?"

Grundel shook his head briskly. "We'll descend the cliff and skirt the water's edge. I have no desire to confront the beasts that live within the lake. I believe we can make our path somewhere above the waterfall, and move on to flatter lands. It appears passable."

Sarion nodded, and the fighters looked weary, but determined. They would answer the call. About to add something, Sarion snapped his head around in surprise as a low hissing broke the air.

The Glefin was speaking.

ᷰ:ᷰ

"Foolishhh..."

The voice was harsh, guttural, the syllables unnatural to the creature's normal tongue.

"You don't realizzze the danger."

Grundel walked towards the Glefin, a look of mild surprise on his face. He stopped in front of its bound form. "So, you've decided to speak at last? Have you considered our offer?"

"Offer...perhapsss. I value my life."

"So do we all," answered Grundel. "Why were you following us?"

Sarion came close, trying to read the truth in the creature's words. They were deceitful and cunning, and he knew better than to let down his guard.

"Found your trail, was curiousss. Trencit warriors in Grammore? Strange..."

"Are there others of your kind nearby? Waiting for you?"

The Glefin spat on the ground. "The lassst one."

"What?" Sarion spoke up. "You are the last of the Glefins?"

The creature nodded, the eyes flashing with anger. "Hunted, sslain."

Sarion considered the answer and he glanced at Grundel, who seemed content to let him take over the questioning, angling his head slightly.

"By who?"

The creature was silent.

"You are unwilling to tell me?"

The Glefin could have been carved from stone as it sat there, granite and immobile.

"Then why speak up now? You lack any credibility with us. Trickery will not work, Glefin."

"Danger," it answered. "Below."

"We can see that, and will take measures to avoid the water beasts," interjected Grundel. "The way is passable, if a bit rough. The cliff levels out somewhat, and we can keep a healthy distance away from the more treacherous areas."

"In the waterfall. A cave."

"There is a cave in the waterfall? Why should that concern us?" Grundel frowned at the creature, a look of impatience crossing his face. "Get to your point, we leave quickly."

The Glefin hissed, narrowing its eyes. "The Jurvech livesss there."

Sarion tensed at the name, although it was unfamiliar to him. He felt a chill crawl along his spine, as the creature appeared disturbed—and that was reason enough for him to feel cautious.

"And what exactly is that?" Grundel peered forward, gazing at the lake, as the sky overhead became brighter with the advent of dawn.

"A great beast, livesss in cave."

"Can we bypass the cave without waking it? It didn't bother us up here last night."

"It sleepsss. Wakesss only to feed. Terrible."

"When? During the day, or just at night? What type of beast is this Jurvech?" Sarion pursued the captain's questioning, dismayed by the revelation of something unknown and powerful lurking in the waterfall.

"Day, night. When it getsss hungry. A monster you have never seeeen before. A great one."

"I don't like the sound of this, Captain. Remember our earlier talk?"

Grundel ordered the fighters to prepare to leave, taking Sarion aside. "The larger beasts of Grammore? Yes, I recall your fears of such creatures, and we would do well to avoid them. But we can't trust the Glefin either. Maybe such a monster dwells here, and maybe not. Who can tell?"

"True, but it could prove disastrous to encounter one of the larger predators. The Glefin chose now to speak up—and that concerns me."

"Let's see if it will reveal anything else." Grundel went back to the captive.

"Are we able to sneak by the monster, passing above the waterfall?"

"Perhapsss. Must be quiet, hope it does not awaken."

"Do you know of a path?"

The Glefin remained unspeaking for several moments, and then nodded.

"You will lead then. If you betray us, your fate will be ours. Give us the knowledge we seek, and we may set you free. If you decide to offer information about the evil in Grammore, I will uphold my gesture."

The captain went back to the men, talking to Chertron about the coming trek. Sarion watched the Glefin's unblinking orbs, wondering what slept in the hidden cave.

⌣∴⌣

In single file the warriors crept along the cliff side, the horses led by hand. The sound of the waterfall rumbled unceasingly below them, filling the humid air around them with a cool spray. Sarion welcomed the soothing moisture on his unshaven face, and he wondered what Edward would say to him at his ragged appearance. Soiled clothes, muddied boots, and grimy skin. He grinned to himself, realizing how much he cared for his nephew. But he snapped out of the daydream, chastising himself against complacency.

The lake below teemed with surface creatures, while fishing herons glided overhead in search of prey, some a brilliant blue, and others a dull green. The foliage was dense, but the vegetation was far from toneless. Jungle flowers flourished in the temperate climate, jutting forth from the ground in dazzling colors of every hue imaginable—bright violet, purple, blazing shades of orange and yellow, everything within the spectrum of man's vision was represented.

At the lead was the Glefin, followed by the hulking form of Chertron, the warrior never taking his eyes from the back of the captive's neck. The slope was strewn with thousands of small rocks at the feet of leaning trees, some of them in danger of succumbing to gravity and tumbling down below where the cliff became ever steeper.

Grundel walked directly behind Sarion, and the others fell into formation after him, with the sturdy Rundin bringing up the rear, many yards after. He purposely dropped back further at times to listen and watch for pursuit, a practice they deemed valuable while traveling in Grammore.

The next hour passed without event as the fighters slowly picked their way steadily downwards, drawing closer to the liquid turbulence issuing forth from the earth. The water exploded from underground sources as it erupted into the lake, cascading over a hundred feet into the depths below. Somewhere nearby lay the cavern, and the lair of the Jurvech—if the Glefin were to be believed.

The noise grew to a deafening blast, and the warriors found themselves moving immediately above the churning waters. Sarion peered down the slope, glancing back at Grundel for his reaction. The captain shook his head slowly, both men knowing that any misstep there could be disastrous. The greatest moment of peril was at hand, and Sarion felt the tension in his shoulders as he struggled to calm his mount. The horses remained in good temper, resulting from generations of breeding as war-steeds—rugged and obedient, but Sarion knew that the hostile environment could shatter those instincts in a second. As an additional caution, Grundel ordered all the horses to be muzzled, although the roaring of the falls drowned out all other noises.

The Glefin moved smoothly across the terrain, having no trouble at all—unlike the encumbered fighters. The creature was at home in Grammore, now the last of its kind. Sarion questioned the notion, but knew it could very well be the truth. The Glefins had always been a scarce race, reproducing infrequently, resulting in their small population. It was a good thing too, he thought. With greater numbers they would have been a real threat to overrun Trencit, aggressive enough to raid at will on the eastern settlements despite the lack of equality in size.

The moisture in the air dampened Sarion's brow, and he stiffened as the Glefin pivoted, Chertron swiftly raising his weapon. The creature hissed at the warrior's movement, staring at Sarion and gesturing directly below them, where a ridge spiked outwards, obscuring what lay below. Sarion knew immediately that the Jurvech's lair was beneath them now, and he shuddered, trying to visualize what the unseen beast looked like. Sarion fervently hoped that he would never see the answer to such a dark thought.

Glancing over one shoulder, Sarion motioned for silence, meeting Grundel's eyes for a moment in unspoken determination. Nodding to Chertron, the signal was given to proceed again, and the men began picking their way carefully forward, all heads on the Glefin. The warriors tred lightly with their tough leather boots, holding their collective breath whenever a chance pebble loosened and slid towards the edge. Some of the horses grew restless, and Sarion knew they were disturbed by the scent of something unfamiliar. Their reaction alone convinced him that the Jurvech was a real creature, and nearby.

The seconds crawled by agonizingly, and the tension continued to mount as the Glefin slowed, at times halting completely and sniffing, a look of unease crossing the reptilian face. The tongue would lap out, vanishing quickly as if probing the very air, tasting and deciding upon the next course of action. Sarion felt the extreme vulnerability of himself and the others, and he searched for any sign of mischief from the captive, or indications of the lurking predator. He wished they had never encountered the Glefin—the creature was a living reminder of harsh memories which now turned uneasily in his mind. But reflection was not a luxury he could afford, for his own sake and the lives of the warriors.

The company trudged onwards, the footing becoming more treacherous by the moment. Sarion realized that if things became any more difficult, passage would prove to be nearly impossible. He shot a quick glance at the captive, looking for any indication as to what it was thinking. The Glefin was a predator in every sense, relying heavily on other senses beside vision. Snuffling at the air, head shifting to accommodate a change in hearing, narrow eyes forward, missing nothing.

To their left, the lake sprawled outwards, the relentless mist lifting into the gloomy sky overhead and obscuring the sun. The view was much more shrouded from their present vantage point, and Sarion couldn't see any of the water beasts, but he knew they were down there, preying upon any vulnerable creature within their wake. It was a region of extreme hostility, with larger species dominating the greater areas of the lake, fighting for supremacy. Sarion wondered if the Jurvech fed on the water serpents. If so, the thing would be incredibly dangerous.

They reached the broadest part of the ridge and the waterfall was directly below them now, the tumult assaulting the side of the cliff and churning into the unknown depths of the lake. The ground vibrated with the thrashing of the unseen river, and Sarion felt uneasy knowing of the fury that raged beneath their feet, which would one day collapse a great area of the cliff as erosion finally took its toll. Rocks slid sideways towards the edge, loosened by the booted feet of the men and the hooves of their steeds. The horses tossed their heads in agitation, and Sarion's greatest fear was that one of them would bolt away, or stumble into a warrior.

As Sarion pondered such grim thoughts, the Glefin stiffened, its head pointing to the ground as if watching something there. Chertron began to raise his hunting knife but the blade never reached above his shoulder as the captive creature turned its head towards him, mouth opened wide. To the surprise of the fighter, it spit something from between its teeth and Sarion felt his spine grow cold as an object struck Chertron in the chest and the man grimaced in pain.

The Glefin leaped forward, the ropes falling to the damp earth in a useless pile. Immediately Sarion sprang in pursuit and Grundel whistled to alert the warriors. Chertron fell to his knees, trying madly to pull a tiny dart from his skin. Sarion knew that the creature had bided its time, concealing a hidden weapon within its mouth and choosing the right moment to act, when the company was off balance. The Glefin was several yards ahead, Sarion swiftly following, when it unexpectedly pivoted, facing him.

"Watch!" The captain shouted a warning, but Sarion was already flattened to the ground. Instead of shooting the dart at Sarion, it spit further into the company, the small weapon cutting through the air and striking Tarral's horse, and the beast reared back in fright, kicking Tarral and sending him tumbling towards the edge. Another dart left the Glefin's mouth, narrowly missing Grundel, and it turned to flee.

It all happened so fast that the rear of the company failed to realize what had just occurred, except for Forlern who was right behind Tarral, and he jumped forward. A glint of steel arced through the air as Forlern whipped out a long knife, throwing it at the retreating Glefin. The weapon sliced into the creature's back, and it howled in rage and pain.

The rest of the warriors were trying to calm their own mounts as Grundel was knocked to the ground by his own horse, unable to reach the struggling form of Tarral, now perched dangerously near the edge, his horse fallen on its side and scrambling wildly to regain its footing. Sarion looked on as the Glefin went down, tumbling forward and sliding towards the ridge, grabbing desperately for a handhold.

Sarion glanced back at the others and watched in horror as Tarral's horse plummeted over the ledge, the helpless warrior crushed beneath the animal's bulk. Grundel dove forward in an attempt to grab the fighter's arm but it was too late. Man and beast hurtled over the cliff, starting a small avalanche which threatened to undermine the ridge itself. A brief scream echoed from below, quickly stifled by the bellowing waters. The Glefin was gone as well.

"Tarral!" The captain clawed his way to the edge, Forlern holding the reins of his own horse and Grundel's. Sarion gestured for the warriors to move ahead, and some of them had controlled their mounts enough to take action. Sarion looped his rope around the bough of a rotten hardwood tree, and worked his way back to the captain's side. Forlern began to lead the others ahead, and Sarion motioned to them for haste. "Hurry. We have to pass this area."

Careful not to further loosen the ground, he reached Grundel, the captain laying face down and peering over the edge. "Look," said Grundel, his words filled with alarm. "At the lip of the rock."

Sarion gazed down the slope, afraid at what the captain saw. Several hundred feet below them another ledge jutted out, the front of what appeared to be an immense cave, resting directly above the raging waterfall. Huge clouds of spray swirled upwards, the rocky outcropping coated in a carpet of thick, green mold. And laying there were two figures --- Tarral and his horse.

"Is he alive?"

Grundel clenched his fists together, and Sarion squinted against the mist, hoping to find any indication that the man could have survived the fall. Tarral had his face turned skyward, but even from their distant vantage point they saw how twisted his body was, and he lay motionless.

"I don't think anything could have made it against the rocks from such a height," said Grundel. "He isn't moving, and the horse is dead." Sarion ground his teeth, peering over his shoulder at the retreating warriors. Rundin had now passed, hesitating as he waited for the two men. There was no sign of Chertron, and a shiver crawled Sarion's spine at the thought of the brave fighter, his fate unknown. Not him too, he thought grimly. Not Chertron.

"I can't leave him down there, unaware of his..."

Grundel's sentence was sharply cut off as a tremendous roar broke above even the turbulence of the waterfall, staggering in its magnitude and ferocity. They lay there in dismay, listening to the dreadful, angry call of something which could only belong to a greater predator of Grammore—the Jurvech. The men stiffened, watching in cold horror for the inevitable approach of the awakened creature.

And the Jurvech came.

A huge shadow appeared below them, dwarfing the still forms of Tarral and the horse. Sarion was stunned by the sheer size of the monster. It was enormous, standing several dozen yards high, a creature of unimaginable bulk, like a walking monolith of stone resurrected from the dark bowels of the mountain. Its hide was a mottled gray, tough and hairless, the huge limbs ringed with crusted scales, dripping ooze and soil as if disturbed from a hidden grave. Great wings stretched outwards, webbed like those of an impossibly monstrous bat, leathery and black. The head was grisly, ridged with a pair of curved horns, both thick, and longer than a spear. Two cavities opened where ears should be, round and covered with a reddish membrane.

The Jurvech reared its snout back and snatched up Tarral and the horse with a swoop of one clawed arm. Sniffing them both, it swallowed man and beast whole, its wings flapping back and forth, crashing against the rocks and sending splintered fragments down the cliff. It roared once more, and the two men slunk backward out of sight, hoping that the creature would not look for the source of its disturbance any further. The warriors had fled along the slope, and even Rundin was beyond sight, needing no further urging after hearing the first howl from the monster.

The Jurvech was now awakened, the taste of flesh unsatiated, fresh in its maw. It crouched down for a moment then leaped forward, hurtling into the air with a mighty kick of its huge legs, through the heavy mist and vanishing with another cry. Then it was gone.

Sarion was utterly horrified.

He stared deeply into the captain's eyes, the same unspoken thought riveted in their minds. The Jurvech was a living behemoth, a creature which defied rationality. How could anything be so impossibly large? Sarion's breathing was ragged, unprepared for the vision of the frightful monster. In all his experience in Grammore from his past venture and the current expedition, nothing compared to the hulking Jurvech, a beast of unsurpassed strength and violence. Something spawned only within nightmares and despair. If it had spotted the hiding men, they would have been annihilated. Nothing could defend against such power—nothing.

They were fortunate.

Sarion felt a pang of bitterness at the loss of Tarral, the eldest of the fighters, someone he had barely talked to since joining the company. But there was no time for regrets at the moment. Not so close to the Jurvech's lair. They crawled away, waiting until they were a safe distance from the edge, both men looking fearfully to the sky for any sign of the hunting monster. No words were spoken as they went higher, following the trail of the departed warriors. They walked only a short hike before the alarmed face of Rundin appeared throughout the gloom, skin pale, his eyes terrified.

He had also seen the flight of the Jurvech.

"Is it gone?" he whispered. "Captain, in my blackest nightmares I could not have imagined such a beast. How can anything be so huge? We haven't a chance against something like that. This land is evil—cursed." He spat upon the ground. The tough warrior's face was drawn, clearly shaken by the appearance of the dreadful Jurvech.

Grundel merely nodded, sighing deeply. Sarion held his breath at the captain's next words, hovering over each syllable. "What about Chertron, how is he?"

Sarion read the relief in Rundin's face before he spoke.

"He'll be fine, it was just a thick dart, although how the creature kept it within its mouth the entire time, and cut the bindings, I'll never know. Fortunately it wasn't poisoned, or so it seems. Chertron was more surprised I think than injured."

"That's good news, at least. Unlike Tarral." The captain sighed, bowing his head.

"It's my fault." Sarion's heart ached at the loss of yet another warrior. "I should have known, me of all people. The Glefins are ruthless, cunning and deadly. It should have been killed from the beginning. I'll take the blame for the loss of Tarral."

Rundin frowned, and Grundel snapped his head up. "It's no one's fault, Sarion. We're trained to anticipate anything, but no rules apply Grammore. You couldn't have suspected, and we were vigilant in our watch. If anything, it was my decision. I'm the leader of this expedition, and all blame rests on my shoulders. You are here voluntarily, and have as much to lose as everyone else. I brought you here. We would never had made it this far without your guidance."

Sarion shook his head sadly. "Regardless, I am the only one here who has faced these creatures before, and should have anticipated trickery. It was no accident that it waited until we were above the Jurvech's cave." Sarion stared towards the slope, and they all looked nervously into the sky.

"I'll hear no more of such talk," said Grundel. "Let's move ahead, we need to leave this region of terror."

They walked forward, Sarion looking regretfully behind them. They had started out a full company, fourteen men strong, and now their numbers were halved. But he was determined not to leave the Lowlands as the only survivor—if he were so fortunate.

Not this time.

⌣∶∿

They shortly caught up with the others, who had resumed at a diminished pace at Rundin's orders. Chertron was walking on his own, recovered from the Glefin's attack. There was no sign of the wicked thing after having fallen over the edge.

Sarion hoped that the creature had indeed spoken the truth concerning its own race—that it had been the last one.

Their trek became easier over the next several hours as they veered away from the lake and the Jurvech's lair. They had seen no other sign of the great beast, Grundel and Sarion both guessing that it hunted deeper into the lake region. The territory of such a creature would be vast, and with the ability of flight it could travel for countless miles in all directions. Unfortunately, that meant they would be within its area of dominion for days at least.

Little conversation passed between the men, who moved once more into their previous positions, Chertron insisting on taking the lead again, Sarion at his side and keeping a close eye on the durable fighter. The landscape gradually flattened, the forest remaining thick yet, the vegetation lush and oppressive. Even to skilled trackers such as Sarion and Chertron it was difficult to pick a clear path. They had remounted the horses when the footing became certain, and the lake was now far behind them as they walked in a northwesterly direction.

The afternoon passed with little event, and Sarion spoke to Grundel during a brief halt, the last one before nightfall. "If anything, we might not see as many larger beasts within this area. I'm sure a monster like the Jurvech has hunted them all down by now."

They both were quiet, contemplating the close brush with the fantastic creature. Sarion was still amazed as he recalled looking down upon the gigantic beast, unable to wipe away the terrible vision of Tarral's broken form laying before the cave entrance. A better thing that he was not able to see the Jurvech before the end, he thought.

"I think you speak the truth, although Grammore holds many other unpleasant creatures as you have so warned us. This land surpasses all my expectations, in both its wondrous beauty and savagery, the vastness of its boundaries, the changing terrain of water and hill. It's an untamed wilderness, and man has no place here. Our best hope in Trencit is for isolation, and vigilance. This country has always been wild, at least for countless centuries. The elder race of giants may have been a dominant species at one time, but I don't see how any species could hold mastery over such chaos and terror."

Sarion sharpened his knife against a stone, and he glanced at the borders of the small clearing in which they'd chosen to pause. The sky was overcast, the air moderate. The forest was vocal, a number of insects droning from the concealing bushes, several brightly-colored birds whistling in the lofty branches overhead. Cerestin and Areck stood guard at opposite ends of their perimeter, the horses tied to a blackened tree stump close to the center of the glade.

"You speak the truth." Sarion's voice was low, and he felt tired, his heart longing for the gentle fields of his home. It was not so much a physical sensation, but more an emptiness, a void left within his chest caused by the loss of the brave warriors who had fallen victim to the horrors of Grammore. Men he had barely known, and some whom he felt he did know, sharing the trials of the dangerous venture, men who gave their lives to protect Trencit from the surrounding evil. Sarion wondered about the families they would never have a chance to see again. How many children would be left fatherless, how many women would find themselves the widow of yet another courageous soldier? He recalled Halgur's red beard, the man killed by the ogre. The brave Kalen, the weathered face of the newly-fallen Tarral, and the other warrior who had succumbed to the wrath of the ogre—Sarion had never even known his name. He hoped Barthuk and Lerion had found safe passage back to the fortress of Nighton, and were without a doubt in a much safer place than the company of warriors. And how far would their quest take them now?

"Thinking about Tarral yet?" Grundel's words were more a statement than question, and Sarion nodded. "It's not your fault. Don't dwell on it. If I took the time to linger on all the men who have been lost while serving under my command, I would despair, and go mad. It is the age of sacrifice, and all our borders are under siege in some form. The arm of evil reaches into the far corners of the world, terror threatens us at every turn. My thoughts are constantly on the eastern front, and I wonder how the war goes."

"You've seen a lot of battles, I'm sure." Sarion sighed, kicking restlessly at a small clump of dirt. The reddish color reminded him of the rich soils of his farm land, and he missed his nephew Edward and the familiar surroundings of home. The boy was quickly growing into a man, and a fine one he would become, possessing the qualities of his father—honesty, reliability, and an inherent sense of right and wrong, with a far-reaching vision of how the world should be, and might be, if the efforts of good men prevailed. But would Sarion ever see him again? His stomach churned at such a grim thought.

The captain rubbed his hands together, then reached for his water flask before responding, Sarion looking up at him as he spoke, breaking from his drifting reverie.

"Too many." Grundel sighed deeply. "More bloodshed than any man deserves to see in a dozen lifetimes. I speak of despair? We can ill afford to tread that road, and there are thousands of people who rely on our servitude, but I wouldn't have it any other way. I love Trencit and its people, the rolling fields, rich meadows, fertile valleys and wooded hillsides. The great fortresses in high places and low. King Gregor is well-loved, and puts all his energy into fighting—and winning, this war. He has entrusted me with discovering the nature of the threat from the west, and I will not let him down."

"And you still think to go further into Grammore, with our numbers sorely reduced?"

"Yes. A larger host would assuredly attract more notice, although I wouldn't turn down an army if I had one now at my disposal. But I still would not feel secure here."

"Hmm, you would be wise to think such," Sarion answered. "Arrows and swords are no match for a creature such as the Jurvech. I'm astounded that something can grow to such size. We were fortunate those seven years ago to have avoided anything so dangerous. If we would have suspected the existence of such monsters, things might have been different. It is beyond bravery to risk confronting one of Grammore's greater beasts. It would be seeking one's own death…Imagine the devastation something like the Jurvech could rein upon Trencit? Entire villages would be destroyed, regiments of fighters vanquished. It could lay siege to our larger cities. What protection could King Gregor offer against such an attack?"

"He is not without weapons, my friend, but few eyes have ever looked upon their likeness. Another time, maybe." Grundel gazed around the clearing, gesturing at the men to break the light camp.

"One day you may see for yourself," he whispered, a glint in his eye.

Sarion held that thought for a long time.

*:~

They rode onward until nightfall, entering a region of tall trees, the species strange and ominous, towering well over a hundred feet above their heads, the upper boughs shrouded in a perpetual mist. Sarion felt uneasy in this area as they traveled in silence, the forest unusually quiet, lacking the incessant chirping and buzzing which filled many parts of the Lowlands. Sarion found himself peering upwards into the gloom, remembering the earlier encounter with the deadly tree-dweller which had snatched up Chertron's horse with blinding speed. The variety of creatures living in Grammore was incredible, and he'd discussed the matter many times with Grundel during their travels. It was a land filled with stark beauty, wondrous plants and creatures, and also a haven for the most ghastly and monstrous beasts in the known world. No one really knew the expanse of the region, and what lay past its borders. Trencit was a sizable kingdom, but Grammore was far larger, and much more deadly.

Twilight was nigh, and Grundel let out a low whistle, signaling for a halt. They had not passed any clearings for what seemed like hours, so it was up to Chertron and Sarion to find a suitable spot to make camp. They spoke in hushed tones for several moments, deciding to push further. Sarion rode back to the captain, conveying his fears that there would be no ideal site for them that evening, and they would continue onward for a short time to find an area where the brush was thinner.

After several minutes they managed to stumble onto a region of fallen trees, and here they stopped for the night. A pair of vast trunks lay in upheaval, the disturbance looking to be fairly recent, and the men tied their horses in the middle, spreading out in careful formation as was their usual routine. Sarion and Forlern were the first to stand watch, finding positions at opposite ends of the chosen area. They lit a small fire, both men carrying brands with them for light.

As their numbers continued to dwindle, it proved to be a greater strain on the seasoned fighters, and the demands placed on every man became more strenuous. Five men slept, two men stood guard—and the nights could be terrifying. Countless times since entering Grammore the entire company would be awakened, placed on alert, as possible dangers lurked nearby, or someone heard anything unusual. But as powerful as the physical horrors were, the psychological aspect could be even more horrific. The deeper they traveled inside the lowlands, the more visible the land left its mark upon the men, an imprint of resounding terror that could never be completely wiped away or forgotten in their lifetimes. Sarion read the concern and doubt within the eyes of the warriors, the only exceptions being himself and Grundel. Seven years ago Sarion had faced the perils of the wilderland—faced them, and survived. He emerged a changed man, but in a positive way. The experience was always fresh in his memory, and he walked the world with a higher level of awareness, caution, and respect. His abilities and instincts were uncanny, his prowess as a fighter and tracker unmatched in the west, and perhaps beyond. Sarion now pondered the enigmatic captain, who was another survivor. The qualities he had displayed both in leadership and combat placed him among the highest possible echelon of officers, enabling him to obtain the rank of a Captain in Trencit's elite Home Guard, a position of unequaled prominence and confidence. The titles were impressive in their own right, but Sarion was more taken by the man's determination and spirit. Grundel was someone who demanded allegiance, not just because of his ranking, but in his mannerisms and understanding—and even more so, his vision.

Sarion yawned, feeling weary from the long day. It was hard to believe that they had stood above the magnificent but dangerous lake earlier that morning, scaled the hazardous slope led by the deceitful Glefin, and looked upon the overwhelming figure of the incredible Jurvech, all within that same day. He wondered if the monster was even now gliding above the jungle canopy, searching for fresh prey. As fearsome as the creature was, they knew nothing about its habits and other capabilities. It was a most unpleasant thought.

He glanced over his shoulder where he discerned the huddled forms of the horses, restless in their sleep. The fire burned low, and Forlern stood silently past the men who were wrapped tightly in hunting blankets. The man possessed a striking intensity, elevating him over the others in this respect. At times he appeared rash, impatient, but never fearful. He was a natural fighter, and his quickness to depose of the Glefin showed an ability to take action when the unexpected materialized. The Glefin had caught the men by surprise, even the reliable Chertron, but Forlern was ready for anything, and unafraid to take the appropriate measure of response.

Sarion listened to the woods, straining to detect the approach of any wandering predator, but the forest was deathly quiet. Restless, his apprehension continued to grow, enough so that he raised his weapon higher, placing his own brand into the soil, surrounded by several other fixed pieces of burning wood. Something was nearby—he could feel it. His instincts called to him, that refined inner sense which defied rationalization, but existed.

He sensed something—a lurking presence, malevolent, and intelligent. But what was the source of his anxiety—was it somewhere beyond the visible eaves, waiting, perhaps watching him even now? He almost signaled an alarm, but thought better of it. He realized that not every creature in Grammore attacked without provocation. They were still a formidable group even in their diminished numbers, and unfamiliar to the dwellers of the Lowlands. Many beasts would back away unless they spotted an easy kill, and not all predators were large, or unique like the Jurvech. Smaller ones existed, swift and crafty, others roamed in hunting packs, while yet some were solitary animals, surviving on special abilities or living inside a particular environment, be it plant, earth, or water.

Nothing stirred in the forest, no creature visible to his keen hearing or vision. Maybe his natural caution was remaining high-strung, unable to ease down. Sarion looked up into the dark trees, and went cold with dread.

A pair of yellow eyes were staring directly at him.

༝ː༚

It was one of Sarion's most terrifying moments as he locked gazes with the unknown creature overhead. He hardly dared to breathe, matching the stare of whatever perched above him, maybe twenty feet into the tree. The body of the thing was invisible, obscured by darkness, and Sarion knew it was by design. The eyes were reflective, the orange from the fire gleaming within its orbs, and the first thing which came to Sarion's mind were the eyes of an insect, lifeless and alien. He was being observed, and the creature was fully aware of his own scrutiny as they measured each other. Sarion held his weapon higher, gauging the thing for a reaction. It remained there for several more seconds, then the eyes blinked once and were gone.

He heard a faint rustling as the creature moved away, climbing higher into the tree. Was it gone for good, though? There was no way of telling, or knowing if more of the things lurked overhead. Sarion felt a cold shiver cross his back at the notion of a colony of such creatures living in the vast canopy, like a nest of giant spiders. It was a hideous thought, and he looked over to Forlern, letting out a low whistle. The man snapped his head around immediately, and Sarion gave a curt hand signal upwards, a caution to be on the alert for possible danger overhead. The warrior nodded back, bringing his own weapon up.

On watch now in all directions, time dragged by slowly that night for Sarion until he relieved a groggy Areck later on, telling him what he'd seen. Sarion stayed up late with the fighter, until he was convinced that the creature was not threatening an imminent attack. It may have simply been curious, examining the intruders below, and had went off in search of easier prey. The questions were all disturbing, but no answers appeared to be forthcoming, and the night passed without further event.

The morning dawned slowly, gloomy and oppressive. The warriors had passed through many harrowing encounters while in the Lowlands, barely surviving. They were a tough and durable breed of men, some of them quick to laughter, much swifter to the sword, but the relentless gray which accompanied their travels weighed heavily upon their shoulders, offering no gleam of brightness from the hidden sun. It was a lost friend, a companion from better days and much more hospitable lands. Sarion knew the dreary weather was yet another enemy, one which battled against their fortitude, striving for them to give into despair and panic. Little could be done except to maintain his own hope, encourage the fighters, lend assistance wherever needed, and the men respected him for it.

Cerestin was adjusting a broken harness on his steed, and Sarion walked over, helping him fasten the leather bindings until they were tight. He grinned in satisfaction at Sarion and picked up his helm, which was stained and discolored from their trials in the wilderness.

"I remember a silver glint to this helmet when we first met, Cerestin. Maybe we can polish it up a bit later, what do you think?" Sarion patted the metal, fingers rubbing one of the larger dents.

"I say it's a fine idea, and long overdue," replied the warrior, a smirk covering his lightly-bearded face. "Sorely is it in need of a good cleaning—and myself, I might add." He rubbed his whiskers, and Sarion chuckled.

"I also recall a face fresh as an infant's, hairless as a woman's. Sharpen that knife for later, when we pause for a rest. We'll both look like civilized men again, once we've had a decent scrub."

"Aye, Sarion. If this forsaken land permits us, that is. After seeing that beast yesterday, I'll never sleep well again,

I'm afraid. The night-wings haunt my rest, chasing me like a frightened child in my slumber. I am shamed."

Sarion held up a hand. "I would disagree with you there, Cerestin. You've faced great evil and come through unscathed. Lesser men than our group would have fallen long ago to the sights of what you have borne witness to." He looked intently into the man's gray eyes. "You have stared at the face of horror and evil, undaunted. Take heart from your experience, my friend. You have shown the ability to confront anything—your nightmares have already been revealed. Darkness is the cloak of ignorance and hopelessness. You have thrown off this burden from your own strong shoulders. And you'll continue to ride with head held high, sword arm ready. I for one am glad to have you at my side."

The warrior nodded, gazing respectfully at Sarion. The words were brave, even though they walked within a den of madness and terror. He inclined his head to Sarion, who walked away. Grundel watched, listening to Sarion's words from a short distance, his head motionless, but his eyes following the man's back, a faint gleam of admiration visible within his orbs.

"Well said, Sarion," he whispered. "The words of a leader."

⌁

There was little to distinguish this particular day from any other, and the company rode on late into the morning, their clothes damp from the relentless humidity. Dense foliage surrounded the men in every direction, exotic and colorful flowers appearing in scattered patches, while other areas swarmed with the tendrils of green vines which latched onto any wood within their grasp. The sun was still invisible, blanketed above by towering trees shooting upwards into the gloom. They were of a strange variety, and Sarion spoke to Grundel concerning his encounter with the unseen creature, and their mutual observation the previous night.

"It was measuring me, gauging myself as a threat—or lack of being a threat, perhaps. The orbs reminded me of an insect's, like it was a huge spider waiting at the borders of its web. Flat, expressionless in themselves, but I perceived intelligence in that gaze. It seemed unwilling to press our advantage in numbers, or else I believe it would have attacked."

The captain arched his neck upwards, peering into the sprawling canopy overhead. "A most unpleasant thought, the notion of predators crawling above us, shrouded by night and these abysmally large trees. There's not one region of Grammore I would feel safe in, but this area seems more perilous than some, although I haven't reason to confirm my suspicions. If there is indeed a host of such creatures lurking within the forest eaves, we should make haste to move on. If they mass for an assault, we will be hard put for a pitched battle under the cloak of darkness."

Sarion nodded, his face grim as he stared at Chertron's horse before him. "Even considering all the tragic events which have befallen our quest, it's fortunate that we have not been attacked at night. This may change soon, though."

Grundel paused, his voice lower. "Sarion, I have also decided to make due east, and leave the Lowlands."

Sarion gave him a sharp glance, surprised at the resignation in the captain's voice. Grundel met his gaze, unflinching and determined despite his words. Even after the harrowing brush with the Jurvech, Grundel had remained resolute in his conviction for the company to push deeper into the Lowlands. And now he had changed his mind.

"I can read your thoughts, my friend. Yes, I stated a differing opinion yesterday, confirming the thrust of our mission. But we tread upon delicate ground. Our numbers have dwindled, and the danger grows with each further step into this terrible country, and still there is no sign of our quarry, or anything which could lend us hope for things to change."

The captain gave a curt whistle, signaling for a halt. The afternoon was lengthening, and the terrain had not altered since earlier the previous day, and now a light drizzle had begun to fall, adding to their discomfort and dampening the overall mood of the warriors. Forlern and Chertron acted as watch, while the others dismounted and foraged for nuts and berries. Many of the common fruits and edible plants were numerous in the moisture-rich Lowlands, and they filled their food sacks at nearly every rest. A small spring trickled several yards to their right, and the men led the horses for a drink. Brooks and water holes were plentiful, and they avoided only the larger ponds, fearing for what might be living nearby, or possibly within the unseen depths. Such areas were quickly bypassed, and more than once Sarion had seen footprints within the yielding turf, some of insignificant size, others very large, left by unknown beasts.

Sarion approached Grundel as the men went about various tasks or chose to rest, and he was eager to discover the reasoning behind the man's decision. The captain sat upon a moss-coated log, which had at one time plunged high into the forest canopy, recently fallen by its fresh-looking appearance, lacking any visible decay on the slimy bark. A gray salamander perched near one of the captain's booted feet, scurrying away as Sarion drew close.

"Sit down, Sarion. I understand your confusion, but I'm convinced that we need to leave Grammore."

"Surely I see the reasons for either course of action, but what has changed since yesterday?" Sarion joined Grundel on the log.

"Much, or little, depending on which perspective you use. Maybe it's an accumulation of everything that's happened to us. The loss of my men, watching the monstrous evil which lives within this accursed land, the overwhelming odds facing us. My orders are clear, but the means of carrying them out are not. I've done a lot of thinking, torn between the need to uncover the secrets buried within the Lowlands, learn as to why the ogre marauded the borders of Trencit, and who sent it. I am certain of this last fact, but have not the power to discover the answer."

"And what of the King, will he be content with the knowledge you bring him?"

Grundel nodded his head, looking weary.

"He will understand. I can't ask anymore from the men, they've already far surpassed many of their peers in bravery, endurance, and combat. They have faced creatures which are only legend back in Trencit, demons whispered around a warm bonfire on a cold night, and some of them will not see their beloved homeland again, claimed by the cruelty of Grammore. But we are fighters, and readily accept our fate. None loyal to Trencit would question their command."

"Nor I, Captain. King Gregor is respected and loved by the people, fair and just. He does not act on anything which is not of grave consequence to the survival of our land and its people. What will be his next course of action, do you think?"

Grundel patted the hilt of his blade. "It's hard to be sure, but additional patrols will already be in place by now, scouting parties foraging past our borders, attempting to form a network of protection and communication between the outlying territories and the interior strongholds. The Western Guard is being mobilized as we speak. He may even assign a larger war party to probe the reaches of Grammore. Of course, he will consider our venture foremost, but there is a need for additional knowledge, and he will not be satisfied until more is learned."

"I wonder how the war in the east goes?" Sarion stared off in the direction where he believed their own country lay, but he couldn't be sure. Things were changing, and he would be changing with them. Trencit required his service, and he would answer to his own call—a position in the Western Watch, Grundel had said. His mind drifted to Edward and the farm, both familiar dream-fragments, constant companions to him whether he slept or walked the earth. He knew the boy would be greatly concerned for his safety, but Sarion had told him to have courage, and remember what he had been taught. Edward would not falter.

"The thought dwells heavily upon my heart," replied the captain. "Trencit requires my services on every border, at each conflict. I held a high command on the eastern front, but was called back for this quest. I was unwilling to go at first, but the King cannot be denied."

"You argued against his orders?" Sarion was a bit surprised by Grundel's statement.

"Not in the manner you might think. He is always open to disagreement and ideas opposite of his own, especially to those he holds within his confidence—such as myself." He winked at Sarion, who now wondered just how powerful a position Grundel held in the Home Guard. Much more than he let people know, he decided. And how much did the fighters really know about him?

"And you attempted to persuade him otherwise?" Sarion glanced over at Rundin, the bearish man restlessly practicing with his long sword.

"Against sending me...yes. I was needed on the frontier, near the fortress of Druhil, where the fighting has been fierce. When he told me that he would be sending a command off regardless of my decision, then I agreed to lead the company. I knew how hazardous such an expedition would be, and volunteered in the end."

He seemed ready to say something else, but hesitated. Sarion wanted to pursue the matter, but Grundel stood up, gesturing to Rundin.

"Time grows late, and we're still beneath these forsaken trees. Let's make haste and leave this region behind."

Sarion followed him, more curious than ever about the mysterious captain.

⌇⁚⌇

Twilight had captured the day early, and the rain continued to fall upon them from the lofty boughs overhead. The forest was a shimmering haze of gray, a sluggish mist curling between the vast trunks and limiting their vision to scarcely a dozen yards. Grundel pushed them onwards in an easterly direction, and Sarion felt confident of their progress even in the immense wilderness. He read much from simple things, like where moss grew on trees, the positioning of stars, although the latter had been severely hampered since entering the Lowlands. But the task of leading them back to their own lands was a daunting one, and he confided with Chertron at many points.

One disturbing thing he noticed was the amount of trees that were laying on the ground, the great roots sticking upright from the moist soil, as if having been torn apart at the hands of some enormous creature. They seemed to be finally leaving the area of tall trees, and he was slightly relieved by this, but he also knew that the dangers of Grammore were everywhere, the only difference being the shape and manner.

At times they would catch glimpses of wandering herds of stag, one of the more common and harmless types of animal, similar to the beasts of Trencit, but these were stouter and more cautious. Other times they heard the passing of some unknown creature, but as the rain increased the forest grew still once more. The air had an unpleasant chill to it, heavy with the dampness from the precipitation, and Sarion realized that it would soon be impossible to maintain a fire. The warriors carried small lanterns for such dismal situations, and had relied upon them many times within the Lowlands. Tonight would be no exception.

At the lead along with Chertron on his right, Sarion swept his gaze front and to his left side, trying to cover as much of the perimeter as possible. Forlern rode immediately behind him, followed by Grundel, Cerestin and Areck, and the reliable Rundin bringing up the rear. Only seven of us left, thought

Sarion. Seven against all the countless horrors of Grammore. Bad, but it could have been much worse, he knew.

The trees loomed menacingly on every side, the mist trailing along the forest floor in swirling miniature clouds, hindering their speed. To move any faster would hamper their ability to react quickly, but they also would face danger without any warning due to their slower pace. With such reduced numbers, they all needed to be alert at every moment—the night watchers doubly vigilant. It was a good thing they were departing the Lowlands, Sarion knew. The men had been pushed far beyond reasonable limits, even for highly-trained fighters that they were. The factors which existed in battle along their other borders were of no consequence here. Grammore was like one monstrous beast, patiently waiting to devour the weak and unwary. They had been neither so far, but things had changed. Fatigue and loss were now their enemies as well.

The rain fell in fat droplets from the invisible heights above, splattering off the green, leafy branches of the mixed hardwood trees enveloping them. Sarion struggled to maintain a sense of their general direction, but the conditions were deteriorating swiftly. Soon, the jungle canopy glittered eerily as lightning flashes seared the evening sky. Several of the warriors had already lighted their lanterns, and Chertron glanced uneasily over at Sarion.

Without speaking, Sarion nodded his head, gesturing to the woods which lay before them. He felt a sense of dread, although he couldn't locate the source, or any reason for his disquiet, but he had learned at an early age to trust his instincts, and his were exceptional. The storm raged overhead, great claps of thunder now bellowing through the trees. The rainfall was coming down harder, and the horses lifted their hooves higher as the already soft ground transformed into a mud pit, marked with small rocks, dead leaves, and scattered twigs poking out of the soil like the crooked hands of diminutive creatures. The warriors were clothed in hunting cloaks, the finest available in Trencit, but nothing could entirely keep the moisture from seeping through, soaking them all to the skin.

The jungle was silent—no insect or animal called out, or moved nearby as the rain overwhelmed everything. There had been little change in the gloom the day long, but now, as nightfall descended, the blanket of darkness consumed the half-light, throwing the Lowlands into blackness. The lanterns were water-proof, and the fighters appeared as a line of forsaken will-o-wisps, riding along in the inhospitable terrain. Sarion listened to the peals of thunder rumbling in the heavens, and at times a single loud crash would echo through the forest, fading within a few seconds. As they continued, he grew increasingly nervous about the sound, which now stood out above the background thunder in its intensity.

Sarion pursed his lips together, soon realizing that the noise did not originate from the storm at all—it was coming from the forest floor, somewhere in the distance, but drawing nearer. It was a tremendous booming, as of something large making its way through the trees. He knew instantly that it was something very huge, and extremely dangerous. Was he the only one to notice? He peered over at Chertron, but the warrior rode with his head bowed, eyes alert to the trees and bushes ahead of them, apparently oblivious to the approaching threat.

Sarion looked back, reining in his horse. Forlern halted as well, reading the concern in Sarion's face. The warriors had long ago come to respect Sarion without hesitation, and Forlern's hand immediately went to the haft of his sword.

"What is it?" Chertron hissed over to him, his voice muffled by the folds of his cloak. The company held their steeds at bay, and Grundel trotted forward. Even through the drenching rain and relentless thunder, Sarion clearly heard the noise, which would cease for long moments before picking up again.

"Listen." He held up his hand, gesturing as the noise sounded, ominous and dreadful in the distance. "Do you hear it? It's not from the storm—something comes."

The captain's face was grave, and he gave a light nod of recognition. "I hear it, although I thought it was the storm at first, but you're right. It's from the forest, but from what direction..."

His words abruptly ended as another crash was heard, loud and powerful. The horses grew restless, nickering about in agitation. "Muffle the beasts," he commanded. "They can't give us away."

The men acted at once, pulling out the soft leather straps to quiet the animals. The creatures were invaluable to the group, considering all the distance they had so far traveled, although at times they needed to be silenced for fear of attracting unwanted attention. Sarion perched high on his own horse after securing the muzzle, trying to pinpoint the source of the noise. After waiting over a minute, he heard the sound twice, and decided it was coming from behind them.

"We're being hunted." Sarion's face was grim, but certain, as he spoke the chilling words. "Something picked up our scent, or trail, after we left the region of high trees, tracking us even through the rain and mud." He looked around. The warriors were ready for battle, and many of them held weapons in their grips, but also Sarion read the terror in some of their faces, the haunted gazes, and knew that they had to escape whatever was stalking them. Tired and on the run, they were in no condition for a battle in the darkness. The approaching beast had to be formidable, and he hoped it was not one of the stronger predators of the Lowlands, but in his heart he had a sinking feeling that it was exactly that.

"Let's move, keeping in this direction." Grundel thrust his hand forward, balled into a tight fist, the other hand holding the horse in check. "We stop for nothing until we lose the beast. With luck, our trail will be washed away, or confused from this abominable weather. Rundin, keep a close watch behind, and stay near. I want everyone to ride together. To separate in here means death. Go!"

He had to shout so the men could hear his words above the enraged storm. Trees whipped and cracked, and branches began dropping heavily to the ground, some of them striking the warriors. The booming sound still continued, and Sarion doubted that the creature would be so easily lost. The hunters of Grammore relied on finely-developed senses, of sight, smell, and hearing. If it had followed them this far, it would have little difficulty in continuing after them. The men urged their steeds onward, and Grundel called for a brisk pace. Sarion knew the hazards of moving swiftly through the jungle, but the greater risk was evident behind them. They would have to take the chance that the rain and approach of the unseen predator would deter any other marauders from attacking.

It was a nightmarish flight. The horses breathed raggedly, straining through the muzzles, steam pouring forth and curling around their heads. The riders were trying desperately to see through the mist and rain, but the entire forest was shrouded in a thick, billowing fog. The storm seemed to be intensifying even more, and great rumbles of thunder shook the very earth, lightning snaking between the trees and casting the woods in brief sparks of white illumination. In these scant moments, the jungle was electrified, and Sarion used the opportunity to scan his surroundings. At one point, he looked to his left and gasped in surprise.

A huge creature stood upright, crouched behind a vine-strangled oak. Its hide was shaggy, long, trailing tufts of hair covering its entire body, as if it had grown up from the mossy ground. The face was small, with two black openings for eye slots, lacking ears or nose. A thin line creased the lower part of the head, and the rest of its features remained obscured as the lightning dimmed.

It made no move against the men, but stood with head tilted, facing towards the direction where the warriors had come from. Shambling off into the shadows, the creature vanished as quickly as it appeared. The men rode past it, all of them unaware of its presence except for Sarion. The creature had looked deadly, standing at least a dozen feet high, its hair camouflaged within the trunks and moss.

Sarion knew that the strange beast was more concerned with what was approaching, just as they were, choosing to escape instead of attacking. As startled as he was by the unexpected vision of the thing, he was much more anxious about the unknown pursuer. For something as large as the weird creature appeared to be, it had disappeared quickly into the wilderness, and Sarion shivered, trying to imagine what was hunting them.

He didn't want to think about it. A battle in the dark and rain, against something fierce enough to scare away other larger predators, was too much for them to challenge. Flight was their only chance, and a grim one at that. The fighters were weary, suffering from a lack of sleep, warmth, and plagued by the constant terror of Grammore, which was like a hangman's noose, squeezing them ever-so-slowly, bearing down upon their collective endurance and determination. The minutes dragged by, the horses picking their way carefully through the thickets and dead wood, sloshing through patches of mud and small pebbles.

Sarion and Chertron were still riding in brisk stride as the woods unexpectedly gave way, and the two trackers were surprised at the sudden change in terrain. A river lay before them, the far shore invisible in the murkiness, the waters brown and swollen from the heavy rainfall. Branches floated along the surface, carried away by the current, fading from view as quickly as they appeared. The fog curled above the river in a swirling haze, and the other warriors came forward, Rundin dropping back in the woods to listen for sounds of the inevitable pursuit.

Grundel stared deeply into Sarion's eyes, the unspoken thought plaguing both their hearts. There wasn't any way of knowing how far off the opposite shore sat, or even the depth of the angry waters. A loud crash echoed from behind them— the loudest they had heard. The thing was closing swiftly, moving with amazing speed through the undergrowth. It would be upon them within a few minutes, and they were faced with an unpleasant choice. Sarion decided immediately their course of action. They could not face whatever pursued them. He glanced sideways at the captain.

"We have no other option. The beast is nearly upon us. The river must be attempted."

Grundel nodded. "Secure your packs and weapons, we must hope the water is not too deep or too swift."

"And let's hope we're not heading into a watery grave," answered Forlern beneath his breath.

⌣·∾

Areck headed into the woods after Rundin, and the fighters prepared to enter the river. The current flowed to their left, in a westerly direction, and deeper into Grammore. Sarion was moving, leading his horse into the waters, and finding the current alarmingly strong already. It would take a tremendous stroke of luck for them to pass unharmed and without mishap, and he made certain his belongings were strapped tight.

"Do you think there be water beasts living here?" Cerestin passed alongside of him, and Sarion fell silent at the man's words. It was a terrible thought, but he couldn't offer any comfort to the grim-faced warrior.

"Let's not think such black things. I believe it flows too swiftly for it to hide anything dangerous, but have a care. Evil lodges where it may. Watch your steed."

The men were up to their knees in the river, pushing steadily downstream and across at the same time. The others entered, with Rundin and Areck bringing up the rear. The horses seemed to be alright, their war training coming to light, unafraid of water and able to swim strongly if necessary.

The river felt cool, the sensation not altogether unpleasant. The rain hammered full force into the churning waters, and the sky crackled with lightning spears. Occasionally a particularly strong one would strike nearby, startling man and horse alike. The noise from their pursuer continued to grow louder and more frequent, and Sarion knew that the creature was excited, knowing its quarry was near. How ironic, he thought. The company had entered Grammore as the hunters, chasing the trail of the elusive ogre, but had increasingly become prey themselves to the horrors dwelling in the Lowlands. Men were severely outmatched against the much larger and stronger natives of the wilderland, and only a combination of their tracking and survival skills had brought them this far. Fortune had been on their side many times as well, and Sarion did not like to rely on luck—it would not always prove to be so generous. The faces of the fallen warriors passed before his gaze, spectral and sad, reminding him of those who had not been so fortunate in their quest.

He shrugged aside such dismal thoughts, concentrating on keeping his balance and guiding his horse, which was moving with little difficulty. He praised the breeding of the species as well as its training, knowing that they were among the finest to be found anywhere. They had drifted a good distance downstream and away from shore but were still only about three dozen yards from the bank. The bottom of the river was gravelly, and they were able to secure decent footing. If it had been soft muck, the going would have been extremely hazardous and Sarion dared not think of what might have happened.

The men were in a fairly close circle, staying together and remaining alert. The storm raged furiously overhead, the wind blowing with gale-like force. Sarion could not have imagined a worse scenario. The booming sound blasted from just off the shore and he realized the creature was trying to pinpoint their location. The wind screamed, and they were picking up speed, carried in the formidable current and struggling to keep from dipping under.

The water lapped over their chests now, and the horses were swimming alongside them, their powerful legs thrusting them onward. The fog descended like a vast blanket of gray, neither shore visible. They were in a vulnerable position, especially if the river dropped significantly, or the current continued to increase. After a few short minutes, they had put a fair amount of distance between themselves and the bank, but were growing tired, their bodies reaching the limits of their endurance. Another crash came from upstream, and Sarion watched his companions, knowing they wouldn't make it much further in the rising current. Suddenly a dark shape appeared from the gloom, and Sarion felt a glimmer of hope. An island lay before them, maybe thirty yards from their position.

"Captain Grundel," he gasped. "Head for the island, it's our only chance."

He shouted to be heard above the clamor of the river and the storm, and the captain waved an arm in a gesture of recognition, a short distance behind him. Chertron surged ahead with his horse, gaining momentum as the current arced before nearing the island, and Sarion followed his lead. They splashed ahead, the water growing shallower and the force of the current receding as they walked knee deep, leaving the main part of the river behind them.

The warriors emerged from the waters intact, if weary and soaked, the horses appearing unharmed. The island was covered in thick brush and scraggy trees, several yards wide and the length shrouded in mist. The banks were at a slight angle, but the animals had no difficulty ascending the incline. Rundin was the last one to step on shore, and he motioned the others to move deeper into the brush.

"Something was making a lot of noise before we drew nigh to the island. I'm unsure if the river thwarted our pursuer, but it has made no attempt to conceal its presence ever since picking up our trail."

Grundel said "Maybe its size will act against it here, not wishing to try and cross after us. The water will have extinguished all scent of our passing, for sure. And it can't be certain of our direction regardless."

"All unknown factors." Sarion walked in front of them, turning his head to respond. "If the thing is highly intelligent, it will undoubtedly know that we couldn't force our way upstream in such a short span of time. Also, if it's familiar with the territory, it might even know all the shallower channels, crossing at will. We also cannot comprehend its sense of smell, maybe a small trace of us can still be found. Too many questions."

"Sarion, you never fail to make me rethink all my schemes and assumptions, as well as increasing my own uncertainties." Grundel frowned, while Rundin looked behind his shoulder nervously, adding " I fervently hope you're wrong on all accounts."

"Well, right or wrong, we make a stand here." The captain's voice was confident, brimming with leadership and determination. "The men are near exhaustion, and we all need food and dry clothes. I wish this blasted rain would let up."

Sarion stared upwards as another shard of lightning streaked across the air, giving the landscape an eerie look. The burdens of the journey weighed heavily upon his heart and limbs, and he trudged along behind Areck's tired frame, wondering how it would all end.

�⋅

The rain ended sometime after midnight, although it was impossible to be sure what hour it was in the perpetual gloom of Grammore. The men huddled close together, unable to light a fire and draw notice to their position. It would have been unlikely in any case, in the drenching downpour, although the lanterns remained waterproof for limited lighting if needed.

The rest of the evening passed uneventfully, and Sarion believed they had finally shaken off their pursuit. He thought the creature might have searched the shores of the river for a while, prying about for signs of their passage. Something as large as what pursued them would have great need for a constant supply of prey, and couldn't waste time on something as elusive as their group. He was thankful they hadn't been forced to fight against it, their chances would have been slim. Whatever manner of creature it was, there could be no doubt it would have been a disastrous event.

The morning eventually arrived, drier but remaining dusky. The mist rolled along the edges of the island, billowing towards the far shores, both of which were invisible. Grundel decided to wait until late morning before attempting the waters, no one looking forward to immersing themselves again.

"Captain, another thought for our next move." Sarion drew near, his face excited.

"I'm listening. Not very eager for another swim myself, but we can't stay here too much longer."

"My plan calls for exactly that, though."

"Let's hear it."

"There is plenty of wood here, sturdy vines, spare rope. We'll fasten logs together, creating makeshift rafts. We can at least keep our supplies dry for the next crossing, and have something to hold onto, in case the river is deeper on the opposite side."

Grundel paused. "Hmm, that's a good idea. Give us some additional leverage. It was becoming dangerous before we breached the island. This way, we can use the rafts to lighten our burdens. I'll have the others start immediately, and take the watch. Have at it."

They both stood, going about the task at hand. The fighters were rested, although stiff and miserable. They were also eager for action, and this helped distract their wandering imaginations from blacker thoughts.

Several hours later they had completed enough small rafts to assist them when they crossed the river once more. They prepared to enter the swollen turbulence, the far side appearing swifter and deeper. "When we gain the opposite side, immediately take up fighting stances, Chertron and Sarion foremost, while the others untie our belongings. Move in." Grundel gave the signal to advance, and the fighters pushed the logs into the river, the horses at their sides.

Man and beast waded into the gravelly shallows, trying to maintain their balance. It was fortunate they had made the rafts, because the going was even more difficult this time. They floated downstream several dozen yards, and moved further into the current. Shortly, they were beyond sight of the island, and the far shore loomed in the distance across the wide channel. In waters up to their chest, the fighters gasped and splashed, forcing themselves against the strong flow and keeping tight grip on the reins of their steeds.

They had passed over nearly half a mile downstream from the island before they finally started wading into the shoal of the opposite shore. Their feet sank in the muck, and they avoided larger branches drifting close by, newly fallen from the previous night's storm. The approaching forest was dark and even denser on this side, gnarled trees hovering above the murky waters like bent old men, moss and vines dipping within reach of the muddy surface. Huge roots erupted above steeper banks, and the men searched for an accessible path to clamber up from the river. Another stream spilled into the channel from a small waterfall and they made for it, as the ground leveled off. Soon, they found themselves on firmer ground and finally out of the tenacious current.

The men went about unpacking their belongings, Chertron and Sarion moving inland to watch for danger. Grundel wanted them well-past the river in short notice, unwilling to tempt a brush with any lurking shoreline predators. The woods here seemed normal enough, squirrels and colorful birds poking around above their heads, insects droning in clumps of scattered thickets and weeds.

The men pushed the rafts back into the river and they scurried off in the current, Grundel thinking it best to leave no indication of their passing. Not even giving the fighters time to unbundle drier clothes, the company moved quickly through the brush and made decent time, hoping that the horrors of the past night would not be soon rekindled. Sarion knew they were still no closer to the edge of the Lowlands, increasingly concerned that they were becoming further entangled within the dark woods.

They rode silently for the most part, Sarion and Chertron murmuring between themselves about the proposed direction. "I wish we could reach some point of higher ground, out of this forsaken fog even for a few seconds." Chertron muttered, shivering as they trotted along.

"It would indeed be a wonderful thing. Sunshine, a pleasant breeze. Such matters we deem of little consequence back in Trencit, galloping along a bright meadow or country pathway. None of us will take these small things for granted once we return to our homelands." Sarion gazed into the canopy above, eyeing nothing suspicious, which only made him more watchful. The subtle dangers were the ones he feared the most, and he did not want to be caught off guard.

"This area appears less sinister to my senses, but that only serves to increase my caution. Keep a sharp look out for trouble, Chertron."

"Aye. Although I can't help wishing for a cheerful blaze to warm my bones."

Sarion nodded, and they rode quietly for the remainder of the afternoon, their fortune seeming to hold out for the moment. But would it last, he wondered?

⤳:⤳

The forest grew thinner as the day wore on, the ground becoming harder and rocks appearing with greater frequency, smooth dull-gray pebbles scattered among them. They picked a suitable spot for camp that evening, a cluster of large boulders stained with lichen and pocked with small openings, many of these filled with water from the recent rains.

The mist was a familiar companion, at times breaking up, but never disappearing altogether.

Forlern and Cerestin had the first watch, taking up strategic positions at the edge of two outcroppings, both stretching out like the rocky arm from the main cluster, large enough to offer a haven on three sides for the men and horses alike. Sarion was restless, staying up late with Grundel, discussing the past events and immediate plans. The other men lay wrapped in blankets, and Sarion discerned Forlern's lean figure wielding a long knife in one hand.

"Circumstances have been chaotic ever since we entered the Lowlands." The captain leaned back against the stone, eyes staring intently at the small fire they had started earlier. "There are some things I have wanted to tell you, and now seems as good a time as any."

Curious, Sarion wondered what was on the captain's mind.

"Have a look at this. I had almost forgotten about it."

Grundel pulled out a small obsidian wand fixed with a red orb at the top from beneath his cloak. It seemed to be made from a finely wrought metal, tube-like but strong. He handed it to Sarion, who touched it wonderingly, surprised at the warmth he felt coming from the rod.

"Beautiful little thing, don't you think?" Grundel smiled appreciatively at Sarion's confused expression.

"Where did you come across this wand?" asked Sarion, admiring the texture and design of the object. "I've never seen the like before. Did King Gregor give this to you?"

Grundel shook his head. "No, I found it within the lair of the Killworm. Among piles of bones, weapons, armor, and untold other items. A treasure trove, all buried beneath the remains of the creature's victims. It seemed to glow when I first spotted it, and I took it with me. I've kept it hidden since then, and safe."

"Any idea of its purpose or maker?"

Grundel hesitated. "No, but I am certain it is very old, and was created by skillful hands. I have no recollection of anything with this description from what I've read in the ancient tomes at the palace. I wish to bring it to King Gregor, to see what he can make of it, or any of his elders. My feeling is that it served some purpose in a time long ago— and still may, for that matter. There's something about it— something very special."

Sarion agreed. Holding it in his grip he felt a faint sensation, almost a vitality of sorts, from somewhere deep inside the rod, energy that lay dormant. Grundel was right—there was something peculiar about it, and he was fascinated by the simplistic beauty it possessed.

"You were wise to keep it safe. I would not bring it to anyone's attention either. It might be a divination wand of some kind, or perhaps even an ancient weapon." Sarion was chilled by his own words. A talisman from a lost age? It was a striking notion, but the idea held certain grains of truth, and dread.

The captain agreed. "Hmm, I thought the same. Maybe it's just a pretty artifact, once kept on the person of an unfortunate victim of the Killworm. However, if it is a weapon, or contains any magic, it could prove quite beneficial to the king at some later point—if its secret can be unlocked, of course..."

"Beneficial, or dangerous." Sarion and Grundel stared at the wand for long moments before the captain concealed it once more.

⌇⁚⁘

The night prowlers were active, and Sarion took his turn to watch along with Areck into the early morning hours. Howls and yelps disturbed the forest, shrill cries from far off, and some closer. Sarion believed they were from wolves and similar animals, others were of unknown species and a more sinister nature. In the unforgiving Lowlands, you were either the hunted or the hunter. Their company had been both.

Dawn arrived, somewhat less dreary than the other mornings. The fighters were soon ready to be off, their spirits elevated by the drier weather and the uneventfullness of the previous day. Would that the same could be said until they left the Lowlands, Sarion mused.

The forest continued to clear, the trees thinning, patches of grass cropping up, as they moved on in what they hoped was a true easterly direction, the ground sloping gradually beneath their feet. Sarion knew they had not gone nearly far enough to be entering the edges of Grammore, but the change in terrain lightened his heart somewhat. The day brightened, but the sun remained hidden by the ever-present mist, although it was considerably less thick. The forest contained a mixture of hardwoods and other strange varieties, and Sarion was quick to avoid anything suspicious looking, or dense.

At one point, they entered a glade filled with a species of dazzling purple flowers, their petals stretching outwards for several feet. A sweet perfume smell wafted from the unusual plants, and Sarion immediately halted, pressing the company back and taking another path. He was not going to take any chances. He knew that beauty and death could take the same form in the inhospitable Lowlands.

As the land continued to climb, Sarion wondered if they were approaching a ridge, or even a line of low foothills. They still had to be a number of miles away from the borders, perhaps two or three days at least. They traveled using their skills of tracking and instinct, without anything else to go on, lacking maps or experience. The air turned slightly cooler, but still was heavy with the permanent humidity and dampness of the Lowlands. By afternoon it was evident that their surroundings had significantly changed, and the denser jungle was left behind. A line of boulders appeared just ahead, the trees fewer and smaller. Sarion was naturally cautious, and he slowed his horse down, motioning to Chertron. They walked forward carefully, eyeing the terrain ahead. There was a lack of tree tops beyond the rocks, and he was now sure the land would soon drop off.

Sarion decided to dismount, and Chertron followed his example, the other warriors pausing until the leaders could scout ahead. The men crouched low, moving forward with weapons raised. The rocks were high enough to offer concealment, and this was Sarion's fear, that they would be waylaid by something lurking behind the boulders. The rocks were actually smaller than they had appeared from further away, broken slags of chipped stone with larger ones between them, forming a crude ridge line. What struck Sarion was the very existence of a structured design, albeit old and weathered. They found nothing unusual on their initial inspection and pressed onward, the ground leveling off at their feet. It appeared to be the remains of an ancient wall of sorts, cracked and blasted, the larger boulders once part of the main barrier. Through a cleared space, Sarion snaked his way past the greater part of the ruins, and found himself looking down from the rim of a tremendous valley, confirming what he'd originally thought. But he'd never anticipated what lay below...

Chertron now joined his side, his own weapon lowering in astonishment. The two men stared for long moments, until Forlern and Grundel himself came forward, concerned by their absence. No stares were exchanged, only gasps of awe.

An enormous valley lay at their feet, the bottom cloaked within a deep and impenetrable mist. The bottom terrain could only be guessed at, as the view was hazy. Climbing up from the middle of the vale were tiered spires, sprawling skywards and ringed about with vapor. Towering battlements and walls stood immense, distant but clearly visible from where they stood, despite the tenacious fog.

It was a vast fortress, ominous and forbidding.

The men were stunned. Even Grundel seemed to be at a loss for words. Sarion stared down at the impossible castle, dread crawling towards his heart. The sensation of foreboding he felt was powerful, his instincts warning him of certain danger. It was evil, built by evil things, and home to evil still. He had not the slightest doubt about his feelings. But what was it, and who had made it? Grammore was filled with unanswerable questions, and everything he thought he knew about the land, which was little, instantly became nullified by the sight of this fantastic structure, his knowledge ineffectual.

The other three fighters appeared, wondering as to their comrade's fixation. Rundin let out an oath, Areck mumbling something incoherent beneath his breath.

"Shades and devils," Rundin hissed. "'Tis' a castle of death and nightmares, springing to life in this forsaken land. I can feel the power of it from here. Captain Grundel, we must flee before something terrible happens to us."

Sarion said nothing, keen eyes gazing upon the valley for indication of movement or life. The vale was silent, no bird or animal cry reaching their ears. It was like a corrupt sanctuary, haven for the wicked and lost. Who could have made such an enormous fortress in the middle of the world's most hostile country? Grundel leaned on his long sword, nodding grimly. "So, a final surprise for us as we make to leave this wilderland. What fate has brought us within sight of such a dark monument, is it coincidence or manipulation?"

"I don't see how we could have been led here, Captain," answered Forlern. "Our choices, whether through circumstance or plan alike have brought us here, and I don't like the look of this stronghold, I can almost taste the evil."

Grundel hovered there, and Sarion chanced a glance at the man's face. What he saw startled and chilled him—he knew that Grundel fully intended on going down there. The captain turned towards him before speaking.

"Our quest has been rife with pain and sorrow, and King Gregor could not have chosen finer men to serve him. We've come so far, survived many dangers, and a long road home still awaits us. But my orders are clear...even if they seem harsh. I owe allegiance firstly to my king, and the price for servitude and valor has always been high." His voice lowered, and Sarion heard the sadness in his tone. "But too many answers lie within that castle—and they are the ones which I seek. Trencit and King Gregor must have knowledge. I'm going down there."

None of the men stirred, all staring at the glazed look of determination, the unquenched fire, brimming inside of

Captain Grundel's orbs. They knew what was being asked of them, understood the dangers, and some of them realized that they would not all be leaving Grammore, never to see their fair homeland again. It was a powerful moment, emotions soaring, but not one of the warriors looked away from their leader's steely gaze.

"We will persevere, though the way is fraught with peril and madness. Our numbers are sorely reduced, yet no more could I ask for, seeing the bravery which has been shown to me every step of the way from Trencit. You will be enough, and word will get back to the King. The sacrifices of many have preserved our freedom and way of life, and sadly, much more is still needed. Who can envision the defeat of evil, if ever it comes to pass? Yet we must try. And so, your loyalty is required once again."

There was a terrible pause as he held their attention.

"All except for Sarion."

The two men locked gazes, a look of surprise flashing across Sarion's face as he measured the man's words. Except for him—what was he saying?

"You've volunteered for this quest, although the asking was not done mildly, or without regret on my part. Yet you have proven invaluable, a true leader of men. There is not one among this group which would not follow your lead. You held a high position in the Western Watch before, and will again." He swept his gaze across the warriors, several of them nodding, none in disagreement.

"Captain, you honor me—but I have as much to lose as any other, and fight willingly for Trencit. Regardless of these facts, I cannot allow myself to stay behind while you enter this dark domain. You know me too well by now."

Grundel shook his head. "I can't afford to take the risk of having us all becoming trapped inside the walls of this fortress. Your tracking skills are unsurpassed. You alone of our group have a chance to return back to Trencit and give word to King Gregor if disaster falls. You must stay behind."

Sarion's eyes smoldered. "I can't do this, Captain. It might prove to be through my own ability which can help to bring us out of the castle again. Is that another chance you can afford to take?"

The warriors were silent, tense at the war of wills being waged between the two men. Their loyalty to Grundel was unshakable, but their devotion to Sarion had grown quickly since the start of the journey, reaching the point of unquestioning respect and admiration. To any of them, the captain's orders would have been taken without comment, an immediate acceptance of his decision. But Sarion was not one of them.

"I can't read into the future, Sarion. I am neither mage nor sorcerer, but a fighter, and chosen by the king himself to make terrible decisions. This is one of them. My mind is made."

Sarion fumed, biting back an angry retort. He couldn't stay behind! It was outrageous. His mind whirled, battling strong emotions. Part of him wanted to agree with Grundel's choice, comprehend the logic, but it wasn't enough. He looked around at the others, the bitterness evident in his eyes. His gaze was returned with looks of sadness and compassion—none of them envied his position—or there own, for that matter. Sarion made another attempt.

"Captain...please listen to me." Grundel had started to turn away, but he now locked eyes with Sarion, his gaze impassionate. He said nothing, but his look offered no concession.

"We've made it this far as a group, relied on each other's abilities to survive the terrors of Grammore. It doesn't make sense for us to separate now. We should face what's inside this castle together, and we might yet overcome any obstacles. I know more about the Lowlands than any other in Trencit."

"And so you have argued my point. No one questions your skills inside Grammore, or elsewhere. But this is different...You have no more, or less, knowledge of what might dwell within this citadel. It is my belief that our answers do indeed lay inside, and if there is danger, then we will try to prevail. If it proves too powerful, it is quite foolish to take you with us. You must return. I will hear no further argument, time grows short. Men, we take a brief rest, then scale the valley sides under cover of dusk."

Grundel left the edge of the valley, and Sarion's heart grew cold. The shades of his previous visit to the Lowlands swam before his eyes. The only one to return intact of body and mind. Not again, he thought.

Please, not again.

Few words were spoken as the men prepared to leave. The horses were to be left behind, since they could not be taken inside the fortress. Sarion would watch them until the men returned. Grundel told him to wait for one entire day, and be on the alert for anything suspicious from the valley. If anything untoward materialized, he was to flee immediately. There was no way of knowing what manner of creatures dwelt within the walls, although the captain hoped to find it long-abandoned. Even then, it might still conceal traps or wandering predators, he said. But his orders were clear. Sarion must not wait past the next day.

Individually, the fighters approached Sarion, offering words of comfort and hope. He wished them all luck, and to be alert for the smallest of things. Sarion was convinced something monstrous waited down there, and the castle appeared to him as a slumbering beast, patient and deadly.

He embraced Chertron warmly, the fighter clapping him firmly on the back. "I feel your anguish, my friend, but envy you nonetheless. I do not like the look of this fortress, but I understand Captain Grundel's need for knowledge. If he failed to deem it important for the good of Trencit, then he would not choose such a path. Be well, and I'll see you before the morrow's duskfall."

Sarion strongly gripped the man's shoulder. "Trust your hunting instincts, Chertron. You are gifted above the others in this way. Rely on your senses. What others miss, you can see. Be careful."

Chertron walked away, and Sarion couldn't shake the feeling of imminent disaster. Forlern came near, fingering the hilt of one of his long knives. "Although you remain here, I know your heart will be in the valley with the rest of us. I wish you were coming, Sarion." His voice was a whisper. "I fear entering that foul place without you by my side." He hesitated. "I don't think we will be returning."

Sarion's eyes stung at the bluntness and resignation in the man's words. "Have faith in your comrades, Forlern. Trust yourself. You can face anything and survive. Tell me you believe in yourself."

The warrior lifted his head.

"I do, but I'm only one man against the horrors of a strange land, another world, even. I'd hoped to return to my old rank, but the ache in my chest tells me otherwise. Farewell, Sarion. It's not your fate to fall down there also." He pointed to the castle, the incredible structure nearly invisible in the shrinking light. "Greater things await you. You can help save Trencit. Be safe, and if we don't return, tell the king how well we fought the perils of Grammore...and not to take our sacrifice lightly."

Forlern walked away, and Sarion was crushed by the man's demeanor. Forlern felt the same as he did, that some unspeakable terror awaited them below. Why did not Grundel recognize it? What action could he possibly take to stop the captain? But he was not to be dissuaded from his decision, and had already made it clear.

The captain gestured for Sarion to approach as he stood beneath a large, oval-shaped boulder. "I want you to keep this safe." He pulled out the rod. "Take it back to King Gregor if I don't return, along with this package." He handed Sarion a small, tightly-wrapped pouch.

"What is this?"

"A journal, my observations as we traveled throughout Grammore. The king will find it extremely important. It cannot be lost, do you understand?"

Sarion nodded.

"I know you disagree with my decision, but it can't be any other way. The risk is terrible, and I've left the chance for one of us to escape in case something happens down there. You'll know what to do. Your actions have shown us all that Trencit has much to hope for, with men like you fighting for the kingdom. Please do not be too harsh at my judgment.

I dislike such choices, and brave men have died because of them already."

"And what do you think to find in the fortress?" asked Sarion quietly.

Grundel's eyes looked unfocused. "It may prove to be an ancient stronghold of some forgotten race—perhaps men even lived here at one time. It might also be a nesting ground for whatever is responsible for the raids upon our borders. We shall see."

Sarion hesitated before speaking. "Captain—take care. I will wait as long as necessary for your return. Do not take any additional risks. If it's occupied, flee before your presence is revealed. You don't have to go in there."

Grundel gently shook his head. "But I do. The king would expect such a choice from me." He smiled, gripping Sarion's hand. "You are indeed much more than an ordinary farmer, my friend. You are what every man in Trencit strives to be. We will meet again tomorrow. And if we're late—I command you to leave."

The fighters waved sadly to their comrade, and picked their way slowly down the side of the valley. The vale slumbered below, eager to embrace the brave company of warriors. Sarion watched the last man disappear, the hunkering shoulders of Rundin, who turned about for one last look at him before vanishing.

He sat down on a flat rock, his throat dry and his heart numb.

Gone. The fighters were gone.

Overwhelmed with bitter emotions, a single unwanted tear slowly rolled down his cheek. He was now alone in Grammore. The immense boundaries of the Lowlands crushed him where he sat, pushing him towards the brink of despair and frustration.

Sarion felt as if the warriors were already lost to him.

⌣∶⌣

The company of six moved with great care down the sides of the valley, trying to keep their movements quiet and measured. The descent was uneventful as they scrambled over loose rocks and scrub brushes, the lack of trees not going unnoticed beneath Grundel's watchful eye. The mist grew thicker as they went lower, and increasingly gloomy as the day faded into late afternoon. Grundel realized they would need to light their lanterns at some point, but not until they gained the inside of the fortress.

The men were spread out in a position of fighting readiness, the reliable Chertron taking the lead, Forlern behind him, Grundel following, flanked by Cerestin and Areck, and a nervous Rundin bringing up the rear guard. Though unspoken, the warriors all felt the missing presence of Sarion as a physical and mental blow, their spirits disheartened by the absence of their comrade and friend. But they were still a strong fighting unit, and it would have been difficult to find half a dozen men in the entire land of Trencit who could challenge their skills of field and sword.

Piles of stone lay about in scattered heaps, several mounds protruding from the ground, extending upwards several feet in conical shapes like miniature volcanoes. The landscape was desolate, void of any life, animal and insect alike. Grundel hoped that it would prove to be empty of predators as well, considering the lack of game. He also understood that he was placing a considerable amount of trust in good fortune, and it was a disturbing thought. He had always relied on his skills of combat and preparedness, strategies well-laid out and adhered to. Grammore was an unpredictable enemy, impossible to judge, fatal to underestimate. He didn't want to be guilty of such miscalculation down here.

The first sign of trouble appeared as they reached the bottom of the valley. Chertron paused for a moment, whispering back to Forlern, who pointed to something on the ground just ahead. A pile of bones lay broken in a small ditch, the remains of some unknown creature, several times larger than a man. The captain lowered himself, examining the skeleton. "Hmm, looks like a recent victim, but it's hard to say."

"Victim of what, though?" Forlern peered into the haze. "The area appears deserted, but I wouldn't trust that notion."

"And we won't," added Grundel. "Keep your weapons raised at all times, and no more talking. Use the code, and stay alert for anything unusual. Move." The men continued, trying to walk soundlessly across the blasted vale. They had lost sight of the fortress after descending, but Grundel knew they would soon reach it.

When they finally did, it came upon them quite unexpectedly, looming menacingly from out of the mist. Chertron crouched down and the others followed his lead, the captain creeping forward. From the ridge above, they could not appreciate the full immensity of the structure. Concrete walls climbed above their heads, shooting upwards until disappearing into the thickening fog. Barred windows stared outward, forlorn and watchful. The ramparts were unadorned, lacking pennants or other emblems which could have displayed any identity as to who had built the incredible fortress.

The keep was a colossal achievement in architecture, power, and grandeur. A living memorial to its long-lost builders, standing tall and proud in defiance of weather and time. Built to withstand any assault, capable of housing armies along with any populated citizens, it was an incredible sight, and the men could only marvel as to its appearance if the cumbersome mist were not present to quench the full enormity of its magnitude.

The walls were empty, and Grundel half-expected to see phantoms patrolling the catwalks, restlessly guarding against mortal trespassers. It was a lurid thought. He strained his vision, looking for the main gate, but couldn't see it. The captain motioned to his right and the men shuffled along, trying to keep a respectful distance from the citadel. The feeling of dread and awe washed over the entire company, and each were affected in their own way. Trencit was home to many formidable castles, but the sight of this structure in the middle of the accursed Lowlands had a devastating effect upon their moral fabric. They felt effectless and insignificant. Its very existence threatened to extinguish their lives.

They stayed within the cover of the fog bank, glimpses of the castle coming back into view at times and causing them to retreat further. The fighters kept on like this for long moments, all the while the day continuing to fade, the long arms of night claiming the valley as its own. The fortress seemed to go on without end, and Grundel soon began to wonder if indeed there existed any gate, or visible entrance at all. When they ultimately reached the front of the castle, Chertron's face appeared from ahead, his features twisted into an expression of bewilderment. The captain moved forward with him, the men scattering in each direction.

They huddled behind a cluster of rocks, edging towards the castle walls, the massive structure only a distance of several dozen yards from their vantage spot. Chertron pointed. They had found the gate, though as with everything else within the Lowlands, it was not what they'd expected.

Four battlements protruded outwards, each of them immense and unbreachable. It would take the largest siege tower in Trencit to be able to make an attempt upon the seemingly impregnable fortress, thought Grundel. A wide opening, square-shaped and ringed by smooth stone, opened outwards. It was like the maw of a monstrous beast, soaring countless feet into the air. The original gate which once had enclosed the citadel was no longer functional, huge pieces of iron laying bent and rusted on the ground, the chains which served to lower it hanging loose and useless. Two stone guardians sided the gate, massive and ornately carved in the shape of creatures which defied imagination, the heads squid-like with muscular bodies, clawed arms folded over their enormous chests.

Inside the entrance could be seen only blackness, ominous and silent. Grundel squeezed the haft of his sword, nodding to Chertron. The fighter dropped back, gathering the other warriors for the coming assault. They formed a tight group, and Grundel gestured to Forlern and Areck, sending them back and beyond the old causeway which led to the fortress. A road sprawled forth from the teeth of the gate, plunging through the depths of the valley and disappearing in the hazy air. The two men would cross the path, and meet up with them at the gate. There was no sign of movement or recent activity, but Grundel wasn't going to be lured into complacency.

After waiting several minutes for the men to fall into position, the remaining fighters led by Chertron, cautiously approached the entrance. The closer they came, the more amazed they were at the sheer size of the structure and the fantastic architecture. At either side of the gate the pair of stone figures loomed fearfully, skillfully crafted by the hands of ancient, unknown masons. Grundel looked upon them with awe, knowing that the hand of man had no part in their conception.

The men stood beneath the very walls of the gate, joined now by Forlern and Areck. Halting before the entrance, they stared upwards uneasily, knowing that it was impossible to pass inside unnoticed if the guard towers were occupied. Scores of windows were set within the stone walls, each too high to be reached by shaft or arrow, but wide enough for the launching of volleys down upon the heads of intruders. Chertron gazed at the statues, shaking his head in wonderment. Grundel motioned the men forward and they scattered, taking up fighting positions, two to each side, himself, Chertron, and Rundin going down the middle.

Evening had arrived, and it would prove impossible for them to advance without the use of their lamps. When they were beneath the gate itself, Grundel paused, signaling for them to bring out their lanterns. The small lights cast lurid shadows on the walls and they pressed onward, taking careful steps, alert to any traps, listening for noise. Nothing suspicious materialized, and shortly they passed inside the incredible castle, feeling as if they had stepped into another world.

Sarion sat at the lip of the vale, disheartened and confused.

He felt more alone now than he'd ever felt in his entire life. The Grammore Lowlands, he thought. So much of his life with its bitter memories revolved around this enigmatic and dangerous country, home to the vanquished Glefins, the murderers of his closest kinsmen, the final resting place for many of his past comrades—the durable soldiers of the Western Watch, and now more recently, the brave warriors led by Captain Grundel. Tarral and Kalen among them. Good men, worthy men.

Lost.

How long would it be until their families learned of their fate? Would they ever? There was no sure way of knowing if he would emerge from the Lowlands unscathed, or any of the others. And what had befallen them? They should be within the citadel by now, he mused. And Captain Grundel had commanded him to stay behind. That action in itself convinced Sarion that the captain knew more than he led them to believe—he also sensed something might happen down there. What knowledge did Grundel possess, keeping to himself? There was more, certainly. Perhaps he suspected something about this castle, and didn't want to tell the others. Could he have known of its existence even?

Sarion frowned at the notion. If Grundel already was aware of the fortress, then he also knew what possible dangers it concealed. His decision to enter had been a swift one, his mind immediately made up. And there had been no hesitation in keeping Sarion behind, waiting at the lip of the valley.

He looked into the vale, unable to see the fortress anymore. Sarion tried not to think of the warriors ending their journey here, but he couldn't shake the feeling of imminent disaster. He already missed their quiet companionship, Grundel's unflinching but level-headed confidence, Chertron's friendly demeanor, Rundin's gruff mannerisms, and Forlern's eagerness, his taste for adventure. Forlern...yes, he certainly missed him as well, but their last conversation had been a grim one. The change in Forlern's mindset had been drastic, greatly upsetting to Sarion. The fighter's words haunted his mind, his prediction that the company would not be returning. All the men had felt foreboding about the ominous castle, but still it had not stopped Grundel from entering. What did the man know, or at least suspect? He was an elite member of King Gregor's inner circle, a Captain of the Home Guard. No warrior of Trencit could refuse an order from someone of Grundel's ranking, or would question it. But Sarion had tried anyway.

And been denied.

He kicked his boot in frustration, sending tiny pebbles rolling along the uneven ground. The strange rod was secure, tightly packed within the folds of his riding cloak. Sarion gazed down at the packet at his feet, entrusted to him by Grundel in the chance they failed to return. What did it contain—maps and a diary, perhaps?

Answers, maybe?

Curiosity brimmed inside of him as he waited there. He looked around, checking on the horses which were tied in a loose circle, standing above a patch of grass. The animals were highly trained, born and bred for battle. Even more so, they also acted to supplement their rider's abilities. Their senses of smell and hearing were acute, and the beasts would act in agitation if something approached. They had shown such on the journey through the Lowlands, and Sarion knew that he would have to rely on their attentiveness as he rested.

He planned on sleeping among them, letting them serve as his night watch. Sarion didn't relish the notion of being alone in Grammore, but he had no other choice. It was a great concern, but not any greater than the thought of the fighters stranded in the forsaken stronghold below, threatened by a nameless enemy.

And the packet—Grundel had not said he shouldn't look within, only that the king needed to receive it intact. Feeling a twinge of guilt, he picked up the pouch, weighing it in his hand. All he had done for the captain, leading them into the Lowlands, fighting alongside the warriors, perhaps saving them all on more than one occasion—but he wasn't looking for recognition, only answers to his own questions. He deserved at the very least to have some answers, whether Grundel was willing to tell him or not…

Sarion opened the pouch, squinting in the dim light. He reached for his own lantern, the glare illuminating a small area. He didn't want to risk casting more light than was necessary. Untying the leather bindings, Sarion sat down, then gently laid the contents on the rock, examining what he found inside. He paged through a small journal, the pages neatly inscribed in the captain's firm script. Careful attention had been paid to the slightest detail, he realized, browsing the pages. It was a log of their journey, starting from before they had even met Sarion. He quickly skimmed through, noting how Grundel had mentioned the flora and fauna of the Lowlands, missing nothing. Everything of possible benefit was there—the terrible creatures, questions about their habits and environment, the extent of their threat, and additional notes. Flowers and plants, weather conditions and temperature fluctuations—Grundel had been extremely precise.

Sarion was impressed. The man had given a written account, first hand knowledge of the dangers and terrain of Grammore. It was indeed an invaluable collection. He sighed, putting down the journal, and looking over the crude map of their quest as drawn by the captain, finished to where they now found themselves, at the lip of the mysterious valley. Various notes were scribbled down, references to events which had befallen them. The valley was noted, and there was a name following its placement—Gorothagled, with a question mark after it.

A name?

How had Grundel known of the fortress?

Sarion's eyes narrowed. The captain knew many things, or suspected them, it seemed. He felt a surge of anger welling inside. Grundel and the king knew of the existence of such a place. It all seemed to make sense now. Going after the ogre, the notion that raids on the borders of Trencit were somehow connected to a greater scheme, stretching far beyond a marauding predator terrorizing frontiersmen and trappers.

But as much as Grundel and King Gregor might know, there were still many questions remaining. The question mark signified that Grundel wasn't convinced the fortress was actually Gorothagled, whatever that meant. Perhaps the ancient records back at the palace contained reference to certain landmarks, and Grundel was trying to discover the truth for himself. Maybe they had arrived here on chance alone, for the captain had assuredly been unaware of countless other dangers in the Lowlands, relying on Sarion's experience and tracking ability.

No, he decided. Grundel more likely had known of the citadel, and maybe other old fortifications, but no other reference was listed on the map. The journal, however, could prove to shed more insight on the matter. Sarion paged to the end of the written notes, reading the last few paragraphs. Grundel had mentioned the fortress as possibly being Gorothagled, but little else. He described the valley, trying to pinpoint their location, writing down his belief that their questions might be answered by what lay inside.

My hope is that the old fortress remains abandoned, the ancient evil vanquished, its legacy forever silenced. While there may indeed be other malevolent beings using the castle for their own handiwork, I have seen no sign of any recent activity around the valley, only desolation and whispered memories.

If I fail to emerge from the dark fortress, I have placed the contents of this pouch into the reliable hands of Sarion, the most skilled tracker and fighter I have seen in all of the kingdom. He alone of us might be able to escape the foul talons of Grammore and emerge once again into our own lands. His prowess of field and observation is eclipsed only by his ability to inspire and lead others. The land needs Sarion, and I highly recommend him for a position within the Home Guard.

Sarion was shocked as he read the end of the post, and he looked up.

Grundel had been aware of the possible existence of the citadel, but not convinced, and no detail was given as to what might lay inside. And the captain had praised Sarion with the strongest words he could muster, recommending him for a ranking in the Home Guard itself, the most prestigious

Watch in the land, which warded the king himself at Daregil Keep.

But as startling as these things were, they paled in comparison to what followed. Sarion again stared at the book, amazed by the stark revelation laying before his eyes.

For the journal ended in a signature, accompanied by a silver medallion fixed to a golden chain, the ornament taped fast to the page.

General Charadan, King's Champion.

The warriors walked down a long tunnel, their lantern wicks turned high for maximum lighting. Grundel knew the risk of exposing themselves, but he took that chance over being attacked in the twilight. Several doorways opened to either side, most likely leading to the guard turrets immediately above the gate. The corridor could have housed scores of men walking abreast, constructed in such a way as to make any attackers vulnerable from the sides and above, as he caught glimpses of shadowed balconies looming in the dim heights. The fortress was created to be virtually impregnable, and Grundel realized that an enemy could hold off immense armies for an indefinite amount of time if properly garrisoned and stocked with food.

He knew that the citadel was huge, and he needed to decide quickly where to search. The men moved forward, bleak phantoms in the murky light, anxious and bewildered by the incredible fortress. Grundel knew that time was against him, and he had no desire to remain inside any longer than was necessary. But he wasn't even sure what that meant. Answers lay within, he was convinced, as to the history of Grammore, and possibly relating to the unrest in the borderlands. What-ever had created the castle had also left behind hints and se-crets as to their legacy, and he needed to find them. They could prove invaluable.

They approached the end of the tunnel, and Chertron waved to him from ahead. Hurrying to the warrior's side, Grundel crouched down, examining what the man was pointing to. He felt a chill. There were tracks in the dusty stone. The prints of recent passing, but they were large and obscure. Definitely not made by any man.

The captain straightened, peering intently into the gloom. Something had been prowling the fortress, and was possibly still inside. And he did not know what manner of creature it was, although everything in Grammore could be considered potentially dangerous, even extremely so.

Chertron was clearly disturbed, glancing nervously about. Grundel hesitated…They were in a hostile land, tres-passers with no friend, or help to be found anywhere. Alone and many times hunted. Would it prove to be the same in here? There was no way of knowing for sure. He was torn between his instinctive feeling of preserving his men, and the strong nature of the king's orders. They knew of the ex-istence of such ancient citadels, the by-product of long-for-gotten races. The history annals of Trencit contained much knowledge, although the details were uncertain, the passages incomplete. Names were recorded, possible locations, some of them destroyed from time and other factors, while others remained intact, as was this fortress. It pained him to keep things from Sarion, but he himself knew little else. What could he have told him? And he didn't want to alarm the men further—their abilities had already been strained to the limit.

But his orders were clear. To investigate anything of the old world in Grammore, and to bring back as much knowledge as possible. King Gregor had cautioned him, but told him also to take chances as needed, despite any hazards. He had to continue, although the choice weighed heavily on his heart and conscience.

Trencit and the king demanded no less.

Motioning them onward, the warriors passed through a massive archway, entering into the castle proper. The walls rolled outwards on either side, revealing a courtyard large enough to house a thousand men strong with their horses. Grundel knew the peril was great as they hovered there near the entrance, but he led them further. Staying near the left wall, they veered away from the exposed center, keeping their backs against the stone for a better defensive position, although he hoped none would be needed. In single file now the warriors trotted along, increasing their pace, alert to anything.

But nothing materialized. The courtyard rested in quiet, aged slumber, dream-fragments of forgotten beings the only remaining vestige of existence. Chalky dust swirled up around their boots, and the silence was oppressive. Rundin brought up the rear, staying close to Areck in front of him. Parts of the wall showed signs of old battle scars, cracked in spots, piles of rocks scattered in clumps, but most of the structure was remarkably well-intact, defying the relentless grip of antiquity. The makers had been skilled craftsmen the like of which the world had not seen in centuries, or longer, thought Grundel. He suspected more, but needed all his focus on the matter at hand, and not wandering conjecture. They could not afford any mistakes inside the castle.

Smaller buildings sat behind the courtyard proper, at one time housing supplies or soldiers. Or maybe something entirely unknown. Grundel decided to pass these by, thinking they would prove to be of minor significance. They needed to search the main keep itself, which lay in the center of the structure, still some distance away. The warriors skirted the outlying buildings, moving in-between the stone walls in pairs of two, listening and watching for pursuit or movement. The great fortress echoed lightly with their passing, and Grundel knew this could work in their favor, alerting them of anything approaching—but could also give away their own position, an unpleasant thought.

Time dragged on slowly as they made their circumspect way deeper into the heart of the castle, at every turn expecting their fears to be realized and discovering themselves not to be alone. Above their heads sloped long curving arches, ornately carved figurines, their features and limbs vague, stretching away from view, the vision completed only by the warrior's fractured imaginations. Statues sat at varying intervals, some of them similar to the pair at the front gate, menacing and terrible to behold. Grundel tried to ignore his fantastic surroundings and architecture, things better left to future memories than to current inspection.

The pathways of the citadel were all wide and high, as if monstrous creatures had once walked the stone streets and intersections. And Grundel suspected that they had at one time…It was a nightmare city in itself, a vast graveyard from a terrible time, populated by terrible beings. It was not a place for men, or the living. The fighters were uneasy, feeling the dread watchfulness of the fortress, the eyes of the dead fixed upon them. The energy was still there, slumbering and latent. Some of the more sensitive men keenly felt this power, the others struggled against an overwhelming fear which threatened to drown them.

Grundel knew he had to keep the men from slipping, hold them together by exerting his own will and confidence. They rounded the corner of a rectangular building, and the captain called for a halt. Gesturing for them to stay near he spoke, his voice soft but filled with conviction.

"I can feel it as you all do—this place is haunted by creatures of another age, long forgotten. It is a city of the dead." He paused, looking into their eyes, challenging their courage.

"This company has been through much. You have survived horrors which would have defeated lesser men. Instead of cowering in dismay, you have stood tall, and faced the terror. We fought when it was needed, fled when it was wise. Do not forget our fallen comrades. Their legacy must never be forgotten, and we will make them proud. You were hand-picked—some of the finest warriors in the land. Hold your heart, remain alert, and do not give your fear a handhold to latch onto. The main palace lies ahead. Once inside, we will scour the upper chambers, giving it a quick search. We will not delay any longer than necessary, but we have come too far to turn back. Let's move on, and watch for anything out of the ordinary. Use our signal for danger, and stay close at all times."

The fighters nodded, some of them appearing a bit calmer than they were scant moments ago. Grundel knew he could not hope to quench the blanket of dread which loomed over the fortress, but he could try and sustain his men, lending them as much courage as he had to give.

Several minutes passed and the fighters hurried forward, a group of phantoms themselves, garbed in dark cloaks holding sharp teeth of steel, appearing as a company of the dead, awakened from their slumber and once more stalking the streets of the dusty citadel.

The main building was now before them, fronted by great steps of concrete, large enough so that the men had to take long strides to advance. Two gargantuan statues sat to either side of an enormous door, likened to those which guarded the front gate. Grundel began to think that he actually looked upon the visage of the crafters of the ancient citadel themselves—a race of huge, monstrous beings, fearsome and grisly to behold. Could this indeed be the legendary race of giants that were recorded in the royal archives? He'd suspected this earlier, but there was no way to be certain. At least yet.

Chertron hovered near the entrance, his sword glinting coldly in the dim light. Grundel waved his hand, and Forlern moved with him to join the tracker, both of them searching along the doorway. To their surprise, a square latch protruded from the middle, and with scant effort they were able to open the panels. They shuddered apart, creaking ominously in the black solitude of the fortress and the men looked about nervously, the sound an unwelcome harbinger as to their presence. Grundel was startled as to how loud it was, but knew it was too late for other options.

"Can't be helped. If anything lurks nearby, then it is assuredly alerted as to our presence. Our task lies before us. If we fail to uncover anything useful inside, we will depart the fortress immediately. The night grows late, and with the coming dawn, we will at least have some more light above to guide us."

"Captain Grundel, I've searched the steps in front of the door, and there are no signs I can see of anything passing this way." Chertron pointed to the flat area of stone which lay before the doors, Areck and Forlern already partly inside, watching for movement.

"So the building might be empty, you think?"

Chertron nodded grimly. "It would be my hope. This seems to be the only entrance as well, and there are no windows in sight. The outer wall confines the structure."

"A logical notion, but we can't be sure there doesn't exist another access passage, perhaps secret, or even underground."

"Not certain, but I have a greater fear. We know something stalks the streets of the citadel, and I would not like to emerge from here only to be waylaid by whatever waits outside. That might be exactly its ploy. A trap."

Grundel considered. The idea had already occurred to him. He didn't make decisions based on coincidence, or good fortune. The signs showed that some type of creature had recently entered the fortress, maybe even waiting for this very opportunity, to trap them inside. It was a terrible risk, but one he'd been willing to take. Their venture inside the citadel had so far been uneventful, although he felt certain that something would happen before they left—an attack by the unknown lurker. It could have wandered in here foraging for food, or it could have even been hunting them. That possibility was alarming, but all he could do was remain prepared. The element of surprise must not be lost.

"And what is your suggestion?" asked Grundel.

Chertron frowned. "All of my ideas sound weak in my own mind." He hesitated. "I thought we might post someone here at the door, while the others search the interior."

The fighters watched in every direction, all of them close enough to hear the exchange. It was a frightening position they held, knowing they were not alone in the fortress. Which of them wanted to stand watch though? And was it any safer to forage inside?

Grundel disliked the idea immensely—separating his men further, with the ranks already depleted. And who would he choose to stay? He scanned the group, his gaze a lance of ice upon their unyielding figures.

"All right, I'll leave a guard behind. But I refuse to leave any man alone inside here. Areck and Cerestin will await us outside. Have a care, and keep a sharp lookout. If something approaches, you are to seal the doors immediately and go inside—use this warning horn as a signal."

Grundel handed Areck a small, curved horn. Himself and Rundin each had one to use when the group needed to separate, although they had not been necessary yet—until now.

"Have a care, Captain Grundel." Cerestin saluted him, a trace of his cheerful humor briefly mirrored in his boyish demeanor. But it was forced. "Find what you seek swiftly. I can't wait to see the look on Sarion's face when we return carrying a trunk full of diamonds."

Grundel grinned mildly, the first one in a long time. "Not quite what I hope to find, but if we do, we'll bring back what we can. Give us three hours, and if we do not return, I command you to leave the fortress. Understood?"

The fighters nodded.

"Farewell."

The others entered inside, the darkness swallowing them whole.

⋌⁝∾

General Charadan and Captain Grundel. The same person? Impossible! They would have known.

But as he sat there, trying to make sense of it all, several realizations dawned on him. From everything he'd ever heard, General Charadan was a most elusive leader, constantly in counsel with King Gregor or other top commanders, splitting his time at crucial locations on the eastern war front. The common soldier, or even officer, would most likely never have seen the man. The armies of Trencit were vast, its territory large. No, it's possible that this group of fighters had no knowledge of who their leader really was. Maybe…

He pondered this astounding revelation in his head for long minutes. And the minutes grew longer as all possibilities waged maddeningly inside his mind.

For long hours Sarion stalked the ridge line, disbelief etched over his handsome face. Charadan—the King's Champion. Captain Grundel did not exist, serving instead as a disguise for the land's greatest war general and hero.

Charadan, whose name alone served to inspire hope and determination for the embattled people of Trencit to continue on, sacrificing life and limb to thwart the enemies of the kingdom. Charadan, the dominant figure in the war against the Devlents, denying the constant assaults thrown at them on the eastern borders, rallying the warriors to countless victories against the rampaging invaders.

And now he led a small company of men hand-picked from the ranks at Daregil Keep as a new threat plagued the western frontiers of Trencit, a danger which was so important that King Gregor had commanded his top advisor and general to withdraw from the field of battle to embark on a quest into the deadliest hinterland known to man, the Grammore Lowlands.

Sarion was shocked. Charadan. He kept repeating the name to himself, rationalizing all that had transpired in the past two weeks. Was that it? It seemed like months since they'd left their homeland. And the fighters? Did any of them really suspect? He kept wondering this one, and finally decided they didn't realize it. Except maybe for Rundin. The durable fighter was Grundel's second, and the two were extremely fluid in communication and counsel, as if they had been together for a long period of time. Yes, Rundin certainly knew. The man always stayed close to Grundel, his eyes looking out for potential danger. Rundin always brought up the rearguard as well, serving to give him a better outlook for the man's protection. Rundin knew the truth. But the others? No.

If he'd been uncertain earlier, this revelation surely convinced him. But he needed to act. Soon…Despite the orders, he couldn't abandon the men. Tomorrow he would go in search of the company in defiance of his charge. Let the captain try to chastise him, once the truth was known. Sarion could not afford to take a chance with the man's safety— Trencit could not afford it.

General Charadan. Impossible.

But it seemed instead that everything was now quite possible, he thought. And the stakes had been raised to an alarming new height.

It was later in the evening when Sarion finally rested, laying amongst the horses, a blanket pulled over him, using a bundle of clothes for a pillow. At first he resisted sleep, chastising himself of even this small luxury while the others searched the mysterious fortress below. Torn between honor and guilt, he had ended his inner turmoil, wrestling with his conscience, determining his course of action if the fighters failed to return the next day. He already knew what his decision would be. There was no way that he could abandon Charadan and the men, even if King Gregor himself had given the orders. His own conscience and loyalty made him incapable of such inaction.

He drifted off despite his concern for both the warriors and his own security, and he had no choice but to trust in the animals, using their abilities to warn him of any approaching threats. His dreams were terrible, a growing anxiety weighing heavily upon him, preventing deeper or relaxed sleep to come. A cloud of doom hovered over him, insubstantial except within his fears, but stronger while beneath the cloaks of slumber.

Sarion awoke with a start, his eyes adjusting to the small flare of his lantern several feet away, dawn still in its infancy, struggling to crack the darkness. The horses appeared relaxed, most of them laying on the ground, although one was standing along the larger cluster of stones which faced the forest. It was his own steed, and he jumped in surprise as he saw a slim figure standing there, caressing the animal's head.

Immediately he held his sword high, springing to his feet and taking a defensive posture. How had he been tricked?

"Fear not, I mean you no harm."

Sarion gasped. It was a woman!

But no ordinary woman by any means, instead the most stunning creature he'd ever seen before.

She was slender and looked fairly young, perhaps close to his own age. She stepped closer, the horse nuzzling her with its head. Dressed in a tunic of brown, she seemed to have emerged from the heart of the forest itself. Her eyes glazed with a burning intensity, emerald ice glittering deep within the incredible orbs. Upon her long auburn tresses lay a circlet of flowers like a primeval crown. Her skin was darker than his own, flawless and smooth.

"Who are you? And why are you here, in the middle of the Lowlands?" Sarion asked. He wasn't afraid, but felt instead curious, almost in awe.

She smiled, and Sarion hesitated, lowering his weapon a notch.

"I could ask the same of you. My name would be Alayian in your tongue."

Confusion clouded Sarion's mind, and he knew that this was no common girl in the wilderness of Grammore. She was something very special, and different.

"My name is Sarion, from Trencit."

"I knew that much already." She approached Sarion, and he was enthralled by her beauty and manner. "Wonderful creatures, from your land. There are no native horses in Grammore..."

"You live here then? In these woods?" Sarion shook his head in wonder. Alayian laughed, the sound gentle and mirthful, like a spring shower dancing upon a meadow of grass.

"You are so surprised? Did you think the Lowlands are filled only with wicked beasts? There are many others dwelling here, although few would reveal themselves by choice. And many would not consider you a friend, regardless of your actions or intentions."

"And what are you? I've never seen a woman—such as yourself." Sarion stammered, searching for the proper words.

"But tell me," she continued. "Where are your companions? I see the horses, and heard whisperings of your company passing through the Sedge Wood. Where are they now?"

Sarion frowned. He pointed towards the valley, steeped within the darkness and crawling mist. "We're on a quest, and they search the citadel which lies below."

Alayian's face darkened. "There is great evil and peril down there. Why would any venture inside?"

Sarion felt claws of anguish gripping his chest, and he tightened the grip on the pommel of his sword. "What is down there that you know of?"

"Only death and despair. Their need must have been desperate to enter that dread valley." She paused. "I can read the torment in your face—you wished to go also, or persuaded them not to, and were denied?"

"Yes." He grated the words, his frustration and concern raging inside. "It was not my choice for either. A great leader of Trencit has led them, in search of answers. Our borders are being raided, and we entered the Lowlands in pursuit of an ogre. I was commanded to remain behind, and leave for my own lands if they failed to return."

Her face softened in sadness. "That is terrible. Your leader has led them to their deaths then."

Sarion felt as if his body was encased in fire, so tense that he was ready to shriek. "What is the danger—I must leave now to help them!"

"No," she whispered. "A great evil seeps like a poison across the Lowlands, and beyond."

"What is the nature of this evil?" Sarion moved forward, staring into her incredible eyes. "You must tell me what it is, so I can fight it."

"You cannot go down there!" she insisted. "I do not know his origin, the one who wrecks havoc upon Grammore, but his is a power of blackness, trying to enslave the inhabitants, forcing dominion over them for his own needs."

"And the fortress?"

"An ancient stronghold from centuries past. This usurper, which we call only the Dark Mage, attempts to instill life into the creations of the dead giants which once ruled Grammore. He is searching and securing all their abandoned dwellings, fortifying them with horrible beings, fierce and deadly, of the living and dead alike. If your friends entered into this citadel, then they walked into a trap."

Sarion hurried over to his pack of supplies, mind racing, his blood cold. "I must make haste. Can you stay here and watch the horses, or are you also in danger?"

Alayian hesitated. "I am in no danger, but my powers are of concealment—not combat. You must not go below. I can lead you safely to your own lands."

"I can't. Not without my friends." Sarion reached out, gently touching her hand. "You've helped me enough already, and I wish no harm to befall you."

"The Grammore Lowlands are my home. You are a stranger here. I am aware of the dangers. But you must not go down there. The Dark Mage has claimed the old strongholds as his own, setting in place dreadful guardians. My people have knowledge of this, and avoid the accursed places, but have no power to affect them. Please." She gazed into his eyes, holding him briefly under her sway. "Do not go."

"But I must. Good-bye, Alayian. I will return." Sarion spun around, hastening towards the side of the valley.

Alayian watched him disappear, a tear rolling down her cheek. "Humans are so foolish—and brave. Sarion..."

She knelt to the ground, staring into the night.

⁓

Chertron stiffened, examining the intricately carved doors before them. It looked like it had once held something of importance, and still might. He glanced over his shoulder to Grundel, who nodded. "This looks to be an archive chamber of some sort. Most of the building has been gutted, whether by the hand of war or calculated act by the original occupants, who can say. We've found little so far, maybe this will be different."

The company had scoured the upper chambers of the building, probing the cavernous rooms and corridors, finding them empty except for dust and broken furniture. The citadel was a vast tomb, silent and ominous. The warriors had felt uncomfortable the entire time in which they foraged throughout the structure, and there had been no sign of danger. But the captain knew that time was slipping, and he hoped to discover something of importance soon within the great hall, the central building of the fortress. His frustration and anxiety continued to grow.

The men spread out, Forlern remaining near the doorway, vigilant against any possible pursuit, Grundel, Rundin, and Chertron moving deeper into the huge room. An enor-

mous stone table lay in the center of the chamber, and Grundel perceived it to have once been a meeting place, housing
the large inhabitants. Their lanterns failed to breach the recesses of the vaulted ceiling, shadows quenching the light,
obscuring the lofty heights. Along the walls were square
niches, each of them indented into the sides of the chamber,
and the captain moved to investigate.

Shelves were fixed into the walls, deep and wide. Iron
torch racks were set above a single stone table, the fixtures
once serving as lighting for the compartment. It appeared
to have been a crude library, but there was no sign of any
records or tomes. Everything had been removed. The captain continued searching each section, but the result was the
same. The chamber was now empty, although it at one time
had been heavily used in the capacity of record storing.

He smacked one hand against his leg. The search was
getting them nowhere, and he felt increasingly nervous
about the whole expedition. He'd entered with an expecta-
tion of bringing to light questions which needed answering,
instead finding an abandoned stronghold of a forgotten race,
desolate and brooding.

"Captain Grundel."

He swung around, looking over at Chertron's lantern
which the man held aloft from the opposite side of the room.
He walked towards the fighter, shaking his head at his own
inability to discover anything useful. "I've found nothing
over here, it's all been taken away. Yourself?"

Chertron was stooped down, looking at the floor. "Yes,
but not what we were expecting."

"What is it?" The captain leaned over to him, squinting
in the half-light.

"Tracks. Someone has been inside here, fairly recently. I should have been watching more closely, but didn't think of it inside this building. Activity, footprints. They appear man-sized too."

Grundel whispered. "Men, in here? But who, and why? The more we seek, the less we seem to know. And if they were in here recently, their purpose is certainly not in our better interest. It's time we left this place. Come on."

They walked back across the still chamber, anxious and weary. Forlern waited for them by the door, staring into the corridor.

"What is it, Forlern? Something wrong?" The captain raised his weapon as he noticed Forlern's combative stance. The fighter waved a cautious finger, then shrugged.

"Thought I heard something, but I'm not certain. This place gives rise to one's imagination. Shades walk the passages—I can feel it. This is a vault of the dead."

Grundel pressed him. "Nevertheless, your ears are sharp, and maybe you did indeed notice something. We must leave, our search has proven fruitless, and the night grows long. Maybe the dawn will bolster our hopes."

They moved onwards down the hallway, their boots thudding dully on the hard, stone flooring. Past rotted shards of tapestries they went, chewed apart by moths centuries ago, broken urns and oddly-shaped furniture, massive and molded from hard mud. Large doorways loomed to either side, chambers which they had searched earlier and found to be empty. Some looked to be lodging chambers, fixed with curious furnishings, the legacy of the extinct beings which built the fortress. Viewing their dwellings did little to enlighten what they were like, or what their habits had been. Mysteries with no easy answer, and none seemed to be forthcoming. The men reached a huge balcony which overlooked the floor levels of the building, cascading above a staircase of steps hewn into the living bedrock. The structure appeared to be carved from a small hill of rock, crafted masterfully into a living and command quarters, geographically central within the main citadel. The fortress itself was vast, comparable in magnitude to some of Trencit's own cities, and its architecture and scale in height was astounding, making it a formidable defensive fortification, able to house tens of thousands.

The captain believed it to be Gorothagled, an eastern stronghold as mentioned in the archives of Trencit. Unfortunately, little else was recorded, except that it had been a surviving fortress created by the lost race of giants which had once been dominant in the Grammore Lowlands. The significance of finding it was remarkable in itself, although the captain had failed to discover anything which benefited their present circumstance.

The front doors waited below, and he debated on delving deeper into the structure and search the lower regions, although he wasn't sure there existed much below ground level. There were one or two staircases leading down, all the others ascending. Regardless, they had to alert the others guarding outside. They couldn't wait much longer, and he had given them orders to depart if they didn't return.

Mind swirling in indecision, Grundel and the others headed for the entrance.

෴

Sarion moved swiftly down the gently sloping sides of the valley, careful of any misstep in the gloom. He held the lantern in one hand, his blade in the other, heading in the general direction of the fortress, which was invisible within the billowing clouds of low-hanging fog. The silence was profound and he heard his own breath, loud and penetrating in the quiet air of his surroundings. Sarion thought about the strange and lovely Alayian, waiting with the horses above. She was certainly an enigmatic figure, unlike any woman he'd ever laid eyes on. A girl of stunning beauty, soft spoken but strong of will, her eyes enchanting. He could not stop thinking about her, who she was. What she was.

Sarion frowned, searching for the truth. He'd asked the question to her, but she hadn't answered to his satisfaction, only that she lived in Grammore, and there were others. He knew this could very well be true, as countless species of animals and other creatures were native to the Lowlands. But human types? And the Glefins were also unique—and if their former captive was to be believed, possibly extinct. What had it told him? That they had been hunted by something, killing them off and it was the last of its kind?

Sarion frowned. He hoped that part at least was true. The creatures had brutally raided the frontiers of Trencit years ago, and he himself led an expedition to thwart more such incursions, a journey which led them into the danger and chaos of Grammore's edge, where they fought a pitched battle with the crafty Glefins, slaying them to the last. Sarion recalled his own harrowing escapades on that fateful trip, when he was the youngest ever afforded such a high ranking in the Western Watch, and he set out with a party of fighters after months of clashes and killings.

The leader of the Glefins had stood alone against Sarion, who had watched his comrades fall prey to the horrors of the Lowlands. It appeared that the Glefins had suffered terrible misfortune, trespassing into the lair of a huge beast, one of the larger predators of Grammore, and forced to backtrack into the arms of the remaining Trencit fighters. The whole trek had been a nightmare, and Sarion barely escaped with his own life.

He shuddered, trying to focus on his present task. He could ill afford any distractions—not if he were to find the warriors, and keep himself prepared against any attack. Keep himself alive…Alone and in the shrouded vale he was extremely vulnerable, and he knew that a chance encounter with a deadly predator could spell the end of him.

No, he must not dwell on his past journeys, or the mysterious Alayian. The captain and the warriors needed him. He still thought of him as Grundel, and would find it hard to call him otherwise until the truth was admitted.

He crept onward. The early morning was like a living beast to Sarion, oppressive and cunning to his perception, concealing his hopes and fears beneath the cumbrous and damp mist. Time was meaningless to him as he hurried across the dismal landscape, tracking the men and listening for sounds at the same time. He knew that sight alone would not protect him in the valley, and he needed to rely on other senses. If anything dangerous lurked nearby, he would not see it until it was nearly upon him, and then it would be too late.

Few men could have made the trek, struggling against the pervasive haze and the shrouded landscape. It was a monumental task, one that could make even the most stalwart and trained of fighters go either mad or desperate, succumbing to fear and hopelessness, but Sarion was above these things. And his companions had walked into a trap.

A trap!

The words stung him bitterly, and he gritted his teeth in anguish, wishing again that the captain had listened to him, or taken him along at the very least. No time for regrets, he chided himself. It was time for concentration and determination—time for action. These he could deal with better, never being one to gnaw on the wounds of resentment or indecision. Alert to his environment, he took in the texture of his surroundings, noticing the blasted rocks, the protruding mounds, and kept his distance from them. He immediately didn't trust them. Sarion didn't know what had formed them, but his instincts told him they were potentially dangerous, and that was enough. Nothing threatening had materialized as of yet, but it was a meaningless and false hope to cling to, especially while in the Lowlands.

Impatience ate away at him, a growing sense of danger which had been building steadily after the fighters left, and Sarion moved with stealthy deliberateness, feline-quick and acute to anything abnormal. Daybreak approached in earnest when he finally breached the persistent gloom and came into view of the citadel, the huge structure looming menacingly before him like a titan awakened from oblivious slumber. He halted, crouching down as he surveyed the landscape.

The men had angled away here, moving to their left. Searching for an entrance, of course, Sarion nodded to himself. He followed the fresh trail, making care to keep attentive for anything moving beneath the high walls. Several minutes later he emerged closer to the stronghold, coming within sight of the enormous gate and its silent watchers. He hesitated only for a moment, knowing now that the warriors had made it this far, and beyond. The tracks led directly into the fortress and he looked upon the mangled remains of the gate, the twisted and aged iron, now useless. What an incredible achievement, he thought. The citadel was terrible and wondrous in the same breath, ornately carved, and designed foremost with defensive capabilities in mind.

He trotted along with weapon held ready, scanning the entrance for movement. The warriors were inside, and as of yet, he'd not seen any sign of danger. It seemed they'd entered unhindered, and he also noticed the spreading out again of their tracks, a move to enhance their flexibility and observation. Fanning into forward and side positions, the captain had followed all normal strategies scouting potential hazards. Sarion crept forward, standing within reach of the large statues, gazing on their hideous likeness.

They were the giants—he knew it beyond doubt. The legendary dwellers of Grammore, once a dominant race, and now another forgotten species. But their handiwork had survived the ages, intact and dreadful. The captain had realized the unique opportunity, one which he might never have a chance at again, and went searching for clues to elusive answers. And Sarion could not bring himself to feel total rebuke against the man. King Gregor entrusted his Champion to take any action he deemed fit in the protection of Trencit. But prices had been paid—extremely high ones. The captain was a man placed in impossible circumstances, acting as eyes and swordsman for Trencit and the king.

He'd undertaken a terrible chance going into the dark valley, and if Alayian was right, a trap had been placed by the Dark Mage, whoever that being was. Had it been sprung yet?

Maybe they might still escape unnoticed. Sarion needed to find his own answers, and swiftly. He moved forward, feeling a sense of overwhelming urgency.

Then he saw a figure appear from out of the gloom.

⌣⋮⋏

"They're gone." Chertron's voice drifted back to the others, the words tortured and low.

"What?"

Grundel snapped forward, pushing through the opening. Forlern quickly joined him before the great doors where they found Chertron standing alone on the platform between the stone guardians.

"Search below, but have a care." He motioned for the others to spread out, Rundin watching the door and the manor they had left behind. The fortress was a shade brighter as the new day dawned, the shadows pulling back somewhat, but not enough for them to see very far as the murkiness still held sway. The men had vanished, and Grundel was chilled by the implications. Areck and Cerestin had remained on guard, and should not have left for any reason. Certainly a while had passed, but not enough for them to have already left the stronghold.

Unless they were driven off by something...

He knew immediately that's what had happened.

The captain stared at his surroundings, looking for signs of danger. Chertron was on the steps, crouching down. Forlern was at his side, gazing into the depths of the fortress, his lantern sitting on the ground while he hefted his bow.

Rundin looked uncertain, unable to decide where the greatest potential threat lay—behind or before him.

"Captain Grundel, I can't tell where they went. The stone shows traces of dirt, but that could have been from any or our boots. I don't know where they could have gone..." Chertron's face was grim and confused, his words tinged with a hint of desperation. Grundel needed to make a swift decision, but there was no indication as to where the fighters had fled.

"No sign of flight—anything left behind?"

Chertron and Forlern continued to search the steps, and the captain stalked the upper platform in front of the building. "Nothing. They couldn't have just disappeared. There has to be some sign they left behind—of a struggle, or anything..."

But the men could find no hint as to where their comrades had gone to. It was as if they'd vanished into the night. No belongings, weapons, or clothing remained. It was a frightening turn of events, and Grundel instantly regretted bringing his group into the valley. It smelled of a trap.

Rundin whispered from the doorway. "We must make haste, Captain, lest we confront a similar fate."

Grundel pivoted towards him as if he'd been struck a blow. "And leave them behind, ignorant of their whereabouts?" His words were iron, and he stared terribly at Rundin, whose face was impassive.

"Think. Something either caused them to flee, or took them here where they waited. It is perilous to stay, regardless of searching them out or otherwise. The creatures of Grammore do not take hostages, only victims. If this happened to them, they are beyond our help. No answers are to be found here—only a chance to share their doom..."

Grundel hated the cold words, and he knew the pain it cost the fighter to utter them. But Rundin spoke the truth, harsh and bitter as it was, and beyond argument. They had to leave quickly.

He whistled softly to the others, pointing down the steps. Rundin joined him, and Grundel peered upwards at the watchful guardians, trying to find the truth within their stony faces. Areck and Cerestin, both gone. He swallowed heavily, but realized their position on the steps was extremely vulnerable—they were in total ignorance of their danger, of its direction or nature. They moved downward, Forlern's expression one of silent rage and frustration. "And leave them behind without searching, Captain? Madness. They don't have a chance."

"If they are indeed alive, then they chose the wisest course—to leave here. And if they are not, then it places a greater risk for us to share their fate. Move on."

Forlern looked as if he were ready to challenge the man further, and they measured each other, theirs eyes clashing momentarily. Rundin loomed behind Grundel, motioning the fighter into action. "Forlern, that's an order. Captain Grundel has spoken, now hurry before it's too late." Forlern stared at them both for a few seconds, then turned to follow Chertron, who waited just ahead.

"I don't like this decision at all!" He snarled, brandishing his sword as he descended.

"Neither do I, but I have to try and save the rest of us." Grundel's voice was laced with anguish, but he did not falter. They moved at a brisk pace, and the captain felt unseen eyes boring into his back. The fortress seemed awake, and watching them. They scurried back through the citadel, expecting attack around every corner and from any shadow. The light failed to grow any brighter, instead shifting back into the perpetual twilight which lay claim to most of the Lowlands. No words were spoken, only furtive glances at each other and their surroundings. They could have gone mad or despaired, but Grundel's will and unshakable countenance held them firm, the alignment of his shoulders speaking encouragement, displaying his determination to prevail, even in the face of terrible uncertainty and impossible odds.

Chertron paused several times, trying to recall their earlier passage, staring into the high walls as if questioning his next step. Forlern was restless and weary, emotionally drained, struggling to fight an invisible enemy which remained hidden. And even stronger than before, they all felt the presence of the unspeakable company around them, the essence of the fallen dwellers of the fortress gathering from slumber, awakened as to the trespassers who dared enter into the sacred grounds of their ancient stronghold. This sensation grew to a new level of horror, for at times the air itself seemed to quiver, and Grundel gasped as figures moved within the shadows, dim suggestions, blurred and insubstantial, appearing at the corner of vision and swiftly disappearing. The others certainly felt the phantoms nearby, but how they dealt individually with them the captain could only guess, hoping they remained strong enough of will to escape the cursed place.

The dead paraded around the grim warriors, tall forms shimmering in the half-light, behind their shoulders, at their sides, between the blink of an eye, and within their minds. Grundel wondered how much a threat they actually were, believing them to be more dangerous psychologically than physically. If the men should waver and give in to their fears, he thought the specters might then strike, instilling consternation into a weak heart and tearing down the walls of their very spirit, leaving them vulnerable and lost, ultimately to join the grisly ranks. An utterly horrific thought.

Their pace remained steady, and the fighters seemed incapable of moving at any other speed, trotting along numbly, running from the horrors behind, hurtling towards the unknown, in whatever sinister form it would take. The captain was vigilant, more concerned with the condition of his men than about himself. He was not frightened by the unnatural observers, and recognized them for what they were—another pawn set in place by something far greater and more terrible than themselves, disturbed from their slumber to act as a ward against intruders. Someone, or something, possessed incredible power, enough to raise the grim shades of the dead themselves as a mechanism for their own manipulation.

The truth was staggering...

They were dealing with an enemy whose capabilities were profound. Grundel now began to understand the beginnings of a monstrous scheme, one which underlined everything they had been seeking. An evil power was coursing its way throughout the Lowlands, attempting to manipulate those which would serve its purpose. Sorcery was afoot, ancient and potent. The handiwork was evident in many places. The ogre and other marauders, possibly the genocide of the Glefins, the habitation of the stronghold. There was a pattern to these events, and they had barely scraped the surface of the entirety. Grundel knew little, and guessed at much more. He believed the power behind these things was expanding, flexing its muscles inside Grammore, and beyond. The raids upon Trencit's borders were significant. It was perhaps a test, a flexing of might.

But to what deadly endgame—to see how King Gregor would react? Or something more devious yet? He possessed no facts concerning any of these things, all was conjecture. But the captain was a shrewd man, highly-trained and educated. And far more than he appeared to be. He even wondered if the Devlents were involved. This was his greatest fear, and King Gregor's as well. A connection linking the unrest in Grammore to the fierce conflict in the east, one which was increasing in intensity. An alliance of dark forces? The possibility was chilling, and he wished desperately for something more substantial to take back with him to Trencit. They rounded a bend and found themselves facing a narrow corridor, one unfamiliar to Chertron who remained in the lead. He paused, and the captain called for a halt. He needed to reassure his men, although he was uncertain of anything himself. "Water, men. Take a quick drink."

Grundel tried to pretend nothing was unusual, but Forlern shook his head. "What are these hideous shadows which accompany us? Am I going mad, or do the dead walk the streets of this cursed fortress?"

"You are not going insane, Forlern." Grundel's voice was calm, hushed. "Ignore them. They will not harm us. Awakened for this very purpose, to antagonize and frighten the living who dare to enter. A powerful enchantment is at work, to cause such things to be possible. Do not stare at them, or try to look at them directly. You will fail and become distracted. This is what they want. You must be strong."

Forlern looked at him questioningly, trying to comprehend the captain's words. "Then what have we discovered here? What manner of evil so infests this land that the dead wander the earth? Can we fight creatures not of flesh and bone? If so, I know not the means."

"I don't know for certain, but I feel the stench of necromancy hovers above us. I have considered much, guessing more. I may be wrong. I fear a power grows within the Lowlands, spreading outwards, moving east. Towards Trencit… My feeling is that events are taking shape, molding into a cohesive structure. A combination of energy and beings—their goal certainly is malicious, maybe for domination, but over what, and where, I can't say. We must think that the westland, perhaps even Trencit, are targets."

"They will not find us an easy adversary." Chertron hunkered before them, looking weary, but his eyes shining with his determination. Grundel knew he would never give into despair. It was one of the reasons why Chertron had been chosen for this venture. There had been no haphazard choices, but careful discussions with a number of commanders. And he had made the final decision, taking them into a nightmarish land far from their homeland.

He answered. "No, our kingdom will not be overcome—starting with us. I can only guess their motivation. Perhaps I misinterpret much. We've only seen hints and subtleties. My hope was to find something of proof inside this stronghold, and I still think it hides secrets. But they are well-hidden. Great care was taken to remove items of importance from within the manor. Guardians are in place against intruders. The dead walk the pathways, surrounding us. I sense their presence, and malevolence. They are beings of terror because of their nature, but it is my belief that they are unwilling pawns. They may despise us, and desire our essence. Whether they can act is another thing. Fear not, and hold strong. Let's be off."

The warriors nodded, and Grundel felt their strength of mind and heart to be sound. He thought of the two missing fighters, and his anguish was great. Where were they?

Chertron led the way, his silhouette a reassurance in itself, although the captain keenly felt the absence of Sarion, who had served faithfully in leading them through the wilderness. Keeping to the left side, the men hurried along, Grundel fairly certain that the entrance couldn't be too much further. With luck, they should reach it within the hour, he told himself.

But the fighters stiffened as a sound broke the deadness of the citadel's streets. A high-pitched droning, shrill and terrifying...

"Run! Make for the front of this building and inside!" Grundel screamed the command, pointing forward and urging his men on. They scrambled ahead, running as if pursued by demons. The noise was hideous, raking across their hearts and minds, piercing the walls of the stronghold as if calling forth the legions of the netherworld.

The captain knew the deadly hunt was now on, as the creature had made its presence known. He glanced upwards, horrified by what he saw. "Go—don't stop!" They bounded past the corner of the building, an oblong-shaped structure, one of many they had seen, drab and gray. He knew that if the door was locked they were all dead men. Chertron was the first to gain the steps, lunging furiously up the broad casing and onto a sunken platform. He threw himself against the panel, the hinges creaking in warped protest as they surged open. The captain pushed the fighters in, Rundin on his heel.

The huge man was the last to enter, and Grundel slammed the door shut with the help of Forlern. The younger man glared at the captain, the unspoken words frozen on his lips as he saw the glint of silver descending from above.

Grundel's face was impassionate, a mask of dark thoughts. He immediately knew the fate of Cerestin and Areck, and was crushed by the realization that they were both certainly dead. Now he understood why there had been no trace of their flight, or even a struggle. The warriors had been taken from above.

By a Killworm.

⌣⋮⌣

Sarion froze.

Something emerged from the gloom, a hunched-over form, its features indiscernible in the twilight. He heard heavy rasping, a low snarling, and Sarion instantly knew this thing could not possibly be human. He gauged the creature for any reaction, trying to measure its quickness and danger. The thing was deliberate, skulking forward, making no sudden movements. Another figure appeared from inside, followed by two more, and Sarion knew he had walked right into a trap.

Just as the captain and the others.

He lowered the lantern and reached carefully behind him, placing one hand on his bow. Leaning his sword against one knee, he grabbed several arrows, detecting movement from along the walls of the fortress. There were at least six of the creatures, and he saw their faces as they approached. Wolf-like they appeared, walking erect at times, and some of them lowering to the ground. They most likely ran after prey, able to rear up on their back legs for short periods of time. They were covered in coarse, gray fur, their forelegs ending in wicked talons. They growled at him, and he saw long incisors from within their wide mouths.

Ready with his arrows he continued to wait, showing no hint of fear or uncertainty. He didn't think they were very intelligent, but he didn't want to underestimate their abilities. Sarion was using the scant time granted to him wisely, sizing up his adversaries and trying to predict their actions. He guessed right as the pack broke for him all at once from several directions.

Two of them crashed to the ground in agony as Sarion fired a pair of volleys with incredible speed. The others shrieked in rage, ignoring their fallen kindred. The rest were two dozen yards away and Sarion knew he had time for one more volley before they would be on him.

Another of the beasts went down, an arrow lodged in its throat and Sarion was out of time. He threw down the bow and picked up his sword, rolling to his right as one of the beasts hurled itself directly at him. He felt the wind of its passing only inches from his head, the claws raking the air savagely as it missed the elusive prey. They were quick, and Sarion knew there could be no mistakes. One of the others sprang at him, and he kicked back to his feet, arcing upwards with his blade. The steel slashed the creature's chest, blood gushing out as it snapped at the air in pain.

The other one circled Sarion, respecting the cold metal that had speared its kin. The first creature reoriented itself, joining the other and pacing around Sarion. The beasts hesitated, and Sarion realized they possessed some measure of cunning, or would have blindly continued to attack him. He was shrewd enough to guess much about their pack mentality, and it saved him from their next move as they both leaped at him from opposite sides. He dove to the right, holding his blade behind to ward off a blow meant to decapitate him. Instead, he connected heavily on one of the creatures, the sword scoring it in the breast, but not before Sarion was cut, and he felt searing pain in his left shoulder.

He staggered to his feet, feeling the warmth of his own blood seeping into his tunic. His arm was grazed, but he was fortunate. If he had been a second slower the beast would have severed his arm.

Sarion swept the blade before him, chasing the uninjured creature back. The other one cantered madly in agony, biting at its wound and rearing its snout upwards, wailing hideously in the dreadful valley. Sarion saw his opportunity and reached into his tunic with his left arm, the movement sending waves of agony through the limb. He whipped out a long knife and the blade flashed through the air, piercing the injured beast through the neck, and it collapsed to the hard ground.

The other one charged Sarion and he swept his blade forward, dodging to the right at the same time. The beast crashed headlong into Sarion, buffeting him mercilessly to the earth and knocking the wind from his chest. As the creature landed, its limbs twitched uncontrollably, as the head was totally severed by Sarion's blade, rolling along the ground and stopping, the body moving for a few seconds before falling lifelessly to the valley floor.

Everything was still.

Sarion gasped, trying to breathe air into his straining lungs. He pushed himself to his knees, keeping the sword upright in anticipation of another attack. The front of the fortress was empty, and he was the only living thing left. He looked down upon the grim carcasses surrounding him, a half-dozen creatures of unknown origin, but their purpose was known to him. They had been set there as guardians, meant to attack any who entered. But what of the warriors? There had been no sign of a struggle, and he knew that the beasts, although ferocious, would need greater numbers to overcome the battle-hardened fighters.

Sarion examined his wound, opening his tunic and aggravating the injury. Not too deep, but it throbbed painfully, the upper part of his shirt soaked with blood. He was ready to make a quick field dressing when he heard the approach of something from behind him in the valley, a low thundering, and he immediately sprinted for cover within the shadows beneath the guardians.

Sword in hand, he knew someone on horseback was drawing near, and moments later a war-horse plunged out from the mist, a familiar figure on top. It was Alayian.

Relieved but confused, Sarion moved from his place of concealment, but she had already steered the horse directly for him as if knowing exactly where he hid. "Sarion." She called out to him, the words weaving a gentle enchantment across his exhausted frame. "Are you all right?"

"Alayian," he answered. "What are you doing down here, I thought you were going to stay back with the horses? You shouldn't be here."

"What happened?" She dismounted, staring at the bloody carnage." The girl scowled in recognition. "More of them, waiting for you. Grimhounds."

"You know of them? They are formidable beasts." He sighed, wincing as he lowered his sword arm. "They almost had me."

She looked at him, concern spilling over her face. "You're injured! Let me see." Alayian rushed towards him, and Sarion was surprised at the intensity he saw within her eyes. Embarrassed and touched at the same time, he held still while her gentle hands probed the skin around his wound, gritting his teeth at the new flare of pain.

"Hold, while I dress the wound."

"No, I must go in search of the others. They passed inside, and I don't know what other evil lurks within these dismal walls."

She frowned, but was persistent. "You won't be of any use if you bleed to death. It will not take long."

He conceded, knowing that if he lost too much blood, he would indeed grow weak. Alayian pulled out a pouch, which appeared to be formed from some unknown type of soft animal skin, and she brought out a packet of dried leaves. Sarion watched as she crinkled them within her smooth hands, whispering beneath her breath as she did so. He felt light-headed for a moment, then studied her closely as she rubbed them along the wound. It tingled for several moments, then slowly grew numb. She wrapped a cloth around his shoulder, and offered him a flask to drink from. "This will sustain you, through dark times. You will need this."

Sarion drank, savoring the splendid taste of the cool fluid, and would have continued, but she pulled it back. "Ah, it is very potent, my brave warrior. Too much and you'll feel the arms of slumber calling." She smiled, and he returned her gaze.

"But why did you follow?"

"To look after you." Her simple answer sounded sincere, but he shook his head.

"I smelled the foul beasts shortly after you left, and knew you were in grave danger, although it seems you certainly know how to take care of yourself. Any ordinary man would not have withstood six Grimhounds. You are strong among men—and foolhardy."

Sarion shrugged. "My friends are in need, and I have to go on."

"I know. When I passed through the valley, I came across more of the beasts. I distracted a larger pack that were heading straight for the fortress."

Sarion's face turned dark. "More of them? You should not have come."

"I lured them elsewhere." Alayian smiled mischievously, her eyes twinkling. "You forget, Grammore is my home. I know many tricks...and secrets," she added.

"Apparently so...I hesitate to think what would have happened if more of them would have found me here. My thanks."

Alayian was silent, and Sarion retrieved his fallen bow and lantern. "I'm going inside—you stay out here."

She pursed her lips in protest, but he was not going to give her a chance to speak. "No, Alayian. I fear the stronghold holds creatures more powerful than these. Too much for even you." He gestured to the slain Grimhounds. "I will not let you follow me. Wait outside, I will need your help once I return."

"But..."

"Alayian, no. Promise me you'll stay. Please?"

She nodded reluctantly. "I will." She tilted her head slightly, then looked at the brooding walls of the fortress. "I've never met anyone like you before, Sarion. My people are scarce, and reclusive. Your kind is so different...determined. Not easily dissuaded."

"Well, you certainly are as well. Maybe we're not so different."

She looked ready to respond, but remained quiet.

"I'll be back. Now I'm the one promising. But I have to go. Don't take any more chances, ride away if anything else appears."

Sarion turned around, wondering what she meant by her kind, but he didn't have time to consider. He hurried into the citadel, leaving the strange girl behind for the second time now, and thinking that she would probably not leave even if a dragon reared its scaly head from out of the mist.

∾∶∾

"Just like the monster from the clearing. Another one of these devils!"

Forlern looked angry, his hand tightly gripping the handle of his sword, trying to contain his tension, control his emotion. The others drew close, unaware of what the two men had glimpsed outside—the falling strands of massive webbing raining silver death upon the spirit-infested lanes of the forsaken stronghold.

"Captain, what's out there?" Chertron's eyes were wide and unblinking, bleary red from lack of proper rest. "It must be bad—what did you see?"

"What is it that stalks this cursed place?" Rundin moved his bearish frame close to Grundel, and the captain looked weary and distraught. His shoulders slumped more so than usual, head bowed, and he leaned tiredly against the stone wall, staring into the darkness.

"A Killworm..."

"What?" Chertron swore beneath his breath, and Rundin simply nodded in understanding.

"You're sure of this?" Chertron glanced over to Forlern, and the younger man agreed.

"Yes, their were countless strands falling, as if a thousand monstrous spiders were out there weaving a tapestry above the buildings themselves, attempting to ensnare us all. I didn't see the creature, but its deadly secretion is unmistakable. And I remember vividly that night which seemed so long ago now. In the clearing, and Captain Grundel chased us off, thundering away in the night. I caught a glimpse of it then, silhouetted against the rocks. The Killworm and its call of death."

Chertron nodded in understanding. "Yes, I heard the noise, just like that other night. I remember." His eyes were glazed over in recollection of the nearly fatal encounter earlier in their venture.

"And that in itself answers several questions." Grundel looked up, his eyes blazing in fury. "Areck and Cerestin were taken—snatched from above. They didn't have a chance... The creature must have crept down from the upper reaches of the manor."

"They're gone, then," Forlern said bitterly. "Good men...I should have been out there with them too!"

"And you would also be dead as well." Grundel replied, matching Forlern's dark look. "No signs of a struggle because there wasn't any. The monster must be incredibly quick. It's a living nightmare bred within this cursed land."

Chertron kept his shoulder against the large door which they had locked, and it seemed sturdy enough. A large metal clasp, rounded and sculpted to fit inhuman hands was fixed into the panel. They had seen many of these before, especially inside the central building, a common fixture used by the extinct giants.

"Worse yet—there could be a connection between the two creatures." The captain peered ahead, a look of concern over his features, and he motioned Rundin to move forward. "I don't want any surprises inside here as well."

The rest of them watched as Rundin cautiously searched about, swinging his light, scattering the shadows into the musty corners. After several long moments, he signaled back as the anteroom appeared empty, but other passages branched off, and a staircase led upwards into blackness.

"I don't believe this is a chance coincidence. Someone has uncovered long-dormant eggs, placing them in certain strategic areas. As guardians…It is clear to me now."

Forlern whistled. "Then the first one may have also been a trap?"

"Yes. The ogre knew about the location, purposely leading us into that clearing. It had to have known, and we barely escaped with our lives."

"And that one was only an infant, didn't you say? Just hatched?" Forlern shuddered. "It was huge at birth. Then how big do they get? How large is this one? Shades…"

The fighters stared at each other. None of them had the answer for the terrible question Forlern posed.

"Too many disturbing events, and they reveal the machinations of a far-reaching strategy. What also is of great concern to me, is the possibility that our quest was known by the enemy before we even left Trencit."

The warriors were silent, struggling with the implications voiced by the captain. Rundin called to him from his position of watch, further off in the entry room, which consisted of drab walls, lacking furniture or aesthetic designs of any type. "What can we do to defeat the creature, Captain? Do you know of its weakness?"

Grundel scowled. "No. And it's my belief that we are unable to kill it, either."

Forlern snarled in response. "What? How can you know such a fact? You admit, there is little you understand about the creature. It is indeed extremely dangerous, but surely we have a fighting chance."

He gently shook his head. "True, I know little. But what I have read in the royal archives seemed clear enough. The Killworm is a monster bred in ancient times, a hybrid of several different unique species. It is lethal, spawned from dark magic. The power needed to control one must be vast, and our adversary has mastered at least two, maybe others. It is also said to be vulnerable only to similar magic. And we have none. It was written that normal steel could not harm the monster."

"Then we must avoid combat at all cost. Flee." Chertron remained poised at the door, but there was no sound from outside. "Will it continue hunting us, I wonder. Are we even safe here?"

Forlern pointed to the staircase. "What if it descends from above?" Chertron's mouth opened in an expression of pure terror. "It will have us all. I wouldn't venture up there for all the gold in the Vanyair Market."

The captain scanned the walls. "We must find a way out then. Perhaps it stays only within the fortress, acting as protector. What more suitable creature could exist for such a task? The giants used them as such, to guard their strongholds and treasures." Grundel walked restlessly about the room, pondering their options.

"Just like now," muttered Forlern. "Well. Let's be off quickly. Maybe there is a tunnel in the lower chambers and we can sneak out another way."

"It's worth a try, Captain Grundel." Rundin nudged his head, gazing upwards at the steps.

"And maybe our only hope," answered Grundel, gesturing to the far wall. "Rundin, try that door. Swiftly."

∽∿

Sarion entered the high walls of the fortress, cautiously working his way beneath the broken gate, alert for any movement or sound. He was sure the warriors had went this far unchallenged, and he wondered if this was by chance or design. He'd slain the Grimhounds single-handedly, although he was not brash about his deed. Good fortune, combined with swift-thinking, both played a role in the outcome. The beasts were certainly formidable, and if he'd been without his bow, things might have turned out terribly. A greater number would have proved too much, and he was thankful that Alayian had distracted the other marauders. What had she done to lure them away?

The girl was as mysterious as she was beautiful. And secrets? She concealed many...He gently shook his head as he passed through the main courtyard, amazed at the height and breadth of the stronghold. It was beyond doubt a place created, and inhabited, by a much larger species than humans. The legendary giants. Their legacy survived, and their structures remained intact. The statues which sat at the entrance showed them to have been a fearsome manner of creature, and he was certain they'd been extremely dangerous, and well-organized also.

The sky overhead was becoming brighter but steeped in twilight, yet accompanied by the incessant mist which curled around the upper turrets and battlements. To see the warm face of the sun again breaking through the dismal atmosphere of the Lowlands, he thought. He wouldn't take a wondrous borderland's sunset for granted ever again...Sarion sighed, feeling the ache in his shoulder, now reduced to a dull throb. The remedy Alayian used on him was potent as she said, taking effect within a short period of time. He felt confident enough to engage in battle again, but desperately hoped none would be necessary. Sarion longed for the sight of the captain and the others. He'd become attached to them throughout the dangerous journey, admiring their courage and loyalty, and yes, he could call them friends. He'd risked his own life to help them, and he knew they would respond in like fashion.

Sarion advanced further, finding himself at the edge of the immense front courtyard. It was an area meant to house thousands strong, a sizable army to support the impregnable fortress. He stooped to the ground, noticing traces of the company's passing. Looking around first to make sure he was alone, he made out the boot prints left by the men, small clods of dirt all the detail he needed to convince himself of their earlier presence. They had continued onward, keeping to the left wall of the courtyard, appearing to have moved in single file along the length, attempting to minimize their vulnerability. Sarion found no fault in their methods, but still was convinced the captain had been wrong to enter the fortress. What else lurked inside?

As if in answer to his unspoken question, Sarion heard a sound echoing from somewhere in the distance which chilled him to the very bone. He listened in horror as a high-pitched droning issued forth from deeper inside the structure, yet not too distant. It was familiar and terrifying. Recent memories gushed to the surface, and he recalled the dreadful encounter at the fringe of the Ridgeline when they were tracking the ogre, hoping to catch up with it soon. He visualized the clearing with the rocky hillock, Grundel's harrowing escape from the hole, and the subsequent frantic departure which had nearly ended in their death.

The Killworm!

Sarion recognized it immediately. The sound was unforgettable, like the buzzing of a thousand angry insects, shrill and unwavering. A Killworm! He couldn't believe it… There was one inside the fortress somewhere. Their situation appeared far deadlier than his worst imagination. His skin crawled at the hideous realization that the creature was aware of the warriors and might be hunting them even now. He shuddered, thinking he would never want to face such a monster under any circumstances. Yet he might very well have to if the warriors were in need.

Sarion tilted his head, trying to determine the exact spot where the droning was coming from, and to figure out how far away the creature might be. He decided to continue along the path the fighters had taken, hurrying over the smooth stone which served as foundation to the tomb-like stronghold. He needed to be extremely cautious. Sarion didn't have any disillusions about what would happen if he confronted the Killworm—his only recourse would be flight. Arrows would be useless, and if drew close enough to draw his blade upon the monster, then it would surely have him regardless. The noise ceased after several tense moments, and he now entered a shadowed corridor, surrounded on every side by solemn, quiet buildings, all of them equal in design and dimension. Sarion glanced about for evidence of the Killworm's secretion—the lattice of deadly silver webs it used to ensnare prey. He hadn't seen anything yet to indicate that the creature lurked near the entrance, but the notion did little to calm his fears. The monster was aroused, and hunting, and these were the only facts that mattered.

Sarion had faced countless hazards before, a staggering amount in the past fortnight alone, and danger was a familiar companion in its many different forms. Yet there was a growing sense of dread pulsing through his body, and he was unable to discover where, or exactly what, the nature of this disquiet was. As he moved into the dark corridor, he suddenly understood the source of this threat. A host of beings loomed menacingly before him—grim shades, large and sinister.

They were spirits of the dead.

He recognized the hulking figures of the giants, their forms shimmering hazily, materializing, and then vanishing within the blink of an eye. It was a company of specters, the creators of the great building, now awakened and disturbed. Sarion was aghast, uncertain as to the danger he faced. They shifted across the stone, squid-like heads swaying to either side, but not advancing. It was a dark moment, and Sarion felt his heart racing in panic. For the first time in his life, he wanted to flee in absolute terror. Run like a child frightened by nightmares. But he knew his friends were in need, and these spirits stood between him and them.

Sarion was assaulted by an overwhelming sense of dread, but also something else—a stark urgency, as if they were trying to communicate with him, but he was ignorant of the words or method being used. Whispered fragments of an ancient tongue trailed through his mind, and he tried to grasp onto the meaning, bewildered and frightened in the same moment.

He felt strong emotions pouring out from their ethereal forms, powerful waves of antagonism, palpable to his senses. He felt ripples of hatred towards him, but also something else—a tolerance? They drifted closer to the walls and he wondered if they meant for him to pass or if it was another trap. Sarion hesitated, unwilling to be so easily fooled. He told himself they were only shades, and he was not afraid of spirits, since they could not physically harm him. But Sarion understood the terror which could ensnare living men when encountering phantoms of the dead, claiming their minds, driving them to madness, and he'd never before been witness to such dread specters himself. But he knew he had to continue—his companions were in grave peril.

Heart stronger, he now walked carefully through their midst, not daring to look directly at their glistening forms. It was not a moment of trust, but necessity, and he didn't know if it was more courage or desperation which propelled him through their ranks. Dreamlike, Sarion found himself surrounded by the implacable spirits, and he willed himself onward as a clear path opened between their tall shapes. He finally reached the end of the grim company when a pair of smaller figures appeared before him. Sarion faltered, gasping in utter horror as they drew closer, and he felt as if a shard of ice had pierced his heart.

For the two shades before him were Areck and Cerestin.

∿∴∾

The warriors trampled along the shrouded corridor, searching for a staircase leading down which hopefully would take them out of the building. Holding their lanterns aloft, the men were at the brink of mental and physical exhaustion. The cares and dangers of their journey had taken a harsh toll upon their collective morale, and it was through the strength of Grundel alone, his determination and confidence, that they still remained a group of cohesive, and capable, fighters.

Chertron again took the lead, the captain next, Forlern at his heels, and Rundin bringing up the rear guard. Now only four. The corridor was high and wide, made to permit the giants to travel with ease. The structure loomed silent and empty about them, just as the other building had been. The entire fortress seemed to have been pillaged, the plunderers leaving behind only death and despair. The captain knew it had been a trap all along, and he wondered if the enemy even suspected his true identity. The implication was ghastly. Could it be possible? He almost stopped in his tracks, Forlern bumping him from behind. "Anything wrong?" The fighter queried him.

"No—keep moving." The captain nodded ahead to Chertron, who had also paused. The men resumed their pace,

Grundel consumed in black thoughts. Chertron whistled, whispering back to the others. "Stairs leading down. Let's hope we find more than just empty chambers."

They bounded down the large steps, hewn from rock, broad and deep, going lower dozens of yards before reaching bottom. They entered a musty room, which may have been used as storage, the length disappearing into shadows, their pale lanterns failing to encompass the full dimensions of the area. Chertron eased ahead with weapon raised, and they walked in single file until they were half-way across.

"Hurry." Rundin whispered. "Something comes."

The captain spun around in alarm, signaling to keep moving. Chertron sprinted towards the far end, gesturing sharply. There was only a blank wall, a dead-end. Chertron spat in frustration as the other warriors joined him.

"Rundin, what did you hear?" Forlern stared into the blackness, waving his sword.

"Echoes from above, it sounded like scratching, but I can't be certain." The captain and Chertron spread out, searching along the walls for another exit.

"Trapped." Forlern patted his blade. "Well, it won't catch us unawares like the others. I'll split its eyes open, whatever Captain Grundel believes."

"That might not be necessary...Over here." Grundel sounded excited and the fighters quickly joined him. "A sewer grate, if I'm not mistaken." He crouched down next to a set of iron bars sunken into the floor, a dark opening lying beneath it. "Our only hope. Let's lift it, and quickly."

Rundin and Chertron immediately assisted him, their strong arms pulling mightily at the fastenings which were loose from centuries of disuse. After several seconds they had it out, and Chertron poked his head inside. "A tunnel, though who can tell where it leads."

"Go." The captain nudged him, following behind. When Rundin had entered, he turned around and pulled the bars tight, trying to find a means to secure it. "I don't know how to hold this down." He looked to Grundel for suggestions, and the captain shook his head.

"We've not the means to secure it tighter. We'll pull it fast, and hope to gain a few moments of time if something pursues." They struggled with the iron until they were satisfied, then fled down the narrow tunnel. It was damp and cool, the top high enough to permit them to move along without hindrance. They scurried along the corridor and soon found themselves to be within a maze-like network, the underground spillway system of the fortress. Time was meaningless inside the tunnels, and they went swiftly, feeling the invisible presence of pursuit behind them. Grundel was fairly sure the Killworm had tracked them into the lower levels of the building, and was hunting them even now. They took several turns, coming at times to branches, Chertron maintaining what he thought was the proper direction, but there was no way to be certain. Some of the corridors were flooded, and he thought it might help to throw off the Killworm. They splashed as quietly as possible, trudging through black water up to their ankles. They soon entered a large corridor, which appeared to be a major runway. Staying to the main tunnel, Grundel realized that the smaller passages were outlets originating from buildings or streets. He recalled seeing several of them as they traveled through the fortress, and his hope was to find a way out near the gates. It was a slim hope, but all his expectations were fragile.

He grew increasingly nervous about staying in there for too long, and he told Chertron to seek another branch. Shortly, they reached a narrow fork, and they chose the right, moving into a smaller tunnel. It was a terrifying flight, oblivious of their true direction or location. The tunnel sloped gradually upwards and they came at last to the end, stopping at the bottom of a well. The captain motioned them upwards, where handholds had been carved into the stone. The rock was moist but the notches were deep, and the fighters ascended.

It was a harrowing climb. They moved higher, to such an extent that a fall would prove fatal. Several times one of them gasped, slipping on the dank walls, but caught himself. Long minutes dragged by and Chertron called back to them, spotting another grate above their heads. They had reached the surface at last, and Chertron pushed heavily up, moving the rusted iron which lay between them and the streets of the fortress. Fortunately, this one was also easily maneuvered due to its age, and the warriors finally breached the sewers, emerging once more into the hazy morning.

Although glad to be out of the tunnels once again, their trepidation was no less. They were far from being out of danger. They didn't know for sure where the Killworm was, either still hunting them in the sewers below, or perhaps it had left also, moving into some other passage. The captain helped Rundin from the hole, and they immediately slapped the grate back in place, knowing that there was no way to fasten it any tighter.

"Did you hear anything as we climbed out?" Grundel looked into the tunnel as he queried the fighter.

"Can't say that I did," replied Rundin. "The creature could be anywhere. Maybe we lost it in the water, but we have to make haste and leave this dreadful city behind. I think we have enough answers to our questions, Captain Grundel."

Their leader looked sad, his eyes narrowing. He keenly felt the loss of his men, and it was as if all the burdens of Trencit now rested upon his shoulders. He was one man, and could only do so much. His mission simply could not end here—King Gregor relied on him, and the demands of his high position commanded him not to fail. His thoughts drifted, swirling in the vortex of recent memories, from the beginning of their quest and the subsequent hazards they had faced. And the catastrophic results. The brave warriors who would not be returning back to their homeland or families. The dead were nearby, and he felt their solemn presence. Their accusations. No, he must not fail.

"Yes, it is time to go. Chertron, that building to our right seems familiar. We may not be too far from the gates. Head for the near side, single file. Keep a sharp lookout to the rooftops, as I believe the creature is more comfortable at higher elevations. It can move quickly and quietly. I don't want any more nasty surprises."

They hurried off, holding the same position of order. The reliable Chertron doused the dangling lantern he yet held, loosening arrows from his pouch, his sword arm ready. The others followed his lead, all of them tired and hungry, but willing to continue onward without either food or rest until they had left the forsaken stronghold far behind.

The air was silent, the mist crouching behind corners, swirling above the turrets and lofty walls, spiraling upwards in lazy circles. It was the most consistent feature of the Lowlands—a wretched, unwelcome companion which served to conceal lurking dangers and to dampen morale. Whether they traveled beneath wood or dale, the mist was there. Grundel felt it to be almost a living entity, constantly prying into their clothes and skin, tugging at their fears, whispering to their minds. Trying to bring them down, give up, admit defeat to Grammore and its sinister denizens. It would be so easy...The magnitude of the Lowlands was staggering. Men and beasts seemed insignificant compared to the immense wilderness and the unspeakable monsters which dwelled there. Visions of the horrendous Jurvech materialized within the captain's mind. A beast of unfathomable violence and destruction. Its very existence alone was a threat to any who dared set foot within the Lowlands. And a more terrible thought was the notion that there might be other creatures of similar power and stature inside Grammore, perhaps ones even deadlier.

This thought had been festering inside Grundel's mind for a while, after he'd realized there might be a concentrated purpose behind the old horrors, manipulating them for unknown reasons. If such energy was directed at Trencit, the kingdom would find war upon all sides, and this was Grundel's greatest fear. And that was why he would never give up.

The fighters rounded a bend, and Chertron snapped his head back. "Captain Grundel, I'm certain we passed this area shortly after entering the city. Unless my memory fails me there is a wide corridor after this section, and then a pathway of several hundred yards leading to the gates. We cannot be very far."

Chertron's face glimmered with hope, and it sent a thrill of warmth throughout Grundel's body, seeing such an indication of the man's unquenchable faith. As long as warriors like Chertron lived and fought, he knew Trencit could not be overcome.

They increased their pace, scurrying forward, eager to put the fortress behind them and make for their own lands once more, but their excitement quickly melted into dread as a huge figure lumbered into view from out of the mist.

꒦ ꒰

Sarion was utterly shocked.

Nothing could have prepared him for the sight of the two fighters, Areck and Cerestin, in the midst of the ghostly company. Their forms were ethereal and hazy, but the faces were unmistakable. He felt as if a lance of ice had just pierced his heart, cold and unforgiving. His eyes stung as tears of bitterness appeared at the corners.

Areck and Cerestin were dead!

Black night wings flapped invisibly around his head, pressing in, threatening to overwhelm and drown him in fear and despair. His throat constricted, and he was unable to swallow. He was crushed. The phantoms hovered before him with vacant orbs, staring through him and beyond, to unspeakable realms past the scope of his human imagination.

Dead!

Sarion shuddered in front of them, and he felt the giant-spirits closing in—watching, and waiting. His sword dropped to his side, and he felt incredibly weak and vulnerable, more so than he had ever felt before. The warriors had met with death and disaster, led by General Charadan, under the direct command of King Gregor. The man had been traveling in disguise as Captain Grundel. And they were gone.

He wept.

The tears rolled down his face, and he sobbed at the loss of his friends. Sarion knew he'd failed them. Despite the captain's arguments, Sarion felt that he should have convinced him otherwise, and they might have avoided entering the citadel. Or another thought occurred to him, that he could have followed after them sooner, and led them away from danger. Anything, except for what he had done.

Waited. He'd waited at the edge of the ridge.

Against his better judgment, staying behind out of the valley. He knew it had been a fateful choice from the beginning. Yet he'd taken no action.

Failed the warriors, failed Trencit—failed himself.

Sarion sunk to his knees, letting the tears wash across his cheeks, cleaning the dirt away. But they could never erase the stain of guilt which twisted his heart in a terrible grip.

The shades remained there, ignoring him, lost. Sarion reached out with his senses, trying to communicate, form a link between worlds. To say he was sorry. The figures seemed to ignore him, appearing sad and forsaken. And they were fading as he looked on, heads moving from side to side. What could he do to reach them, he thought? Was it even possible?

Sarion moved forward, opening his heart and mind fully, letting all his emotions pour forth in the hope of a connection.

The spirits focused on him then, as if for the first time noticing his presence. They were nearly gone. Sarion stared intently at them, helpless and stricken. Words echoed through his mind, faint and elusive, like the dream-fragments scattering when one immediately awakens from a deep sleep, chasing the fantasy-memories until they are forever gone.

Help them, Sarion. It is not your fault. Trencit needs you. Stay true.

Then they vanished.

He staggered back from the force of their touch. They had spoken to him, breached the gap before it had closed. But what did it mean? He was sure it had been a message to him—there was no doubt in his mind. Help them? Help who? Were the others still within the fortress?

Sarion lifted his head upwards and he looked to either side, gazing at the looming shadows of the giants. Is this what they wanted? For him to give up? Areck and Cerestin had come to him, seeking him out. Perhaps in one final warning, but also encouraging him. Sarion felt a fire raging inside, an outlet to his grief and anger. He was a man of action, and the two fighters had sparked the flame within his heart once more. The guilt and hurt remained, but if there was still any chance of helping the others he would pursue it, though it cost him his life as well. Their sacrifice demanded no less.

Sarion glared at the phantoms, scorching their airy figures with his terrible gaze. He would not admit defeat. His eyes challenged their unnatural horror, defying them to renew their assault. Quickly they faded, and Sarion knew it would take more than barren shadows to overcome him. He sprang forward, alone once more.

Alone but determined.

∻

The four warriors stared in disbelief at the huge figure emerging from the mist before them. Grundel's heart sunk, as he knew the entrance to the fortress lay just ahead, within their reach. But now his hopes had been dashed as he recognized the trap which had been carefully set, patiently planned, and cleverly sprung. He didn't know what danger faced them now, but knew it had to be formidable. They'd eluded the Killworm, at least for the moment, and now a new horror faced them. What form would it take this time? Did it even matter anymore, he thought? Many obstacles had been lined up against them, and he felt like a toy within the grips of a monstrously evil and powerful cat's paw.

Grimly, he raised his weapon in resignation, the other men scattering to the side in order to make themselves more difficult as targets. Chertron held his bow, Forlern hefted his blade in one hand, a wicked-looking dagger in the other, his face set and confident. The captain knew this was one man ready to strike blows against the enemy. Rundin flexed his bearish arms, looking eager to fight the entire nation of giants should they appear unearthed from the dank earth for a final battle.

The figure grew larger, moving quietly and boldly forward, and a brutish face leered at them, a large, spiked club held within cruel arms. Cries of astonishment echoed from the fighters, and the captain's mouth opened wide in disbelief.

It was the ogre.

Across hill, swamp, and dale, tracked through the most inhospitable terrain known to them, they had relentlessly pursued the fiercesome beast, and now, impossibly, they faced it once again. Grundel nodded, his face dark and impassive—he knew this would be the last meeting between both adversaries. And the odds were extremely tilted this time—he was not foolish enough to believe otherwise. In their first conflict, they had fought the creature to a stalemate, suffering the loss of two of his men. Now, his force was terribly diminished, and they numbered only four.

Four men, he thought. Against such a savage and powerful foe. But they were four of the finest warriors in all of Trencit, a country of determined fighters, a population of durable people. He lifted his sword, pointing it directly at the ogre in challenge.

"So it has come to this at last. This is what we wanted all along, is it not?"

"Aye." Forlern and Chertron both called over to him, voicing their agreement. Rundin was focused on the enemy, his face implacable.

The captain continued speaking as the monster steadily approached. "Stand fast, men. We meet our quarry again, unexpectedly. Remember those who have fallen because of this foul beast, and let us avenge their sacrifice. Beware its speed and cunning. Spread out."

They formed a semi-circle around the brute, Chertron firing a volley of arrows already, scoring hits on the ogre's chest and neck. The creature roared in fury, charging towards him, the club swinging in a huge sweeping arc. Forlern took an early gamble, waiting until the ogre was only yards from him, sidestepping the club and avoiding a fatal blow by mere inches, and throwing one of his knives at the creature's throat. It cut deeply into the monster's flesh, and the ogre pulled the weapon out, casting it to the side. Chertron and Rundin fired several more arrows, taking advantage of the early distraction.

Grundel's heart leaped at the sight of the ogre's pain and confusion, hope springing within his breast. If they could keep the beast off-guard, they might yet have a chance. He raced forward, flashing his sword before the creature, taunting it by remaining just out of reach. It was a courageous but desperate move, as the ogre continued swinging the club, missing the elusive man by only scant inches with each swipe. Rundin and Chertron closed in from the flanks, each of them attempting to score a direct strike, but the ogre was not to be so easily fooled.

It grunted in fury and hurtled itself to one side, straight at Rundin. The others watched in horror as it heaved the club at the warrior's feet, causing him to lose his balance. For one second, everything seemed to hover precariously in the twilight, the ogre poised to move, then it plummeted forward and smacked Rundin to the ground with one massive arm. The fighter fell hard, a sickening crunch sounding as he hit the stone and lay still.

The captain screamed, barreling forward and catching the ogre in one meaty thigh with his blade. The creature howled in agony, its throaty call echoing hideously through the dead corridors and turrets of the fortress. Livid with rage and pain, it brought the club around and Grundel jumped in the air to avoid having his legs shattered. One of the spikes caught his right leg and he felt a searing fire in his limb, as the metal tore through leather and into his exposed skin. He staggered backwards, crumbling to the ground and gasping for breath.

Chertron and Forlern plunged headlong into the fray, unable to have anticipated the captain's drastic action. Another knife sliced through the air, but the ogre saw it coming, deflecting it to the side with the club. Chertron placed himself within three yards of the lumbering brute, trying to move it away from his fallen comrades. Grundel stood up, heavily favoring his leg, but his sword was lifted high once again. The pain was evident on his face but he refused to concede anything.

The ogre noticed his movement, and leaned to its side, angling steadily towards him. Forlern slashed madly with his weapon, yelling at the beast to anger it further. He feinted to one side, then charged directly for the brute, which was taken by surprise. Forlern dove at the monster, driving his blade into the creature's right arm, the limb which carried the devastating club. Its rage was indescribable, and it pulled away, kicking Forlern in the ribs and grabbing the blade with its left arm. The sword had struck deeply and the ogre removed it, ignoring the volley of arrows fired from Chertron, and cracked the sword in its powerful grip, tossing it aside.

Forlern rolled away from the creature, reaching for another knife, although the short dagger would not be nearly as effective as his sword. Rundin had not moved since being struck by the monster, and the others attempted to lead it away from where he lay. The monster seemed unconcerned with the status of the brave warrior, content for the moment that he was out of the fight.

Grundel moved forward once more, gritting his teeth at the fire in his leg. It was a deep cut, and he was losing blood quickly. He knew they had to find a way to put the beast down, as it showed no sign of weakening. Despite its several injuries, the ogre was a massive and powerful creature, a savage predator of the Lowlands, and a match for most of the other inhabitants. It clearly had the advantage, and knew it.

The captain whistled several times, signaling for his men to fall into one of their field tactics. Chertron and Forlern immediately backed off, giving the ogre leeway, while Grundel held his ground. He was still able to fight and move, and his mind raced, trying to devise a plan which would either drive away or kill the ogre outright. Rundin was seriously hurt, and time was swiftly moving against them. He shuddered to think what would happen if the Killworm emerged from beneath the sewers and found them once more.

A pair of bows sang as Chertron and Forlern released a hail of volleys upon the ogre once more, both men trying to maim the relentless beast, or blind it. Some of the arrows were slapped harmlessly aside, others finding a mark. The creature seemed more annoyed than injured by them, its flesh thick and durable, able to withstand a tremendous amount of suffering. It lunged forward towards Grundel, who instead of engaging it, pivoted to one side, trying to steer the creature away from Rundin, and further into the fortress. The men maintained a good distance between themselves and the ogre, ceaselessly letting fly their shafts and hoping to do some real damage. It was a deadly game of cat and mouse, and the captain used every trick of swordplay he knew to stay just out of reach of the monstrous club. He was tiring from lack of rest and loss of blood. His concentration was slipping, and he knew that his first mistake would be his last.

The ogre was growing increasingly angry, and the effects of its numerous injuries were slowly beginning to take a toll. It bled from over a dozen different spots, its greenish blood oozing from the tough hide like sap squeezed from a tree. The stone pathway of the fortress was stained with small puddles as it loped forward, trying to crush Grundel who taunted it with his blade, slashing quickly when it approached, then sprinting away, maddening the monster further.

A hail of fresh arrows rained down upon the ogre, piercing its leathery skin, causing it to roar in dismay. Hesitating, it looked over at the men, shielding its face with a meaty fist. It was tiring of this game, and the captain paused along with it, waiting to see what the ogre would do next. It reached into a sack tied fast around its midsection, pulling out another war horn. The captain immediately recognized their danger.

"Shoot it! The beast signals something to come!"

Chertron pulled his bow back, firing two quick shots, Forlern releasing one of his own. The first arrow embedded itself into the club, the second striking the creatures fist arm which held the horn. Forlern's shaft landed with an incredible stroke of luck, hitting the horn before the ogre's astonished gaze and cleaving it into two equal parts, now totally useless. Its face smoldered with rage.

The captain was pleased with the accuracy of his men, but was greatly concerned as to what it had attempted to do. There could be no question that other creatures lurked somewhere nearby, and the ogre had tried—and failed, to call them. Whether it was the Killworm or otherwise, he didn't know. It proved beyond doubt that an organized, concerted effort had been put into place to thwart their undertaking, or at least to alert the guardians of the stronghold. He realized that something powerful and deadly was manipulating the creatures—and themselves, for that matter.

"We're almost out of arrows, Captain." Chertron shouted over to him, twenty yards from his left. Forlern knelt another score of yards to Chertron's left side, aiming another shaft as his comrade spoke. The ogre moved steadily forward, not taking its eyes off Grundel's determined form.

Then, to the surprise of them all, it did something completely unexpected.

⌣:∾

Sarion ran like a man possessed.

His boots clicked mutely on the harsh stone, and he plunged deeper into the citadel. He'd raced away from the terrible corridor, where the shades of the two fighters had confronted him. Invigorated by their silent warning, Sarion set off to find his companions, knowing full well that a Killworm was prowling the fortress. It was a chilling thought.

As he turned down another long, narrow pathway, he noticed marks on the stone, fresh ones, created by something large and dangerous. He had seen them before, as they tracked an elusive quarry into the Lowlands, and he was startled, realizing that it matched the prints of their quarry.

The ogre was inside the fortress! Grimhounds, a Killworm, and now the ogre.

Dark thoughts plagued his mind at the implications. Areck and Cerestin were already dead. Time was passing swiftly for the remaining warriors, who had entered the forsaken citadel, falling victim to the dreadful guardians. Hunted by a Killworm, pursued by the ogre.

A terrible yell of anguish echoed along the pathway, and he paused. Battle was being waged somewhere nearby…

Sarion quickened his pace, glancing skyward for any signs of danger from the barren rooftops and towers. He was within a haven of nightmares, populated by the living and dead alike. Shades and monsters. He rounded a curve, his eyes glaring wide at the scene in front of him.

He'd found the warriors at last!

His joy quickly changed to dismay as he surveyed the grim circumstances of their plight. The ogre shambled in the

midst of the three remaining fighters, and he saw a figure laying upon the unforgiving stone. Their situation was desperate. His heart went cold at the sight and he sprang forward,
yelling encouragement to the men.

At the same moment, the ogre swung its club in the air,
releasing it directly at Grundel. Sarion watched, horrified, as
the spiked weapon smashed into the captain's body, hurtling
him several yards through the air from the momentum, and
the man landed on the ground, his sword spinning wildly
along the smooth rock. He lay still.

Forlern shrieked with outrage, yelling oaths at the brute,
which ignored the fallen fighters and now headed for them,
a snarl etched into its hideous features, the mouth gaping,
the crooked teeth grinding together. Their arrows spent, the
warriors drew weapons together, a pair of swords gleaming silver in the air, and they spread apart, anticipating the
deadly clash with their adversary. Concentrating on harry-
ing the ogre, and now devastated by the fall of their leader,
the men were unaware of the figure charging toward them
and directly into the fray.

Sarion flew across the hard path, a fire raging inside his
breast, an emotional storm needing release. So quick and silent
was his approach, that the ogre failed to realize his presence
until he was within arm's reach. The two fighters watched in
disbelief and hope as Sarion emerged from behind the dreadful beast, hefting his sword in a mighty swing. The ogre's keen
hearing alerted it to this new danger, and it turned around,
but not quick enough to avoid Sarion's blow. He flung all his
weight into the monster, cutting deeply into its left shoulder.

His speed was too great for him to change direction, and
he used his leverage to pull the sword away and roll for-

ward, narrowly missing a vicious kick leveled at his head. The ogre bellowed in terrible pain, the blood pouring forth from the angry wound to its limb. It was a fearsome predator, not used to suffering such injuries in battle. It was bred for violence, and it immediately moved to crush its foes. Lunging forward again, it grabbed for Chertron who had closed in, attempting to catch it off-guard. Forlern yelled to his comrade but it was too late.

The ogre grazed the warriors brow, knocking his helm off and smacking him aside. Chertron collapsed onto the stone, and the ogre moved in for the kill. Sarion was on his feet again, but too far away to do anything. Forlern slashed at the creature with his dagger, more as a distraction, knowing that it was virtually useless against such a beast. The ogre swatted at the brave fighter, taking its eye away from Chertron's crumpled form. Sarion rejoined the warrior, grabbing the captain's weapon and heaving it over to Forlern, who retreated as the monster came closer to him now.

Sarion looked in alarm at Grundel's lifeless body—the man's eyes were closed, but his lungs drew breath. With renewed determination, he held his sword high, staring into the ogre's eyes. The creature was wounded in numerous spots, and within its orbs burned a primeval rage, the look of the hunter, and it started forward, but Sarion was undaunted. He would not accept defeat.

Instead of giving himself room to maneuver, Sarion took a step towards the approaching behemoth, and his boot caught in the stone. Stumbling, Forlern screamed to him in warning. "Sarion, no!"

The ogre saw its opportunity and did not hesitate. A survivor of countless fights and hunts, its lunged towards Sarion's bowed head, its good arm clenching the air in fury. Forlern looked on in horror as the monster descended, using its weight to propel itself onto the vulnerable figure in front of it.

At the last second, Sarion moved to the right, lifting his head up and regaining his balance. He swung upwards with the sword, slicing into the ogre's neck, letting the creature's ponderous body work against itself. It caught Sarion sharply with a balled fist, but the sword continued to cut into the monster, slicing through muscle and tendon, and completely severing the head. Eyes still wide open, the ogre's head rolled across the stone and lay still, its body crumbling to the ground, shuddering uncontrollably. It was dead.

Forlern watched in amazement, his face changing to relief, and after several seconds he ran over to his companion. "Are you all right?"

Sarion's head was sore, his body terribly bruised in many areas, including his shoulder from the battle with the Grimhounds, but he'd suffered no major injuries. On the verge of collapsing from weariness and pain, he nodded to Forlern, wincing. The warrior helped him stand.

"What a chance you took—I thought the ogre had you as well."

"It nearly did, but I was desperate—and it was injured. Such a move would not have worked under any other circumstance, I can assure you. What about the others?" He felt a lance of anguish pierce his heart at the sight of the fallen warriors, and he hobbled over to his comrades.

Rundin was dead.

The ogre had struck him a tremendous blow, and he had not moved since. Sarion felt for a pulse but knew instantly there was none to be found. Tears streamed down his face at the white pallor of Rundin's skin, the quenched appearance of the bearish man's face. The warrior had shown his reliability and loyalty countless times on their expedition. Durable, dedicated to his country, comrades, and especially his Captain. One of Trencit's finest.

Gone.

Fallen in an unforgiving and treacherous land, far from home and family.

"Sarion, how is Rundin?" Forlern called from several yards away where he knelt with their fallen leader.

His response was a pained whisper. "Dead...Rundin's dead."

Forlern gasped. "You better come over here, he's asking for you." He faltered. "Sarion...it's not good."

Sarion snapped his head up, staring at Forlern's stricken gaze, the man cradling Grundel's head within his lap. He heard a moan from beyond them both, and Chertron sat up, much to Sarion's surprise.

"Chertron is up—he must not be too badly hurt."

Sarion went over to Forlern. The man's eyes were closed, and his breath was barely noticeable.

"He's dying, Sarion."

Forlern choked back the words, and Sarion felt as if a dagger had been driven through his chest.

Dying!

No, he thought. You don't understand, he can't be dying. It's not Grundel—there is no Grundel. He can't be dying.

Sobbing, he felt the man's brow, whispering gently to him. "It's me, Sarion. I'm here."

The Captain of Trencit lifted one hand, his body wracked by spasms of pain. Forlern shook his head bitterly, grinding his teeth. "By the three... he is going, Sarion—leaving us."

Chertron stood, first looking over at the carcass of the ogre, then at Rundin's body in shock. He moved slowly, joining the others.

"Sarion...go to King Gregor. He'll know what to do." Every syllable was painful, tremendous effort needed to bring them forth from his parched lips.

"You can't leave us—the land needs you." Sarion felt his eyes moistening, and the others watched in deathly silence at his side, Forlern stroking their leader's head.

"Sarion, you have done well, a better man..." Blood trickled from his lips, and Forlern quickly wiped it away. "The best of us..." He finished.

"I know who you are," Sarion hesitated, squeezing his hand, willing life into the man. "I read your journal."

Forlern and Chertron stared at Sarion questioningly. "What do you mean?" Chertron touched Sarion's shoulder. "What do you mean by this? What are you talking about?"

"He goes by another name—there exists no Captain Grundel." Sarion inhaled sharply, the words pouring out like acid on his own lips.

The injured leader weakly lifted his hand. "I thought you might, to understand...I'm sorry I didn't get to know you better. Forgive me." He coughed harshly, a look of agony on his face. He opened his eyes. "Don't forget the king. Have faith in yourself, Sarion. You're the one who can save us." His gray orbs closed, and he lay still.

They all waited in terrible silence. He was dead. Impossible for any of them to accept, they stared at his unmoving form, desperately hoping that their eyes were wrong, his injuries not as serious as they appeared. But they knew the truth, and it was overwhelming.

"He's gone." Chertron mumbled. "Sarion, what did you mean?"

It was a long moment until Sarion spoke, and he felt the weight of their journey resting heavily upon his shoulders. All the fallen warriors, the dangerous times they shared, the companionship—their friendship. Yes, he could call them all his friends, if but for a short time. And now two more were dead.

"He's not Captain Grundel, as I said." Sarion paused for an agonizing moment. He breathed deeply. "You look upon the face of General Charadan, leader of the Trencit royal armies—King's Champion."

"What!" Forlern yelled in shock. "This is Charadan himself? Impossible!"

"Are you mad?" Chertron leaned towards Sarion, probing him with a steely gaze. "Speak not in riddles at such a time!"

Sarion shook his head sadly.

"No, I read his journal. And he left this inside." Sarion reached into his tunic, pulling out the medallion of King's Champion. "Sent by King Gregor, commanded to discover the nature of unrest in the westland and beyond…That is why he went to such lengths in pursuing the ogre. He felt compelled to learn of this new threat to Trencit. He gave his life for the land—and now, we've lost him."

"We are defeated…I cannot believe my eyes. The greatest leader in the land—it doesn't seem possible. And I never suspected it." Chertron rambled on, overcome by fatigue, injury, and bewilderment. He dropped to the ground, face held between his arms. Forlern stared silently at Charadan's unmoving body.

A sound echoed in the distance, instantly putting them all on guard. Forlern gently laid the fallen leader to the stone, cursing. "It seems none of us are yet fated to leave this blasted devil's land. I'll go down fighting like my comrades, at least."

The noise grew louder, but it sounded familiar—the approach of someone on horseback. They watched as the beast reared into view, and the fighters held their weapons ready, but Sarion lowered his own. "Wait, this is no enemy which draws near."

Alayian appeared from the mist, hair flowing free, riding like a warrior maiden. Chertron and Forlern looked on in astonishment as she rode up to them, suddenly materializing from the folds of mist within the forsaken fortress.

Chertron sighed wearily. "I have not the strength or will left to fight one so beautiful as this apparition, evil or not. And she sits upon one of our own horses yet? What witchery is this, a final act of mockery?"

She hailed them. "I'm sorry, Sarion. I had to follow after you. Terror dwells within these walls, and your friends look to have suffered much already."

"You know her? Who in blazes is she?" Forlern shook his head wonderingly.

Alayian dismounted, holding a flask in her hands. "Drink some of this, but we must leave immediately. I feel the presence of other things nearby, hunting for you."

She handed the flask to Sarion, who in turn offered it to Chertron. "She's a friend, I met her upon the ridge. She lives in Grammore—although I know little else about her."

Chertron's brow furrowed and he sniffed the container suspiciously. "Indeed you do not. This is no ordinary girl before us." He drank from the flask, his eyes widening. "Ah, this draught is like no other I've tasted before. If I don't leave this cursed fortress, then at least I will end with such a sweet taste upon my lips." He handed it to Forlern, who sipped warily from it.

"Help me with our comrades, and we'll strap them to the horse." Sarion gestured to the two men.

Alayian looked at the fallen warriors, her eyes pained. "Your friends. Alas, I am sorry for their fate. This was the Captain of Trencit you spoke of?"

Sarion nodded.

"A brave man, to risk this place. Hurry, time grows short."

The three of them gently carried the bodies of Charadan and Rundin, tying them fast to the horse. They were quickly done, and headed off in the direction of the entrance. The streets were silent and deserted, and they made their way back to the immense gates at last, standing between the ancient guardians. Sarion looked upon their dreadful forms, keenly feeling the loss of Charadan and the others. Rundin, Areck, and Cerestin, all victims to the awakening evil known only as the Dark Mage.

The enemy of Trencit now had a name, if not a face. He pondered the path which lay before him. He needed to escape the Grammore Lowlands, undoubtedly facing more hazards in finding their way out again. King Gregor must be told the fate of his Champion, the legacy of horror disturbed from slumber within the bordering wilderness, and the sacrifice of the courageous fighters. And then what? What of his own future?

Sarion could not avoid the question. His peaceful life as a farmer was over. The king would be devastated at the loss of his finest leader, and Trencit would be shaken to its foundation. He still could not believe it himself. He'd traveled Grammore in the presence of Trencit's most famous and charismatic warlord, Charadan. And now Charadan was gone. The ramifications would be catastrophic as word spread out across the land, eventually reaching the battle-front, where his very name could lend inspiration to the most downcast of warriors.

General Charadan. Dead.

Sarion wept. For himself, for the warriors and citizens of Trencit, for Edward. Like an unwelcome companion, misfortune had hovered above their quest since the beginning. They'd been beset with obstacles nearly the entire journey. Some deliberate, others by chance. Lesser men would never have escaped with their lives from the original clash with the ogre. They had survived though, eventually prevailing in the face of terrible odds. At least to this point. And with devastating losses to show.

But Sarion was not defeated.

There was everything to fight for, and he would answer the call, giving all if necessary. First he needed to get his remaining companions back to their own country. Hazards surrounded them at every turn, and their numbers were sorely diminished, losing their leader in the end. And what of the strange newcomer?

Chertron tapped him on the shoulder, nodding to Alayian's slender figure. "Aye, she is no average girl, stranded in the middle of Grammore."

Sarion stared at him. "Who is she really then, do you know?"

Chertron nodded again. "The question is what is she."

They both looked up at her, walking after the horse, Forlern taking the lead. The fortress was behind them now, and Alayian had told the warriors she could help them to leave the valley without encountering the Grimhounds. Sarion didn't ask how she could do it—the look in her eyes was all the convincing he needed.

Chertron leaned close, whispering in Sarion's ear. "I think that the girl is a na-dryad."

Sarion opened his mouth in surprise. "What? How do you know that?"

The warrior pointed towards her. "Subtle things you might notice, the ears, slightly pointed, for one."

Sarion realized this for the first time.

"Mostly from what I recall from stories and such. The powers they possess of concealment and camouflage. A creature of the forest, a legendary species. We're surrounded by legends, it seems. Her intentions remain unclear though. Why has she bothered to help us, as we are stalked by evil at every turn? She seems to have taken a fancy with yourself, but I warn you—beware."

"What else do you know of na-dryads, if this is indeed true?" Sarion kept his voice low.

"Well, she can't leave Grammore, the lands of her birth. Others of her kind are limited to a certain type of tree or landscape. Her kind is far superior, and able to travel forth in greater distances. They have power, old and secret. I don't trust her."

Sarion was quiet, startled by Chertron's words. More puzzles? Where would it all end? He had no reason to distrust her though. She might have killed him while he slept, since the horses were not bothered by her presence. Alayian. Hs spoke the name upon his lips, enchanted by her beauty and wonder. There was much he needed to know about her.

Sarion's mind swam in confusion. And pain. A flood of emotional turmoil. The fortress was now behind him, lost in the haze. Before him the land was a desolation, swirling in chaos and uncertainty, just like his own thoughts. Was this what the Dark Mage had in mind for his own homeland?

No clear road lay in front of him, and danger surrounded them on every side. Their destination now was Trencit, and from there directly to King Gregor. Charadan was gone, and the land would sorely miss their greatest leader. But Sarion knew he could not wallow in misery. Others relied on him. He looked first upon Forlern, thinking how similar he was to himself, especially as a younger man, fresh in the Western Watch. Eager, excitable, and perhaps confrontational. Yet Forlern was a tough survivor, a deadly fighter, battle-sharpened and afraid of nothing. He had faced the same dangers which had slain his companions—faced them and surpassed them. And Chertron? Someone to count on under any circumstances. Skilled as a tracker and warrior, resourceful and good-natured. He could place his life within their protection if needed. And he knew with chilling certainty that he would some day, perhaps sooner than he cared to admit.

With these two men at his side, he felt a tremendous sense of pride and valor, not to be easily quenched. No, they would not give up fighting for what they believed in. The loss of Charadan was bitter and devastating, but the general had shown Sarion immense courage and loyalty. What a terrible command for him, leading his own men into a hostile land filled with countless nightmares, knowing full well that some would not be returning. Including himself in the end. And he had suffered greatly, watching as they fell victim to circumstances beyond his ability to save them, and that was what hurt the most. Sarion had also felt it—and hated it.

Sarion was determined to help the people of Trencit. Not moving forward for vengeance, although he knew there would be a time for him to strike at the Dark Mage and the forces gathered with him, but instead he continued onward driven by the love he felt for his country and its citizens. A hope, to give them a chance to live without the constant threat of war and invasion. He wanted to do his part for Edward, for the lost warriors, for Charadan. Perhaps future generations would know real peace.

Sarion looked into the mist with penetrating eyes, scalding the swirling vapor with his gaze. Head held high, he swore to himself that they were not returning in defeat, but hope. He wiped away the single tear upon his cheek.

There would be other days, other battles.

And they would find him ready.

THE END

This concludes "Ogre's Passing", book one of the Trencit Legacy. Book two, "The Rooting of Evil," will continue with the quest of Sarion and his companions as they confront the growing power of the Dark Mage, and battle against his minions of terror.